NADYA SKYLUNG
and the
CLOUDSHIP RESCUE

Nadya Skylung
and the
Cloudship Rescue

JEFF SEYMOUR

Illustrated by BRETT HELQUIST

G. P. Putnam's Sons

G. P. Putnam's Sons
an imprint of Penguin Random House LLC
375 Hudson Street
New York, NY 10014

Library of Congress Cataloging-in-Publication Data
Names: Seymour, Jeff, author. | Helquist, Brett, illustrator.
Title: Nadya Skylung and the cloudship rescue / Jeff Seymour ; illustrated by Brett Helquist.
Description: New York, NY : G. P. Putnam's Sons, [2018]
Summary: When pirates capture a cloudship and its crew, it is up to young Nadya and her friends,
all orphans, to rescue the only family they have ever known.
Identifiers: LCCN 2017033484 | ISBN 9781524738655 (hardcover)
Subjects: | CYAC: Adventure and adventurers—Fiction. | Airships—Fiction. | Kidnapping—Fiction.
| Pirates—Fiction. | Orphans—Fiction. | Identity—Fiction. | Science fiction.
Classification: LCC PZ7.1.S468 Nad 2018 | DDC [Fic]—dc23
LC record available at https://lccn.loc.gov/2017033484

Printed in the United States of America.
ISBN 9781524738655
1 3 5 7 9 10 8 6 4 2

Design by Marikka Tamura.
Text set in Columbus MT Std.

To Oren—Fly high, little one

CHAPTER 1

IN WHICH WE MEET OUR HEROINE, AND A STORM APPROACHES.

"Nadya!"

Outside the cabin doorway, a distant rumble calls . . .

"Nadya!"

Outside the cabin doorway, a distant rumble mumbles . . . ?

"Nadya!"

There's a loud *crack* and the rumble of thunder, and my whole cabin on the cloudship *Orion* jumps up a few inches and falls back down. I snag my journal and pen before they can slide off my desk, and look out the window again, where the yellow-gold light of afternoon is fading into gray, stormy shadows.

"Darn it," I mutter.

Tam Ban, my greatest nemesis on the ship and as goody-goody a kid as you've ever met, shouts at me through the door. "Nadya! Captain Nic wants you, and he'll give you stripes this time if you're not out here in ten seconds!"

I push back from my writing desk and snort. Nic never hits us. Our first mate, Tall Thom, wants him to sometimes, but Nic's too nice for that. All the same, I open the desk drawer where I keep important stuff and toss my journal into it. I *can* hear the rumble of thunder, after all, and we're halfway across the Cloud Sea, six days from the dusty adobe houses, giant walls, and leafy streets of Vash Abandi in the west, and five days till the ironwork cranes, crooked skyscrapers, zip lines, and grungy alleys of Far Agondy in the east. Out here, the storms are big and mean and fast. So if Nic wants me and there's thunder outside, something exciting's probably about to happen.

My name's Nadya Skylung, and I keep the *Orion* afloat.

I don't do it all by myself, of course, not yet. Mrs. Trachia's still teaching me. But I'll have it figured out soon. I have to. Tall Thom's leaving the ship when we make port in Far Agondy next week, and Nic's going to pick one of the kids on the *Orion* to do his job. I'm gonna make sure it's me and learn how to run a cloudship, and then someday I'll be captain of my own ship, and I'll fly anywhere I want, anytime I want to—Nadya, the greatest skylung of them all!

I'm halfway through closing my desk drawer when the ship gives another huge lurch and there's an ominous creaking from the deck outside. Tam pounds on my door again. I flinch and jump up.

"I'm coming!" I shout.

I open the door and glare at Tam.

A mop of iron-black hair sits on his head like a grumpy

octopus, and he's got on the same black overalls and white shirt he always wears. He thinks his clothes show off his permanently tan skin and the muscles underneath it. I think they show off how dumb he is.

Tam's six months younger than me. But he's also six inches taller, six ways wiser, and six times as quick. Or so he tells me, anyway. He's a stick-in-the-mud about rules and safety and doesn't trust anything he can't take apart with a screwdriver. I know the world's not as scary as he thinks, and that rules were made for reasons and the reasons matter more than the rules. We butt heads over it all the time. Everybody thinks Nic'll pick him or me as first mate when Thom leaves the ship, but I know it'll be me.

Above Tam, the big dark egg of the cloud balloon where I do most of my work twists and creaks at the end of long cables secured to the deck. The storm's not far off now, and it's getting closer. The wind's picking up.

"Get your safety belt on," Tam says. "Nic wanted you ten minutes ago. What're you doing in there?"

I roll my eyes. It didn't look like the storm was that close. I was just gonna finish my page. "None of your business," I say. I like to journal 'cause it reminds me of my mom. I've got a page from one of her old diaries tucked away in my desk, and I try to write like she did.

Tam snorts, but right then a huge gust of wind hits the *Orion*. The whole ship rises up by a couple of feet and slams back down. My stomach jumps into my throat. I just about float off the deck.

Behind me, I hear the *thunk* of something heavy falling out of my desk. The wind pushes down on the aft of the *Orion* and up on its bow, so the deck slants and I have to brace myself to keep from slipping aftward, toward Nic's cabin and the stairway at the other end of the ship.

A black-and-silver flash rolls by my feet through the open door, and my heart tries to swan-dive out of my chest.

I don't remember much about my parents, see. That's why my last name's Skylung, after the way I can breathe the special air in cloud balloons, instead of after their last name. Mrs. T and Nic found me in a crashed ship in the desert outside Vash Abandi when I was three.

Tam says my parents must be dead since nobody's ever seen them, but I don't believe him. I remember my dad standing at the wheel of a cloudship in a sandstorm, shouting directions to the crew. I remember my mom letting me run my fingers over fancy etching on a silver safe and telling me how special it was. I think they're still out there, doing something amazing, and I just have to find them. So I take extra special care of the knickknacks I have left from when Nic and Mrs. T found me.

The most important of all those things is a round, tarnished silver doorknob that I remember my mom pressing into my hands and telling me to keep safe. The same one that just rolled past my feet and is heading for the deck rails, the open sky, and the ocean below.

I elbow Tam out of the way and run after it. There's another *crack* of lightning off the port bow. A gust of wind hits the *Orion* and pushes the doorknob starboard. It skitters toward the rail, where there are little gaps called scuppers that let the rain drain off during big storms. The scuppers are more than big enough for my doorknob to fit through.

"Nadya!" Tam shouts, but I ignore him. I've almost caught up to the doorknob when the wind gusts again, and the knob slips through my fingers and rolls farther toward the rail. The *Orion* levels out, and then her port side lifts, sending everything on deck tumbling starboard again. I get a glimpse into the ocean through one of the scuppers, and the doorknob rolls right toward it. I'm still a couple feet away. I hold my breath, dive, stretch out my fingers, and close my eyes.

I nab the doorknob just as it's sailing into the air.

Half a second later, my shoulder slams into the railing hard enough to rattle my teeth, but I don't lose my grip. I snatch the doorknob back up through the hole, open my eyes, and brush my fingers over it. No damage—Goshend be good—it's the same dusty silver, blackened in some spots with tarnish I can't get off no matter how hard I polish. It's about as big as an undersized orange, with a huge, beautiful tree winding its limbs upward on the front like it's praying and a strange little rod with lots of slots in it coming out the back. I sniff it real quick, just to make sure the smell of home's still there. It is—a spicy, musty aroma that makes my tongue tingle.

"Dang it, Nadya!" Tam shouts. He shuts the door to my cabin and stomps toward me. The wind calms down, and the

Orion stops pitching around so much. I take a deep breath and tuck the doorknob into my pocket, where it'll be safe.

Tam grabs me by the wrist when he gets to me and dumps my safety belt, which he must've nabbed from my cabin, into my lap. "That was the dumbest thing I've ever seen you do," he says. "What if you fell?"

I jerk my wrist free and stick my tongue out at him. "I was fine," I say.

Tam rolls his eyes and nods toward my pocket. "Why do you keep that thing, anyway? It's just a useless piece of junk."

I stand up and toss the safety belt at him. "*You're* a useless piece of junk, Tam!" It's not my best work as insults go, but I'm a little distracted by the storm coming on and the fact I almost lost the thing that's most important to me in the whole world.

So I turn my back on Tam, brush myself off, and head toward Nic's cabin.

My cabin nestles up against the *Orion*'s bow. In order to get to Captain Nic's from it, you've got to cross the whole wooden length of the ship's deck. You go past the stairs that lead down to the ironroom, where the engines that drive our huge metal propellers are. You go past the ladder that shoots up to the metal catwalks and rigging around the cloud balloon. And then you go under the aft deck, where Tall Thom stands like a scarecrow at the ship's wheel.

I suppose I should explain about the catwalks, since I practically live up there. Around the balloon there's a big spiderweb of metal walkways, and inside that's the garden that makes the lighter-than-air gas that keeps us afloat. It's my favorite place on the ship, all bright and steamy and beautiful, and only me and Mrs. T can go in there.

"Nadya," I hear from the aft deck.

Tall Thom has his eyes, bright brown and shining as a Glimmerstreet dollar, on me, and I hunch my shoulders a little. Thom knows more about how a cloudship's designed and run than anyone I've ever met, and he never cuts me any slack when I do something wrong. Nic likes to crew the *Orion* with orphans, train them so they can run their own ships, then set them up somewhere else and get a new batch of kids in. Apparently, Thom was one of Nic's orphans once, but it's hard to believe. He's harder on us than Nic and Mrs. T combined.

Thom's skinny as a switch and has a head the shape of a stovepipe. He dresses like a South Sea pirate—all worn-out trousers and striped shirts and bandanas over black hair and dark brown skin—and his clothes always seem to stick to his body. Sometimes I think he wouldn't mind if he lost an eye, just so he could complete his look.

"What?" I call out.

"You have to listen to Tam when we send him for you. We don't always see trouble coming this far off, and the *Orion* needs all of us to keep her safe."

I wait until he turns back to the storm to roll my eyes, but the thunder gets louder when I do, like it's mad at me for arguing. So I scurry on ahead toward Nic's cabin.

He's right about the *Orion* though. The ship's a big wooden job like the sailing vessels that used to cross the ocean. She's solid as sapphires and Nic keeps her well maintained, but she's one of the oldest cloudships around. Sometimes things break on her, like the cable moorings or the engine housings or the bolts that keep the catwalks steady, and it takes a lot of work to keep her running. Still, I love everything about her. She's got a big cargo hold on her lowest deck, a bunch of rooms, the galley, and the ironroom on the middle deck, and the upper deck, where I'm standing and where Nic's cabin and mine are. She's freedom and safety and home, all wrapped up in a cozy little package.

The wind picks up again. Thirty feet or so above my head, the cloud balloon shifts and the cables that attach it to the *Orion* groan like adults getting up from a nap. I stare up at the balloon and its night-sky design. Every cloudship has a design on its balloon to match its name—it's sort of a point of pride and an identifier all at the same time—and ours is painted to look like the night sky seen through the enormous, swirling ferns of somebody's garden. As I'm looking, the balloon twists in the wind, and I hear a flurry of frightened whispers in my mind as some of the plants around it get tilted down to face the ocean. I pat the ladder up to the cloud balloon as I go by, and I try to think reassuring thoughts in the direction of the plants.

That's a big part of my job, see. We've got a hundred and twenty little bays around the catwalks where we grow plants that gobble up different kinds of cloud and churn out all sorts of stuff. Some of them grow fruits and vegetables, but others make fuels, drinks, iron, plasticose—fluffy bits that they spin into fabric in the cities—and more. We've even got one that spits out a couple real fire opals every month. That one cost Nic a mint, but we get a lot of money for the opals in port, and he says it's just about paid for itself now.

The outerplants, along with the garden inside the balloon, need a skylung to take care of them. All those plants and the animals that live around them come from the Roof of the World, like skylungs do, and I can hear them talking and know what they need. Sometimes it's food or water, or the nutrients in the soil are wrong, but sometimes it's softer than that. Sometimes they need shade, or sun, or just company. Plants and animals get lonely too, you know.

I get to Nic's cabin a few seconds later. We're being pushed forward and starboard by the wind, and storm clouds creased with slick lightning blot out the horizon like the giant black skyscrapers on the Far Agondy waterfront. The storm's still a few miles away, but it's rolling toward us. It's gonna be a bad one. I can feel it.

As I put my hand on the door, I hear a *thump* and look back to see what Tam's doing. He's leaning hard on a winch by one of the cables attached to the cloud balloon—loosening one that was groaning, I think. His hair falls over his eyes as he pushes, and when he swipes it away, he sees me watching him.

I stick out my tongue, open the door to the cabin, and walk in.

I love Nic's cabin. It's lined in sweet-smelling orange cedar, and it's got three huge windows at the back of it. There's a couch under them with big green cushions. The room's got an iron chandelier swinging from the ceiling too, but I've never seen Nic turn it on because of how much the gas costs.

Under the chandelier, Nic keeps a big square table. It's usually covered in charts and maps, but sometimes I see him and Salyeh Abande, the kid he's training as our polymath, squinting at lines of figures on it. They work together, comparing what our plants produce to rumors about what's selling well in the cities around the Cloud Sea, doing complicated math with Mrs. T, and figuring out where we're going next.

"Nadya."

Nic and his soup-kettle belly are standing over the table. Nic's got enormous caterpillar eyebrows and fluffy white sideburns that come almost all the way down to his chin, but other than that, he doesn't have a lick of hair on his head. He's got rosy skin and wears gold-rimmed glasses that cost more than a month's worth of supplies, and he never lets anybody touch them. He only even takes them out of their case in his front shirt pocket when he absolutely has to.

Outside, the thunder rumbles again. The ship rolls a little to starboard, like she's being pushed hard by the wind.

Nic's standing next to Salyeh and Tian Li Chang, our starwinder, peering through his glasses at a map covered in Tian Li's scribbled notes and course plots and a bunch of papers with Salyeh's big, blocky numbers on them. Tian Li reads the winds and stars to see where we are on the Cloud Sea, and they show her things about the past, present, and future, like what the clouds are going to do and what might happen in our next port. We found her in T'an Gaban, begging in the market. Nic stopped, looked into her eyes, and offered her a place on board the *Orion*.

Starwinders have special eyes, see? They're gray and blue and green and brown all at the same time, and when they move, the colors swirl inside them, like they're not attached to anything. You can spot a starwinder a mile away, once you know what to look for.

I guess nobody in that market but Nic did.

Tian Li's short, and she's got long dark hair that waves in the breeze like it's got a mind of its own and sandstone-colored skin. She's steady as a block of rock and cares a lot about what's fair, and I think she's awesome, even though we aren't best friends. I'm pink as a peach, my hair looks like wet straw, and I've got more freckles than a freckle-covered mogwok, but she tells me she likes my style anyway. So we get along pretty well, on the whole of it.

Sal and I get on all right too. He's big—almost as tall as Nic, only thirteen, and still growing—and his black hair's wound in tight curls like the fronds of a fern, and cut real close to his head. He's quiet and skittish as a rabbit too, and his skin's the dark brown of burning paper. He joined the crew the same time me and Mrs. T did, and he comes from the desert city of Vash Abandi like I do.

It's real warm in Nic's cabin. The chandelier swings a little as the ship moves, and the windows rattle as the wind knocks against them. The propellers hum outside, just below.

"Nadya, there's a storm coming," Nic says.

I nod.

"We can't afford to change course and go around it like we usually do," he continues. "It's too big, and we've only got seven days of food for the gormling."

The gormling's a baby leviathan we've got in a big tank down in the hold. Some muckety-muck who lords it over Vash Abandi is giving it to some other muckety-muck who thinks he's king of Far Agondy. Muckety-mucks are real big on having pet leviathans, and this one offered Nic a lot of money to have us make a special run between the cities for him. I like the gormling—it's got long whiskers and rainbow scales that flash colored patterns in the darkness, and it makes neat shapes with its body when it's awake—but it only eats a special kind of pickled deep-sea cuttlefish, and a lot of it, and that means we have to make our run much faster than usual.

"I need you to get up in the cloud balloon with Mrs. Trachia," Nic finishes, "and stay there for the storm."

"Where's Pepper?" I ask.

Pepper Pott's our fireminder in training, the last member of our crew. She's my best friend and my most reliable backup when me and Tam argue. She's got hair the color of sunset, skin like a white-sand beach, and almost as many freckles as I do. Her job's the most dangerous of all: she can reach into the world beyond this one and call up the beings of fire who live there. They have names, apparently, although I can't understand them and sometimes I can't even tell them apart from regular flames. Pepper and Tall Thom, who's teaching her, get them to work in the engines for us, so we burn less coal and oil and whatnot. Keeps costs down, and it's better for the clouds too.

"She's trying to coax a little more speed out of the engines. It's going to be a bad storm, Nadya. I hope you're ready for it."

"I'm always ready." I grin.

Tian Li smiles at me. Salyeh looks up from his figures and shakes his head.

Nic just sighs. "Go on up to the balloon, Nadya," he says. "Mrs. Trachia needs you."

I bob my head and do as he says.

Back out on the deck, the wind's so bad I have to lean into it to stay on my feet. The ship bucks and twists, the sun's all the way gone, and the line of storm clouds has gotten so close I can almost reach out and touch it. Tall Thom's shucked into his black raincoat and hat, and he's wearing a safety belt clipped to two bolts by the ship's wheel.

Tam's wearing his rain slicks too. He's got two ropes running between his belt and the safety lines that run up and down the *Orion*'s deck, each rope clipped to its line by a big metal clasp. We call the belt ropes lobster claws, and they're like our little guardian spirits. We use them so often sometimes it feels like if I'm not wearing them I'm a squirrel without a tail. As I watch, Tam unclips his and ties a longer safety rope to his belt and a deck bolt near the ladder so he can move around more freely.

Tam meets me by the ladder that leads to the cloud balloon. He's holding my safety belt and lobster claws. Below us, the whitecaps on the waves have grown as big as dragons. Maybe there's leviathans down there, watching us hungrily. I hope not.

"Be careful this time, will you?" Tam mutters. He hands me the belt. It's got two leg loops and a waist loop, all tied together. I step through the leg loops and start jerking the rest of it up over my pants.

"I was *fine*, Tam." I grab the lobster claws and clip them to my belt, then to the first section of the safety rod next to the ladder.

Tam snorts, but the storm's getting closer and there's no time to argue. We've got an antenna that's supposed to catch lightning bolts and zap them away from the ladder, but I need to get off the metal and inside the balloon as fast as I can. The wind splatters rain into my eyes, and by the time I blink it clear, Tam's gone.

I work my way up the ladder as quick as I can, but it takes a while. To make sure you're safe while you climb, you slide the claws on your lines along the safety rod, then unclip them and lift them over big rings welded on to the rod every few feet. It's a pretty good system—you'll never fall farther than the space between the rings before the claws stop you.

The cloud balloon shivers and shakes above me as I climb. By the time I clip my claws on to the safety lines around the catwalks, the storm has practically swallowed us. The wind shrieks over the balloon's night-sky paint job and whips water into my face. Lightning flashes faster and faster, and the thunder drums a sheet-metal symphony in my ears.

I hop off the ladder and run for the iron door that leads into the cloud balloon. I have to set my shoulder against it and push with all my weight, but eventually it creaks open.

I unclip from the catwalks and step into a little metal room I call the waiting house. We use it to let people in and out of the balloon without letting a bunch of air escape with them.

The door slams shut behind me, and I crank a wheel inside to ratchet it down airtight. Then I push a big green button. A pump attached to the waiting house whirrs.

The air hisses as the pump sucks it out of the room. My ears pop a couple times, and it gets harder and harder to breathe. And then, when almost all the outside air has been sucked out of the waiting house, a little chime sounds.

The door to the inside of the cloud balloon creaks open. A puff of moist air warms the cramped metal benches around me. It smells of lilac and roses and orange trees and damp, musty plants.

The gills where my neck meets my shoulders flutter open.

I take a deep breath and step into the cloud balloon.

It feels like coming home.

CHAPTER 2

IN WHICH THE STORM HITS, AND NADYA IS RESCUED IN A MOST UNFORTUNATE FASHION.

Inside the cloud balloon, it's like another world.

It's bright, first off: always lit in golden rays from the sun-in-a-jar that hangs in the center of it. And it's damp too. A machine in the catwalks collects water from the clouds all day long. It stores it in a tank along the top of the balloon, then drips it through irrigation lines under the plants inside. Walking into the cloud balloon feels like walking into summer, no matter what time of year it is outside.

The balloon itself is made of aluminum. It's super lightweight and more durable than it looks, with heavier canvas and an aluminum skeleton inside to give it shape. The top of it inflates and deflates to make the ship rise and fall.

And, oh, the plants. There are big ferny ones. There are short, squat ones. There are tall, delicate trees and flowers and fruits and nuts. Bees and flies and beetles in black and gold and lime green buzz between them. The frogs are always chirping and ribbiting from their little mud hideaways, and the birds sing songs that remind me of home, that far-off place I can only remember clearly when I've got my eyes closed and the doorknob in my hand.

The cloud balloon's the only place on the *Orion* where I can breathe through my gills, and it feels *so* good to do it. Sometimes I think that's how I'm meant to breathe, and that my mouth and my nose and my lungs are just to help me fit in with other people. Mrs. Trachia says that's not true. But she also says that at the Roof of the World, where the skylungs came from, all the air was like this, and skylungs breathed with their gills all the time.

The cloud balloon jerks and shudders, and I wipe some rain off the back of my neck. Mrs. T's squatting by the pond underneath the sun-in-a-jar, talking to the frogs on their lily pads with her mind. I can hear the conversation clear as day. Right now I can only talk with plants and animals inside the cloud garden, but Mrs. T says that as I get older, I'll be able to talk to any plant or animal with my mind.

And how are you, my darlings? she asks.

She always calls things darlings. I think it's a bit over the top. I never use pet names with the frogs like that, and they seem to like me just fine anyway.

Happy.

Hungry.

Sleeping, leave me alone . . .

Mrs. T reaches down and strokes the frog I call Goldielocks.

. . . It's not a pet name, okay? It's a true name. We sat and tried on names for hours until I found one she said fit her. Everything has a true name. In Vash Abandi, they say that if you call someone by theirs, they have to listen to you. It's like a fundamental law of the universe, even for cloud frogs.

I understand, my lovelies, and I'll take care of it. But if you could, would you mind sleeping a little long today? We need to be just a little bit lower in the sky, you see.

The frogs grunt back their responses.

Okay.

Sure.

I was *sleeping, Zelda . . .*

"Mrs. T?" I ask. "Nic sent me to help." My voice sounds like it comes from my nose when I'm breathing with my gills. It always takes me a second to get used to it.

Mrs. T straightens up. She looks sort of like a willow tree with mottled bark the color of a golden, sunlit riverbank, and the billowing yellow dress she's wearing makes her look more willowy than usual. Her hair droops over her shoulders in long reddish-brown braids, almost all the way to her waist. A wine-red birthmark flows along her jaw, and her eyes are green as emeralds.

"Ah, Nadya," she says softly. "I'm glad you've come. Nic wants the ship a little lower, you see. I've been bleeding off a bit of the air in here, but I need to persuade our little friends to sleep through the storm, or their excitement will just puff us right back up again." She runs a finger along one of the big leaves next to her and sways as the cloud balloon shakes. "I could use your help with the birds, in particular."

The cloud balloon works by the principle of displacement, or something like that. When the plants and animals are awake and active, they breathe in mist from the Cloud Sea and breathe out a different kind of gas that puffs out the top of the cloud balloon. So when we need to go up, we try to get them excited. And when we need to go down, we let air out of the balloon and get them to sleep.

I look up. The birds come in black, yellow, orange, red, violet, blue, and about a zillion other colors. Most of them are smaller than my hand. They nest in the girders that make up the cloud balloon's skeleton. I only see a few of them flapping around.

"It looks like they're pretty hunkered down already, Mrs. T."

Mrs. T strolls around the edge of the pond, whispering to the ferns and the minnows and the palm trees.

"Hunkered, perhaps. But *hunkered* does not mean 'asleep.'"

I make a face at her, but I don't talk back. It's nice of her to let me talk to the birds, since it means I get to go into the rafters. I like doing that.

The metal girder I have to climb up to get there's warm and slick, but the frame was built with climbing in mind. Little rods stick out from it every foot or two, like wings for me to grab on to, and there are empty spaces in the girder just big enough for me to wedge my feet inside.

I'm about halfway to the first bluebird nest when the cloud balloon gives its biggest shake yet. My foot slips trying to get into the next hold, and then the balloon shakes again. My hand slips too.

The birds go nuts. They pour out of their nests like a flapping neon blizzard and fill the air with warnings.

Something's wrong! Something's wrong! It's wrong! It's wrong! Beware! It's wrong! The sky is falling! It's wrong, it's wrong!

"Nadya, darling," Mrs. Trachia calls from below, "I think perhaps on second thought you'd better come down."

The cloud balloon's canvas underskin pushes in toward the girders, then sucks back out again. It takes a big gust of wind to do that—enough to knock somebody down or throw them across the deck if they're outside.

"I guess so," I mutter, and I start back down the girder.

The balloon keeps shaking. The thunder's gotten loud enough I can hear it through the frame.

We must really be in it, I think as I hit the ground.

Mrs. T clucks at me and clears her throat.

I blush, just a little. I know better than to think stuff like that when I'm supposed to be calming everyone down. The plants and animals can hear me, after all.

Sorry, Mrs. T, I think.

She looks up, pointedly, at the birds.

Hey, everybody! I call out, but they're so worked up they don't seem to notice. They're flying from nest to nest, chirping in each other's faces about how everything's wrong and the sky's falling and the world's going to end.

Harriet! Bluebelly! Purplethroat! Wormgobbler! Butterbeak!

22

That gets their attention. True names, see? Universal law.

The birds I named stop flitting around and look down at me. Their neighbors notice and do the same.

We need everybody to stay calm and try to sleep right now, I tell them. The altitude gauge near the front of the balloon is reading steady, but the pressure gauge next to it is creeping higher. The higher the pressure inside the cloud balloon, the more it expands—and the higher the *Orion* rises.

Sleep!

But, Nadya, the sky . . .

We can't sleep!

The world is ending, Nadya!

Don't you know that everything's wrong?

I put my hands on my hips and give them my first-mate face, which I copied from Thom. *The world's not ending. It's just a little rainstorm. Like you get in here when the water tank gets too full. Think about that. Think about gentle mist and the feeling of being tucked tight in your nests.*

Butterbeak, perched on the edge of her nest with her two chicks peeping around her puffy yellow chest, blinks at me.

When the water tank rains, the world doesn't shake, Nadya.

This is true! This is true! This is true!

The other birds all start chirping again.

It's not the world, Butterbeak, it's just a balloon. The world is a big, round—

It is for us, Bluebelly says. She's got two eggs in her nest, still a week or more away from hatching.

I sigh. Before Nic and Mrs. T found me, I thought the world was a balloon for a while too. I remember them coming through the door that I'd forgotten was a door. Mrs. T seemed huge and alien. The smells that came in with her were so terrifyingly strange that I just screamed and screamed.

I'm sorry, I tell them, and the chirping calms down a little. *I promise the world isn't ending. Nothing bad's going to happen to you. Mrs. T and I won't let it.*

We can hear the outerplants, Wormgobbler says. He's perched on the bright glass rim of the sun-in-a-jar. *They're afraid.*

When I listen, I can hear them too.

They're used to the outside world. They're used to storms, even. But they sound terrified. They're shrieking like little seedlings staring a snake in the face for the first time.

If I make them calm down, I ask the birds, *will you sleep?*

Yes.

Yes!

Make them calm so the little ones don't fear!

Make them calm, Nadya! Make them calm!

Right, I say.

I close my eyes and reach for them with my mind.

It's a funny thing, trying to talk to a plant or animal you can't see. Usually, when you can look at who you're talking to, it's like a door opens in your mind and there's their voice. You watch them and you can hear them just as well as you can somebody talking out loud. But when you can't see them, you have to listen for them first. Then you figure out where their voice is coming from. Then you imagine them perfectly in your mind. And once you've got all that done, you have to get their attention somehow.

The outerplants are so scared I just can't do it. The wind's whipping them around and shaking the cloud balloon too hard. I can barely even figure out which ones are screaming and where they are.

So I open my eyes again, and I walk toward the waiting house.

"Nadya, I don't—" Mrs. T says behind me.

Before she can finish, I'm through the door.

The outside air hits my throat like a broomball going a hundred miles an hour. I'm still inside the waiting house, but my gills squeeze shut, and my lungs start breathing regular air again. The chime sounds. I crank the wheel on the outside door to unlock it. The balloon gives a violent shake, then another. The floor bucks up and plunges downward.

My stomach starts its this-was-a-bad-idea dance.

With the lock released, the door swings open. I stare into thick sheets of rain and lightning. A gust of wind swirls into the waiting house and knocks me forward.

My foot catches on the threshold, and then I'm falling.

Out the door.

Into the sky.

I grab for the railing along the catwalk, but I miss it. The *Orion* floats below me at a funny angle. I'm not in line to hit it. I'm not in line to hit anything. I'm going to fall all the way through the storm and into the ocean.

The sea looks up at me with gray, hungry eyes and opens its heaving mouth. The wind whips rain into my face. I fall faster and faster.

I close my eyes and scream.

All of a sudden something knocks the breath out of me. Someone grabs me around both arms and squeezes tight. There's a short stretch and a sharp tug. I'm not falling or screaming anymore. I can barely move.

I open my eyes and stare into the grungy, rain-covered face of Tam Ban.

There's a rope leading from his safety belt toward the deck of the *Orion*, and we're swinging back and forth on it in the wind. The whole world spins. I can't tell up from down.

"Hold on!" Tall Thom shouts.

The rope jerks. We move over the hull toward Thom's voice inch by inch. He must be hauling in Tam's safety rope.

Tam's crushing my ribs. I can barely breathe. I'm probably going to have a bruise tomorrow. He glares at me. "Didn't I tell you to be careful?" he shouts.

Thom keeps pulling us up, but the wind catches us and sends us skittering along the side of the *Orion*.

My head's still spinning and my chest hurts and I'm scared out of my mind so much I don't even know what to say back. "I—you—" I sputter. "Just because—"

The wind picks us up and slams us against the *Orion*'s battered hull. My doorknob wiggles up partway out of my pocket.

I can't reach it. My hands are pinned to my sides. I can

feel the doorknob getting closer and closer to the top of my pocket, where it'll get loose and fall into the ocean and be gone forever.

"Tam, my doorknob!" I shout.

"What?" Tam says.

"My doorknob, in my pocket! It's coming loose!" The wind picks us up and slams us down again and my heart jumps into my throat. The doorknob wiggles up a little farther.

"So?" Tam says. "Nadya, it's just an old piece of junk! Let it go!"

"If you let it fall, I'll never forgive you, Tam!"

"What do you want me to do, let you go and save your doorknob instead?" he shouts.

The wind keeps tossing us around. We're swinging now, side to side, and each time we get to the end of a swing, the doorknob slips a little farther out.

"Just—loosen your arms for a second!"

"No."

"Tam!"

"No!"

Swing. The doorknob's spilling out. I can feel it. *Swing.* It's going to be gone forever. I'm crying and flailing, trying to get to it, but I can't because Tam's got too tight a hold on me.

"*Tam!*"

Thom hauls us onto the *Orion.*

Tam lets me go just as the doorknob falls out of my pocket onto the deck, and I dive on it and curl around it in a ball. Thom clips our lobster claws to the safety lines. A second

27

later, the ship rolls again and pins all three of us against the portside rail.

When the *Orion* levels out, Thom takes off toward her wheel like a shot. I clutch the doorknob to my chest, shaking, smelling home, remembering a warm voice and a face I can't see clearly, someone pressing the doorknob into my hands and telling me to hold on to it, that they love me, that they'll be right back.

I open my eyes and grab Tam by the collar. Still trembling, I stuff the doorknob back in my pocket and push him against the rail. "You don't understand anything!" I shout. "I *hate* you!"

Tam's face goes gray. He gets up slowly, and then the gray turns darker and he takes a deep breath. "No, *you* don't understand!" he barks. He waves at the cloud balloon. "Life's not some stupid game, Nadya! Just because nothing bad's ever happened to you, just because you're dumb and lucky and Nic and Mrs. T's favorite and people always take care of you, it doesn't mean it'll always be that way!"

"Shut up!" I stand up too, thinking of my parents and losing them and how plenty of bad stuff has happened to me and how I'm not anybody's favorite and I haven't always had people to take care of me at all. "You shut up!"

"No!" he yells back. "Everybody always does what you want, but I don't have to, and I—"

"*Stow it!*" Thom cracks like a thunderclap from the wheel. An icy wash runs down my spine, like a glacier's just broken in half and poured a lake over the top of my head. "Back to your cabins, both of you!"

"But he—"

"But she—"

"*Now!*" Thom snaps. "I don't have time for this! Tam, send Tian Li and Salyeh out to help me when you go."

Tam's mouth drops open. Helping keep the ship safe during a storm is his most important job. It always has been. He glares at me like I've ruined his whole life, and then he staggers across the deck to the stairs by the wheel.

I turn around and stumble toward my cabin. The rain pours over my face and into my eyes. My stomach spins in circles. My chest heaves. I try not to think about the sky and the sea trying to swallow me. I try not to think about what Tam said. I try not to think about Thom scolding me and falling off the balloon and whether I've ruined my shot at being first mate. I try not to think about losing the most precious thing that ties me to home.

I try not to be afraid.

It doesn't really work.

 CHAPTER 3

IN WHICH THE SUN COMES OUT, AND NADYA FEELS LIKE CRYING.

It's morning. The silence of the broken engines after the storm is shattered by the crackling whisper of . . .

"Nadya?"

It's morning. The crispness in the air after the storm is flooded by the savory scent of . . .

"Nadya!"

It's morning. Both engines broke during the storm last night, and it feels silent as a library without them running. But the air isn't really crisp so much as damp. My journal curls up at the edges on my desk. The clothes I was wearing yesterday are wadded in a soggy ball in the corner.

Pepper Pott bangs on my door, and I smell fresh-fried bacon.

I don't have good words for that smell. If I had to name it like I do the plants and animals, I'd call it *fangloose*. And I'd give it a title too, like Bringer of Breakfasty Goodness, or Harbinger of Deliciousity, or That Which I Smell Before Drooling.

So I stand up from my desk and open the door. And there's Pepper. She's wearing blue overalls with yellow stains on them and she smells like fish, which makes me feel a little guilty. It means she's been down feeding the gormling, which was supposed to be my job on this trip. All I've been doing is sitting at a desk, trying to make words come together in a way I think sounds pretty.

"Still scribbling, huh?" she says with a grin, and the blood rushes into my face. Everybody teases me about journaling. They just don't get it.

Pepper's curls are about as foofed as I've ever seen them, and there are puddles on the deck behind her. Some of the wood has dried off, but most of it's still that three-shades-darker-than-usual brown that means it hasn't sweated out the storm yet.

In one hand, Pepper holds a plate with four eggs sunny-side up, six strips of bacon, and a heap of pan-fried potatoes and peppers. In the other, she's got two forks and a bottle of hot sauce.

"This is for both of us," she says. She lets herself into my cabin and shuts the door behind her.

Pepper and I've known each other about three years, since Nic started gathering the crew, and we've been best friends pretty much the whole time. Salyeh's been on the ship longer—as long as I have, actually—but he's always been pretty quiet and mostly spends time with Nic. So when Pep joined up, all fire and curiosity, we just clicked. She followed me around asking questions about the *Orion* whenever she wasn't working, and then she started asking about me, and then I started asking about her, and we found out we both love to play broomball and eat bacon and drop stuff over the side of the ship and watch it hit the water and a million other things, and pretty soon we did everything together. She takes care of me when I'm sad or sick, and I do the same for her. I can't imagine life without her anymore. I haven't told her that, but I think she knows it anyway.

"Thanks, Pep," I mumble.

She plonks down on the floor and shoves a fork in my direction.

"Eat," she says.

I sit down and take the fork and do as she says. I start with a strip of bacon, then crumble another one up and start mixing it into my eggs. She starts by slathering hot sauce all over her half of the plate.

I have to admit, it's a great breakfast. Food's been a big part of our friendship, ever since the beginning. Pep used to live behind a restaurant in the Free City of Myrrh, down by the waterfront where the pearl divers eat on the beaches under big, shady fern trees the size of houses. Nic brought me there for breakfast when we were in port once. While we were waiting for a table, me and her got chatting about whether duck eggs or quail eggs or chicken eggs tasted better (we decided chicken eggs for breakfast, quail eggs for lunch, and duck eggs if you wanted to be fancy). I could see Nic's wheels turning even before he found out she was a fireminder, and when he saw her start talking to the spirits dancing under the range where the restaurant's owners did their cooking, he offered her a spot on the *Orion* right away.

"Everyone was asking where you were," Pep says around a mouthful of potatoes. We usually eat breakfast and dinner as a crew. Sometimes lunches too, if we can swing it.

"I wasn't hungry," I mutter.

Pep looks at me and raises her left eyebrow like halfway up her forehead.

I guess I should have made up a better excuse. I'm *always* hungry. I eat like a horse. A flying horse. And I'm proud of it. I tuck into my potatoes and scrape some hot sauce over from the lake on Pepper's half of the plate.

"When I say everyone, Nadj, I mean everyone but Nic and Thom and Mrs. T. They didn't seem too surprised."

I move on to my eggs. I don't say a thing.

"Tam was acting weird too. Barely touched his breakfast. Had these big purple bags under his eyes, right here." She pokes the soft spot between her cheekbones and her eyeballs with a greasy finger. "He didn't sass anyone. Not once."

When I think of Tam, my gills start to flap a bit and my teeth grind together.

"What happ—"

"He rescued me. And he said my doorknob was just a piece of junk. And he called me dumb and lucky and said nothing bad ever happened to me and everybody always does what I want and he's a first-class stupid moron jerk, in general."

We start to talk at the same time, but Pepper gets cut off when whatever's in her mouth sticks in the wrong pipe. She coughs it out, and a hunk of potato flies past my ear and lands somewhere near my desk.

"He *rescued* you?"

I look at the floor. "I fell off the ship, and he jumped after me and caught me, and then the wind was whipping us around and the doorknob almost fell out of my pocket and I was yelling about it, and then he started yelling back and then Thom got mad at us."

Pepper sets down her fork. She leans back and squints one eye at me, like she's trying to figure out if I'm telling the truth. I huff and raise my eyebrows back at her.

"So he had his arms around you pretty good then, huh?"

I nod and frown. She's focusing on the wrong part of the story, but she does that sometimes.

As I'm frowning, she gets a grin the size of Far Agondy on her face.

"Was it nice?"

"*Pep!*"

I get so frustrated I can't breathe right. My gills start to flap and suck in air, but it's all wrong for them and then I can't get in air through my nose and mouth anymore. I start coughing and spluttering and wheezing.

Pep puts an arm around my shoulders and rubs the back of my neck. "Oh geez, Nadj. I didn't mean to tickle your gills like that. I was just teasing. Sorry."

She rubs my arm. I nod. My gills and lungs start to get

along again, and breathing gets easier. There's snot dripping out of my nose and water coming out of my eyes. I wipe my face with my sleeve.

"S'okay," I mumble. "But can we *please* talk about the stuff that matters now?"

Pepper grins again and monkey-scrambles back to her side of the plate. The lake of hot sauce has flooded all the food that's left, and she watches it slide around for a second before stabbing another potato. "So you're upset because of what Tam said? Or because you fell off the *Orion* and Thom got mad at you?"

I take a second to think over her question. The doorknob's back in my desk, safe and sound, but Tam could've made me lose it. I'm really worried that falling off the ship and Thom getting mad at me means Nic won't choose me as first mate. And as much as I hate to admit it, what Tam said about me being lucky and dumb and everybody doing what I want all the time kinda got to me. I look around at my cabin, the best of the kids' ones. I won it in a coin toss against Salyeh when we came aboard.

"Both, I guess," I say. My stomach feels like it's trying to hide behind my spine. "I mean, what if I ruined my chance to be first mate? And you don't think he's right, do you? About the rest?"

Pep stops shoveling eggs into her mouth and grabs my cheeks to make me look into her eyes. "Of. Course. Not," she says with the food still in her mouth. She swallows and raises an eyebrow, like she's waiting for me to show I believe

35

her, and I nod. "Thom gets mad at us all the time," she says. "If that mattered, Nic couldn't pick anybody as first mate. As for the other stuff . . ." She waves her fork around like she's clearing smoke. "Tam thinks we're all dumb and lucky, including him. He doesn't trust anybody, just like he doesn't trust fireminding and starwinding. He's weird like that."

My chest relaxes. I feel like that invisible smoke she cleared was real, 'cause I can breathe easier all of a sudden. I smile. It's amazing how good she can make me feel just by talking to me, like she takes the big noodle bowl of stuff I'm worried about and untangles it and gets it to make sense. Underneath I'm still a little worried, but I feel a lot better overall.

She puts her hand on top of mine and squeezes, smiling back. "I'm glad you're okay, Nadj."

"Thanks," I say. A second later our forks are back on the plate, fencing over the remaining potatoes. "How's the *Orion*?"

After a bit of swashbuckling, Pep gives up the battle and sucks some hot sauce off her fingers. She shrugs. "I think Mrs. T has things in pretty good shape up in the cloud balloon, but you might want to ask her about it, just in case. Salyeh's in the hold doing inventory, and Nic has Tian Li with him. I think we lost a lot of atmosphere, and he wants to find a good patch of brightcloud to sail into so the plants can get working again."

Brightcloud is the kind of cloud—white, puffy, not too dense—that works best when we need to fill up the cloud balloon. *Atmosphere* is what everyone else calls the air inside the cloud balloon, but I don't like the name. It's too cold and bland for what that air really is—what it feels like.

Not that they'd know.

I sigh and abandon the last potato. Pepper scoops it into her mouth, then lifts the plate and drinks down the hot sauce.

"Nic wants to see you after breakfast," she says when she's done. She puts the plate down. "You gonna be all right, Nadya?" Her eyes are bright and wide, like they are before she calls up fire from the World Beyond.

"Yeah," I say.

"Swear it on a finger?" She holds out her hand, pinky first, and I grasp it with mine and shake.

"Good," she says. "If you need to talk, I'll be down at the engines with Thom, doing my thing."

I nod. Her thing usually means a whole lot of frowning at gauges, talking to herself, making adjustments to a bird's nest of brass and iron valves sticking out of the boilers, and occasionally banging on one with a wrench and shouting at the fire spirits inside to stop slacking off. She smiles, gathers up the plates and forks, and slips out the door.

I shuck out of my nightclothes and into a pair of short pants and a tank top. And then I get to work.

Normally Mrs. T would get us all together for lessons in the morning, but because the ship's so banged up I spend the rest of the day in the cloud balloon checking plants and soil acidity or out on the catwalks spot-welding broken trusses with her. Meanwhile Pep, Tam, and Thom work on the engines, and Sal and Tian Li get the rest of the ship back in order. I'm extra careful with my lobster claws on the catwalks, crawling slow like a first-timer from plant to plant over the warm metal bars. The wind is soft and the sky is clear, but my stomach takes a tumble anytime I look down and see the *Orion* and the blue sweep of the sea below me. It's hard not to imagine falling and falling and falling forever.

Inside the balloon, things are pretty messed up. Some of the plants have shifted around. The frogs have buried themselves in the bottom of the pond. And the air smells wrong. There's too much outside air and not enough garden air. (*That's what I'll call it,* I think. I decide to tell Pepper next time I see her and start using the name in my journal.)

"Everyone got very excited after you fell, Nadya," Mrs. T explains. "I had to vent a lot of air to keep us from rising."

I look at my feet. Mrs. T hasn't said anything yet, but I know it's my fault. I shouldn't have gone outside in the storm. She didn't want me to go, and I knew it, but I moved so fast she didn't have time to stop me. The birds look sick and sleepy up in their nests. Some of the bigger leafy plants have started to turn yellow at the edges.

Mrs. T's arm, draped in soft cloth, wraps around my shoulders, carefully avoiding my gills. I dig my fingernails into my palms.

"It's going to be okay," Mrs. T says. She hugs me close.

But Bluebelly's lying with her head on the edge of her nest and her pulse beating fast in her little neck. Wormgobbler

38

sways bravely on his perch atop the sun-in-a-jar. The fish are barely moving in the pond. I see the yellow tint of the plant next to me, and my lips start to tremble. Maybe Tam was right about me. Maybe I am just dumb and lucky after all.

"Shh, Nadya *rybka*," Mrs. T says. "It's going to be okay."

I know that. The cloud balloon has been through worse before. Much worse. But that doesn't change the fact that it's not okay right now, and it's all my fault.

CHAPTER 4

IN WHICH NADYA ENCOUNTERS TAM, AND NIC PULLS A NASTY TRICK.

The sun's already set by the time I start climbing back to the *Orion*'s deck. My stomach keeps trying to turn inside out when I look down, but I do it anyway. I want my life to go back to normal, and that includes being able to look at the deck and the ocean without thinking I'm going to die.

First things first, I head down to the cargo hold to feed the gormling. The hold's a cavernous space like the belly of a full-grown leviathan, reaching right up through all three decks of the ship to the top. It's usually full of gear and tools and spare parts on long rows of big shelves. We earn most of our money from selling the stuff the plants make and don't take on a lot of extra cargo. Nic says he values the freedom of setting our own schedule and picking our own ports more than the money we make hauling stuff for other people.

But this trip we've cleared a space right near the door for the gormling. Its tank's a little bit taller than I am and twice

as wide and long. The gormling
looks like a mix between a giant catfish
and a huge eel, five feet long and about as wide as my thigh.
I've got no idea where the muckety-mucks got it, but I bet it
wasn't easy to find. Leviathans only live in the deepest parts
of the ocean.

As I get into the hold, I'm greeted by two flashing lines
of bright-sky blue spots just below the row of spines on the
gormling's back, pulsing like little stars. Tonight it's floating
in a figure eight, tumbling slowly end over end, long whiskers trailing down its side like ribbons.

Its whiskers twitch every time I take a step, and when I
pick up its smelly bucket of preserved cuttlefish and uncover
its tank, it uncurls and darts up to the surface. It figured out
the feeding-time routine pretty quick when we got it aboard.

It snarfs down its food and turns its glowing eyes on me, big as walnuts. Then it drifts up to the top of the tank and starts to purr, shivering all down its back and shaking the water with its spines. I'm pretty sure that means it's happy. I press my fingers against the glass, and the gormling rubs its cheek on the other side, and then I head back up on deck.

When I get there, Tian Li's sitting on the aft deck by the wheel, staring upward. She's got three charts, which are like maps of the ocean, a compass, two pencils, and a piece of scrap paper covered in numbers next to her. She's probably been checking our position and planning a course for us, but she must be done now, because she's not writing anything down. The sky's completely clear, and the stars sparkle across it like pieces of diamond winking between the folds of a velvet cape.

I pull my pocket watch from my shorts and decide to join her. It's six past the songbird, which means we've got less than an hour before dinner. I don't want to spend that time alone in my cabin, and everybody else is probably making the meal, including Tam. I'm not quite ready to run into him yet.

I climb the creaky wooden stairs up to the aft deck. Thom has the big wheel that changes the angle of the *Orion*'s propellers to steer her locked in place. Tian Li must be keeping an eye on it while he gets some rest. She does a lot to keep the ship on course. It's possible to navigate without a good starwinder to read the stars and figure out where you are on the Cloud Sea, but nobody likes to. There aren't any landmarks out here, and that can make it hard for even the best navigators to figure out a ship's position. But Tian Li's great at it already and getting better every day.

"Got room for me?" I ask her.

"Sure," she says. She stretches her arms and leans back. She doesn't take her eyes off the stars, though.

I look up with her. I always like comparing the real night sky with the design on the balloon. The biggest difference, other than the ferns, is that the real stars change. Tonight, the long, milky streak of the Cat's River sweeps across the sky over the cloud balloon. The orange trickle of starlight we call the Fruitstream crosses it just above the horizon. The rest of the stars group together in clouds and banks and clusters, like living things huddling for warmth in the cold and lightless void.

Tian Li sighs happily. The night sky is beautiful to me, but I think it's a whole lot more than that to her. She loves being out at sea. T'an Gaban, where she came from, is cloudy and fogged in most of the year, and even when it's not it's full of electric lights and nightclubs and steam and smoke. Last time we went there, I could only find three stars through all the haze. After Tian Li joined the crew, she slept on the *Orion's* deck for a whole week, and the first time she saw the starfilled sky over the deep ocean, she cried with happiness.

"What do you see up there?" I ask. I settle down next to her. Her hair pours down her back in long waves, and her eyes are covered by a cloudy haze. They get like that when she looks at the stars.

"A lot of things," she answers. "I see a thick band of clouds to the east and a wide stretch of empty sea to the south. I see ships north and west of here, flickering. And I see you falling and screaming, and shouting and commanding, and . . ." Her cheeks lose a little bit of color. "And other things."

I take a deep breath. *She doesn't know what happened*, I tell myself. Tian Li sees the future and the past and the present as one big blur when she looks at the sky. I've heard Nic trying to teach her to tell the difference between them. He's not a starwinder, but he's worked with a lot of them, and he does his best to help Tian Li learn to use her gifts.

"Shouting and commanding, huh?" I ask.

She nods.

"Must be the future." I grin. "How old am I? Do I look like I have my own ship yet?"

Tian Li turns her eyes from the stars toward my face. The milky haze swirls and melts away.

"You look the same as you do today, Nadya. I don't think it's a distant future."

I grin bigger. First mate then, I bet.

As I'm thinking that, the lamps start to kindle along the ship's rails. Tall Thom's lanky silhouette moves between them. Every time a new light flares, I get a glimpse of his face. It's all stubbly, like he hasn't shaved yet today, and he's frowning and grumbling. Come to think of it, it's weird to see him calling fire. He almost always makes Pep do it, though he knows a lot about it and she says he's real good at it. Wherever she is, Pep must be pretty busy.

He growls at a fire creature that spits sparks back up at him like it's blowing a raspberry, and I wince, remembering him yelling at me and Tam yesterday. I don't like thinking about that, so I decide to change the subject.

"So other things, huh?" I wiggle my eyebrows at Tian Li. "Like you and Salyeh making out, or what?"

The skin on her cheeks turns darker. "No, Nadya," she says. She sounds a little frustrated. I've been teasing her about Salyeh for most of a month. But it's just so *obvious* they like each other, and neither of them wants to admit it. I can't help myself.

"What happened to you yesterday?" she asks.

My stomach flips. She's getting better. Soon she won't even question what's the past and what's the future. She'll just know.

"I fell off the cloud balloon," I mutter.

"Tam caught you, didn't he?"

Tian Li's looking at the stars again, but her eyes haven't hazed over. She's just watching them, like I do.

"Yes," I mumble. My gills burn. It's not fair that she saw me get humiliated. It's not fair that she knows what happened, even though I never told her.

She turns to me, and her hand sneaks over and touches my shoulder. "Must have been scary," she says.

I nod. Tian Li smiles and rubs my back. My cheeks cool down. For a few minutes, we sit and watch the stars.

Then someone thumps up the stairs to the aft deck. I look over, expecting to see Thom, but it's not Thom.

It's Tam.

"Tian Li, dinner's gonna be in about—" He freezes, one foot still on the steps, when he sees me.

I scowl and wait for him to say something insulting.

He pulls his hair out of his eyes and swallows. "Hi, Nadya," he says.

I just keep on scowling.

Tam's eyes jump over to Tian Li, then back to me. After a second, they get narrow and mad. "Dinner's in ten," he snaps. He stumps back down the stairs to the main deck.

I let out a long, deep breath.

"He saved your life," says Thom's voice behind me. I nearly jump out of my skin. Tian Li chirps in surprise.

I watch Tam on the main deck while I wait for my heart to slow down. He's clipping his lobster claws to the ladder up to the cloud balloon, probably on his way to find Mrs. T. "I know," I mutter.

"You could be a little nicer about it." A lamp ignites near my head. The heat cast by the fire creature inside warms my shoulders. "Off this ship, there aren't many people who would jump into the blue like that for you. Have you thanked him yet?"

"No," I say quietly. I don't want to. Not till he apologizes to me.

Halfway up to the cloud balloon, Tam stops and looks in my direction. I don't think he realizes we can see him as well as we can in the starlight. And I'm sure he's too far away to see that we're watching.

Tian Li gets up. "I'm going down to the galley," she announces, and then she walks away.

"Thom," I ask when she's gone, "did you hear what he said—"

"I heard him get frustrated. He'd just jumped off the ship for you, Nadya. He was still scared, and fear makes people say things they regret. It was wrong of him, but he'll realize that eventually. It's not worth fighting over."

I squirm. Thom's smart, and what he says sounds right. I know I should listen to him if I want to make first mate. But when I think about Tam calling me dumb and lucky, saying that the stuff I care about is just junk, my stomach clenches around itself. I don't know if I want to get along with someone like that.

But I don't tell Thom that. I just follow Tian Li to the galley.

The galley's one of my favorite places on the *Orion*.

It's right near the heart of the ship—on the middle deck, smack dab in the center. It's got a great big table down the spine of it, bolted to the floor with long benches on the sides. The walls have sketches and paintings and knickknacks from the ports we visit, plus orange-tinted brass lamps from T'an Gaban that give off cozy, homey light. There's room for everybody and then some, and we always end up clustered at one end, sitting next to our best friends. Me and Pep. Tian Li and Salyeh. I guess Tam doesn't really have a best friend on the ship, but that's his own fault as far as I'm concerned.

Tian Li's and Pepper's cabins are real close to the galley. Tall Thom's and Salyeh's aren't far away either. Sometimes I'm a little jealous of them—I can only imagine what it's like to wake up with the smell of food in your nostrils most mornings. Nic does all the cooking, and he's great at it.

You have to go through the dining room to get to the kitchen, and when I do, Salyeh's putting the finishing touches on the table settings, and Pepper and Tian Li are bringing out the serving dishes. There's a big pot full of chewy sweet-potato noodles and a pan that's got broccoli and water chestnuts and string beans and sweet peppers covered in thick orange sauce. Another pan has egg-fried brown rice in it, and there are plates full of diced oranges and bite-sized pieces of pineapple scattered around the table.

I follow Pep into the kitchen to see if I can help, but Nic's already wiping down dishes. He just shoos me back into the dining room.

The rest of the gang trickles in one by one. Tall Thom's already there when I get back from the kitchen, and Mrs. T shows up a few seconds later.

Tam comes in last. He flashes me a glare before lowering his head and slinking to the seat farthest away from me. I end up sitting between Pepper and Salyeh and make a point of not looking in his direction.

Nic says a quick prayer to Goshend, the seaweed-bearded god of the oceans, and then we tuck in. The food tastes every bit as good as it looks. The sauce is tangy and sweet, the rice is sticky and moist, and the noodles cling to my ribs and make me feel warm and full.

We eat every last bite. That's one of my favorite things about living on the *Orion*: We have two big ice chests to store supplies in, but there's no room for leftovers unless we're running real skinny at the end of a voyage. Almost everything we eat is grown right here in the cloud garden, and we have to eat it all so that it doesn't spoil.

There's no dessert, since we had fruit with dinner, but I don't mind that. We pass the pineapple and orange around until there's nothing left.

"So," Nic says when the food's gone.

The chatter around the table lurches to a stop in fits and whispers. When nobody's talking, Nic continues.

"We took some damage during the storm, and it's going to make our schedule tight. We've got six days of food left for the gormling and we're still four and a half days from Far Agondy. That means we need to get moving as soon as possible so we maintain some margin for error. I want to thank Salyeh and Tian Li for stepping up to help Thom on deck yesterday. It would've been much worse without them. And Tam deserves special mention for his bravery during the earlier stages of the storm." He nods toward the three of them. "Nice job, all of you."

I clap along with everyone else, but I feel my heart clambering down toward my stomach. Maybe he'll pick one of them as first mate, or Tam because he saved me. Salyeh smiles bashfully, and Tian Li takes a little mock bow. Tam looks relieved. My gills burn. I should be happy for them. We're supposed to be friends, supposed to be a team. But I just wish it was me Nic was thanking for good work instead.

Nic clears his throat. "Repairs on the engines are almost complete, but the housing on one of them got bent, and we can't use that engine safely until it's fixed. Tomorrow morning, Tam, Thom, Nadya, and I will go out and hammer it back into place. I want us under way by tomorrow afternoon."

Tam jerks his head up. I sink a little lower in my chair. Nic plows right on talking, like he hasn't noticed.

I'm sure he has, though. I bet he put us on the same team on purpose. Nic doesn't miss a thing that happens on the *Orion*.

"The rest of you will be on normal duties," he says. He looks around the table. Each of us nods when his eyes reach us.

"Our biggest concern other than the engine is the state of the cloud balloon. We lost a lot of atmosphere—"

"Garden air," I mumble under my breath. Pepper elbows me below the table.

"—during the storm, and the plants on the catwalks are in pretty rough shape. Tian Li has found a pocket of brightcloud just off the fastest route to Far Agondy, and we're going to head into it as soon as the engines are working again. We'll head through the clouds and get everything back in shipshape, and then we'll continue east across the Cloud Sea and make port."

I scrape my fork over my plate trying to get up a last little nibble of sauce. The kind of runs we make used to be impossible. Waterships took weeks to get across the Cloud Sea, and a lot of them never made it—they got wrecked by reefs and whirlpools or gobbled by leviathans and giant squid in the deep water. It was like that as far back as anyone knows, but a couple decades ago some skylung engineers and the scientists in T'an Gaban figured out how to make balloons lift ships into the air, and then the whole world opened up. Everybody who can takes to the skies these days. It's faster and safer than travel by land or sea.

Nic's always telling us it's amazing what cloudships have done for the world and how important we are—that each of the six big cities around the Cloud Sea has things the others need, but they're so far apart with so few people in between that it used to be really hard for them to trade those things. I guess it's true, when I think about it. Vash Abandi sends fuel and spices and medicine to Far Agondy, which sends back silver and maple syrup and coal. T'an Gaban trades fruits, vegetables, gold, and livestock. Myrrh sells timber and makes the best musical instruments and barbecue sauce. Deepwater has different timber and medicine, and Nash Valour has fruit you can't find anywhere else and the best schools in the world.

The cities trade ideas too, I think. Each one's ruled by a different government: there's the merchant lords in Vash Abandi and Far Agondy, elected representatives in T'an Gaban, the Free City of Myrrh, and Nash Valour, and a council of hereditary lords in Deepwater. They don't compete much,

51

except in trade, and they're all benefiting now that they can move goods, people, and information so easily. Ships like ours make it happen, and I'm proud of that.

Nic looks around the table again. "Do you all understand what we need to do?"

There are more nods.

"Thom, Zelda, anything to contribute?"

Mrs. T looks hard at me for a second, but shakes her head. Thom, on the other hand, stands up.

"Look," he says gruffly. "You all know I'm leaving for a while after we make port in Far Agondy, and I've heard you whispering about who's going to take my place. So I just want to make things clear. First off: I'll only be away a few months, so don't get too excited. Second: Nic, Mrs. T, and I will pick whoever we think displays the best leadership over the rest of the voyage. If you've got questions about what that means, come and ask us." He sits back down and drums his fingers on the table edge, then glances up at Nic. "That's all from me," he finishes.

Nic nods. "Then you're dismissed, everyone. Nadya and Tam, I want you in work clothes and safety belts by ten after morningdove tomorrow. Thom and I will see you in the iron-room."

I glance at Tam, but he's back to staring at the wall. So I sigh and nod in Nic's direction, and then I help clear the table.

Since he didn't help with cooking or setting up either, Tam

should wash dishes with me. To be honest, I'm looking forward to it. I'd rather finish our fight now, without Nic and Thom watching, than tomorrow out on the engines. And I need to show my leadership too. Prove I'm right.

But Tam doesn't show up. Instead, Salyeh shoulders through the kitchen door, rolls up his sleeves, and handles the rinsing and drying while I do the scrubbing. It reminds me of the first month or so of my time on the ship, before we picked up anybody else, when it was just me, him, and the grown-ups.

"Things go okay today?" I ask.

He shrugs. "Mostly. The parts we're using to fix the engines will set us back a bit, but if we can deliver the gormling on time and get a good price for our fire opals, we should still earn enough to make a deposit at Farsky and Sons after we resupply. How's the plant that makes the opals?"

I clear my throat, remembering my visit to the outerplants in the afternoon. "A little beat up, but she'll hang in there." Opal's hard to hurt—a big, thorny purple vine that takes up two full bays and crawls across about six feet of the frame around them. She lost a few leaves in the storm, and she was wailing like a little kid whose fingernails are sore after they've been trimmed too close, but she kept all her buds, and she wasn't any more hurt than that kid would be, really. She can be a bit dramatic sometimes.

When I ask Sal what Tam's doing, he shrugs.

"He said he'd take my deck-scrubbing duties this week if

I handled dishes for him tonight. I know a good deal when I see one." He grins, but when he turns to put a plate away, his eyes get serious.

He and Tam aren't the best of friends, but they're the only two boys on the ship. I know they talk. I bet Tam's running his mouth off behind my back already.

Sal and I are just finishing up the dishes when we hear a sharp, high whistle from the deck, followed by Tian Li's voice, shouting.

"Ship ahoy!" she yells. A moment later, the horn on the back of the *Orion*, loud enough to make the walls rattle, blares out our identifying code, two short blasts at one note followed by two long ones at a slightly lower note.

Sal and I freeze, and then we cram the remaining dishes in their racks, still wet, and run up the stairs to see who's coming.

CHAPTER 5

IN WHICH ANOTHER SHIP IS ENCOUNTERED, AND NADYA LEARNS A FEW THINGS OF GREAT IMPORTANCE.

By the time Sal and I get topside, Tam and Pepper are already at the rail. The fire spirits glitter brightly in their lamps, and out in the distance, it's easy to make out the shape of a ship coming toward us by the outline of her deck lights and the catwalks around her cloud balloon. There's a pretty lively guessing game going on about who it might be while we wait for her to signal with her horn or get close enough we can spot her balloon design.

"It's the *Walrus*," Pepper says. "See how wide the deck is?"

"No," Tam says, "it's *Sandskimmer*. The deck's not that wide—it just looks that way 'cause she's turning toward us."

Most of us cloudscrapers know each other pretty well. There are a lot of traders, but not that many who grow their own cargo on catwalks, and only the Six Cities have markets big enough to bother flying between—most of the rest of the

55

world's just wild spaces dotted with tiny villages. So scrapers see each other fairly often when we're heading in and out of port. It's a little more unusual to see a ship out here in the middle of the ocean, and we always jump at the chance to swap news and talk with old friends.

I don't think the ship headed toward us looks like either the *Walrus*—a wallowing old cog with a scary-big cloud balloon painted with a giant, lounging walrus that usually just flies between T'an Gaban and the Free City of Myrrh on the western continent—or the *Sandskimmer*, a fast little needle of a ship that mostly runs courier routes between the merchants in Far Agondy and Vash Abandi, with occasional trips farther inland on either side. It's more like . . .

"*Emerald Dream*," I breathe. It's getting closer, and I think I can see its jade railing glowing in the light of its deck lamps.

"It can't be *Dream*," Tam says. "We just saw her in Vash Abandi, and she was headed south to T'an Gaban. It's got to be *Sandskimmer*."

I'm about to remind him that ships can change course, but then the incoming ship blasts out her code, and I don't have to. Two long, low notes, followed by a long note a little higher and then a long note back at the low pitch.

I grin. "*Emerald Dream*," I say again. "Just like I told you."

Tam opens his mouth, shuts it again, and then stomps up toward the aft deck. *Score!* I think. One point for Nadya.

Then I turn and watch the *Dream* come up alongside us, and I forget all about Tam.

She's a beautiful ship. *Dream* is balanced like the *Orion* in terms of height and width, but she's a little bit longer, and it makes her look fast and sleek. Her cloud balloon's sort of cigar shaped to match, and it's got a design that fits her name perfectly: swirling clouds in a dozen shades of green, with little people and creatures and scenes poking out of the gaps between the clouds, painted so small you have to get right up in the catwalks to see them. *Dream*'s skylungs invited me over once to show me, and I found a little girl with sage-green skin and tiny black horns and a tail in one of those gaps, smiling softly and clutching an emerald the size of my fist. Discovering her felt like finding a real live gemstone all for myself.

I'm pretty sure *Dream*'s the most luxurious ship in the world. On her mid-deck, she has glittering windows, and on top of them she's got that railing of dark green, luminous jade. All the metal on her, from her lamps to her hinges, is shining, polished brass. She used to be the personal yacht of one of the lords in Deepwater. Word is Carla Lanza, her captain, won the ship from him in some kind of bet, and he was so mad she couldn't put into the port there for two years, until she got on the good side of a couple of the other lords.

Dream swoops toward us, flying across a black sky speckled with stars, the ocean swelling calmly beneath her. Soon she's close enough that we can see her crew on the deck. I squint at the cloud balloon, trying to spot Amy and Amber, the twins

who take care of it. I can't find them, but I think
I see their fireminder and polymath waving
from the railings.

"*Orion* ahoy!" booms a woman's voice
from *Dream*'s aft deck.

"*Dream* ahoy!" Thom shouts back.

Dream's propellers slow down, and the
ship sheds its speed quickly. On its aft
deck, I can see its pilot making quick adjustments at the wheel. She brings her ship in
slowly and tightly, and me and Pepper run along
the deck throwing out the little rubber bumpers that
will keep the ships from damaging each other once they're
alongside. *Dream*'s crew does the same, and a moment later
we're tossing ropes to each other and tying the ships together
while Thom and *Dream*'s pilot chat with each other and laugh.

We've just barely got the ships lashed
together when a door leading under
the aft deck of *Dream* opens, and
Carla Lanza steps into the night.

She's short and kind of squat, and she's got skin the color of a faded old playing card and long black hair. Her brown eyes glitter in the light of *Dream*'s lamps. She moves like a cat, each footstep quick like she could change directions and jump ten feet in a heartbeat. She wears black pantaloons and a black shirt with long, lacy cuffs, and she leans against the rail of her ship and raises an eyebrow at Thom.

"Permission to come aboard?" she asks bluntly. Her voice sounds like a hammer, all business.

"Denied," Thom says, but he winks at her. "Until the captain's out of the head, anyway."

Carla's businesslike manner evaporates into a grin, and a second later the door to Nic's cabin opens and he steps out, shaking his head. "A little decorum, please, Thom," he says softly.

Thom coughs. "Sorry, Nic," he says.

Nic nods and walks over to the rail. "As for you, you always have permission to come aboard this ship, Carla *tesorita*. I told you when you left, it would never stop being home."

Carla blushes a little and vaults over the railing, and she and Nic hug each other and talk too softly for me to hear. She used to be one of Nic's orphans too, part of his first crew like Thom was. Me and the others are the third set he's trained up. He's never told me why he does it, but I'll wheedle it out of him someday. Carla hands Tam, who's sitting on the stairs to the aft deck, a package, and then she, Thom, and Nic walk into Nic's cabin, and I'm back to staring at *Emerald Dream*'s stone railings and brass lamps and sleek, shimmering cloud balloon.

A sharp whistle gets me to look up just in time to see a comet with brown hair and brown leather boots plunging toward me from *Dream*'s balloon. My heart flies into my throat, and for a second I'm back staring down at the ocean, missing my grip on the catwalk's railing and plummeting over the side, until I realize the comet is Amber sliding down a rope, not someone falling toward me.

Amber lands with a *thump* and a grin in front of me. "Hey, Nadj," she says. She heard Pepper use the nickname once and she's never called me by my full name since. "You look green as a fish. You sick?"

I shake my head, trying to find my voice. Amber intimidates the heck out of me. She's tall and beautiful and smart and seventeen. She's dark like Thom, and has eyes that match her name. "No, I'm fine," I say finally, wishing something a whole lot snappier had come out instead.

"Your outerplants are looking pretty good," Amber says, nodding toward the *Orion*'s cloud balloon. "You guys miss the storm?"

I look up, trying to see what she's seeing. I thought the plants looked terrible this afternoon. "No, we got hit pretty hard."

Amber whistles. "Wo-ow," she says. "Man, that was a big one. You must be doing a great job up there."

I blush, thinking of falling off the cloud balloon and how embarrassed I'd be if Amber found out about it. "I do my best," I mumble. "Mrs. T's a good teacher."

Amber grins. "A good teacher's nothing without a good

student. That's what I always told mine, anyways." She barks a laugh and reaches over to ruffle my hair. "Listen, I gotta get back up to the garden and help Amy out. We really did a number on it trying to run around the edge of that storm last night. But she wanted me to tell you hi and give you this." She reaches into her jacket pocket, pulls out a little leather medallion on a black thong, and hands it to me. A pretty good line drawing of the *Dream* has been scored into it on one side with something sharp, and on the back it says, *To our "little sister." Keep Dreaming.*

My throat closes up, and my gills start flapping, but I do my best not to let Amber see. I grin ear to ear, though. I can't help it. "Thanks," I choke out when I can breathe again. "Thanks a lot."

Amber chucks me on the chin. "Aw, heck. We skylungs gotta stick together, y'know? See if you can have something ready for us next time we meet. We can make it a tradition." She pauses for a second, and a little flash of worry crosses her face like the shadow of a fast-moving cloud. "And be careful, okay? Stay away from strangers in port."

I nod, totally caught up in the leather coin and the idea of making something for her and Amy even though I'm terrible at making things. Maybe Pep can help me. "I will." Amber turns and walks toward the ladder back up to her cloud balloon. "Tell Amy thanks!" I shout after her. She waves without turning around.

I hold the little leather coin and look at the line drawing, then the inscription. *Little sister,* it says, like we're real family, and I feel like a bird soaring over the sea with the sun rising in front of me. I walk back toward my cabin, head in the clouds, and smack right into Tam as I'm passing in front of the door to Nic's cabin.

The impact knocks me down, and I nearly lose my grip on the coin. "Darn it, Tam!" I shout. "Watch where you're—"

But when I look up, he's gone. There's just the closed door to Nic's cabin and the sounds of three adults talking. They're not laughing anymore. Their voices are serious as a winter squall, and hearing them makes the hair go up on the back of my neck.

I head slowly to my cabin, clutching the leather coin that Amber gave me and hoping that whatever they're talking about is far, far away.

I'm all ready for bed and about to slide underneath the covers and extinguish the little oil lamp on my desk when there's a knock at my door. Outside I hear murmurs and shouts as the *Dream* casts off and heads on her way, and I wonder who's helping. Pepper? Tam?

I open the door and find Mrs. Trachia.

She's wearing a different dress, a bright white one that looks sleek like wind-twisted clouds, and she's carrying a tray with two cups on it. I catch a thoughtful look on her face just as it's being chased off by a smile. "Hello, Nadya dear," she says softly. "I'm glad I caught you. May I come in?"

I nod and back away from the door. Mrs. T walks in, frowns briefly at the still-soggy lump of wadded-up clothes in the corner, and sets her tray down on my desk. I can smell what's in the cups now: chamomile tea with honey. One of my favorite things in the world. We used to grow chamomile back in Vash Abandi, in the little apartment Mrs. T raised me in during the years between when she and Nic found me and when Nic came back for us with the *Orion*.

"I've been thinking, Nadya," she says, handing me the tea. She's got a bandage on one of her fingers from burning it with the welding torch today. "And I want to show you something tonight, if you're awake enough. Something new."

My heart beats faster. I love it when Mrs. T shows me new things. She knows so much about the world and being a skylung—what we can do, where we're from, what happened to drive us all away from home—but she's been drip-feeding things to me for years, like I'm some little plant in the cloud garden that can't handle too much water all at once without drowning.

"I'm awake," I say, and I hop up on my bed and sit cross-legged. "What is it?"

Mrs. T frowns, tapping her finger on her lips like she's afraid maybe she's made a mistake and I'm not ready yet, and I try to calm down, or at least to look like I've calmed down.

"Do you ever see the plants in your head, when you try to speak with them?" she asks.

I start to chew on one of my nails as I think about it, then stop. Mrs. T hates it when I do that. "Yeah," I say. "I mean, I picture them. Like if I'm talking to Opal, I try to remember what she looks like. It helps me hear her."

Mrs. T leans her hip against the desk. "What does she look like?"

I shrug. "Like she does when I see her with my eyes open, I guess."

"Exactly the same?"

I shake my head, trying to remember the last time I talked to Opal with my eyes closed. It's a bit fuzzy. I was pretty busy that day, trying to talk to all the plants at once as we got ready to head out of port. "I guess not. She was sort of . . . glowing."

It sounds like I'm making it up, and I blush a bit when I say it, but Mrs. T just smiles and lets out a deep breath, like she's relieved. "Good. I thought you might be getting there." She reaches down and puts the snuffer over my oil lamp, and the cabin plunges into deep shadows. There's a little moonlight coming in from the window at the fore and a little firelight coming in through the other windows from the deck lamps, but it's not much. Mrs. T looks like a ghost. "Close your eyes," she says softly.

I do as she asks, so excited I'm practically bouncing. "Okay. Closed."

"Now reach out toward the cloud garden with your mind, like you were going to talk to the plants. Tell me what you see."

I try to do what she's asking, but it's hard. "They're too far away," I say. "I can't talk to them."

"What do you *see* though, Nadya?"

I frown. Usually I don't pay a lot of attention to what I'm

seeing when I try to talk to the plants. I figure I'm just imagining it. "Some bright little dots, I guess. Like when you close your eyes and rub them too hard."

"Is there a pattern to the dots?"

I focus on them, and they get bigger and brighter. The more I pay attention to them, the more I can see. There are dozens. A hundred or more, maybe. Too many to count, like the stars in their clouds on the horizon. They're clustered in a big egglike outline. Some dots are on the outside of the egg, and others are on the inside. It almost looks like . . .

"The cloud garden," I breathe. "They look like the cloud garden."

"Excellent, Nadya." Mrs. T comes over and puts her hand on my shoulder. "Now try to stretch your mind farther. What's off the port bow in front of us, moving away?"

I try to turn my mind away from the constellation of glowing dots that looks like the *Orion's* cloud garden and see what she told me to. For a moment I don't find anything, but as I push harder I spot the dim outline of a long, cigarlike cloud of other dots. Like before, the more I focus on them, the brighter they get. "It's the *Dream!*" I shout. "I can see the *Dream's* garden!"

"Splendidly done. One more thing and then I'll explain what you're seeing. Are there any especially bright lights in the garden of the *Emerald Dream?*"

I push my mind closer, past the bright cloud of *Dream's* outerplants and into the heart of her garden. "Yes," I say. "Two of them." They're much bigger than the other lights, and much brighter. They glow like the sun-in-a-jar, or like Pepper's fire spirits.

"Can you talk to them, like you do to the plants?"

I try. It feels weird because I can't picture what they'd look like if I saw them with my eyes. But the more I think about the way Opal glowed the last time I talked to her, the more I understand. I've never been talking to the *outside* of the plants. It's not like they have ears to hear it. I've been talking to what's *inside* them. The glowing part. *Hello?* I ask. *Can you hear me?*

. . . llo? . . . not qui . . . a voice says back. It crackles and hisses, fading in and out of my hearing . . . *ocus harder?*

My head's starting to hurt like I've been trying to read in the dark, little needles poking the backs of my eyes, but I ignore it. I have a hunch. *Hello?* I try again. *Hello? Who are you?*

This time the voice is clear as a singing songbird. *Hey, little sister!* The picture in my mind flares into bright life, and I see Amber smiling, crossing her arms and leaning against something inside her cloud garden. *Goshend's toes, Nadj. You know how old I was before I learned to do this?*

I get so excited my gills start flapping again, and while I'm thinking about breathing, I lose my connection to Amber. It's sort of like getting shaken off a rope in the dark and not being able to find it. I know she's there somewhere, but I can't figure out where. The pain in my head gets sharper and sharper, and eventually I give up and open my eyes.

They're watery from the headache, but when I blink through the tears, I see Mrs. Trachia standing at the side of my bed and holding a cup of tea out to me. She's lit my oil lamp again, and she smiles real big. "Well?" she asks.

"It was Amber!" I blurt out. "I saw Amber! I could talk to her, and she could talk back!"

Mrs. T nods toward the tea. "Drink this," she says. Gently, she wipes some of the tears off my cheeks with her thumb. "It'll help with the headache."

I pick up the tea and take a big gulp. It's wonderful. Light and sweet and warm but not hot, just the way I like it. Mrs. T pulls the chair from my desk over to the side of the bed and sits in it.

"What you just saw, Nadya, is known as the Panpathia. It's like a web—a network of light called lifebond stretching between the hearts and minds of everything in the world. As you learn to use it, you'll get better at seeing what's on it clearly and connecting to it, even over great distances. The strongest skylungs can communicate all the way across the Cloud Sea, and even farther."

"You mean I can talk to any skylung? Any plant in a cloud garden?"

Mrs. T nods. "Yes, and eventually with most plants and animals." Her face grows darker. "Other things too," she says. She glances at my desk drawer, the one where I keep my doorknob. "The Panpathia can be dangerous. I want you to promise me you won't go out on it without me there with you."

I frown. "Why not? What other things are on it? Are there other people?"

Mrs. T taps her finger against her lips again, and I know

I'm only going to get half an answer. She does that when she's figuring out how to talk to me without lying or telling the whole truth. "Most people can't use the Panpathia, and nobody knows quite why, though a doctor in T'an Gaban once suggested something to me about brain structure. But there are others who can do what we do. They call themselves cloudlings, and they used to live at the Roof of the World alongside us. They don't have gills, but their lungs can breathe the air from cloudplants. Most of them lived differently from us, preferring smaller communities." She smiles, like she's remembering something pleasant. "I was friends with some of them. But very few cloudlings lived in the cities or used cloudships, so not many made it out when . . ." Her smile disappears. "When we left."

Another flash of pain streaks through my head, and I grimace and sip my tea again and try to dig for what she wasn't telling me. "Are they dangerous or something?"

Mrs. T blinks and touches her hand to her chest. "Heavens no, child. No more than other people. Where did—? Ah." She looks at me sharply. "My warning, of course. No, Nadya. There's something else on the Panpathia. Something dark and cold. You must promise me to stay far, far away from it."

"Why?" I ask. My heart pounds. Maybe she's finally going to tell me what happened to the skylungs, why we're scattered all over the place, why there are so few of us and why we don't have a place to call our own.

She looks at me for a second as if she's thinking about it, and then she sighs and strokes my hair. "I'm glad you and the

69

doorknob are safe, *rybka*," she says softly. "Will you promise me to be more careful in the future?"

My heart shrivels up. I remember my mother, telling me to hold on to the doorknob, and I feel like crying. "I will," I rasp. "I'm sorry."

Mrs. T keeps stroking my hair. "I didn't mean to make you feel guilty. But the doorknob is important. Keep it protected." She sits on the bed next to me and looks out the window, peering at the stars. "Do you know why Nic and I do all this?" she asks after a moment.

My heart starts beating faster again. Maybe this has to do with what Nic, Thom, and Carla talked about. Maybe I'm old enough to know too. "No."

"Nic used to live at the Roof of the World," she says. "In the same city I lived in. It was on the edge of the continent, where the inland air mixed with the air from the sea and anyone could breathe easily. He was a doctor there, and he loved it." She picks idly at a loose thread on the top of my comforter. "He is a kind man, one of the kindest I have ever known, and when the continent was lost, it hit him hard. Many people didn't make it out on the cloudships, and he feels guilty that he did and they didn't. So he tries to help people now, skylungs and cloudlings especially, however he can. If someone offers him a lot of money, like they did to deliver the gormling, he doesn't think of what it will buy him. He thinks of what it will do for others. He is trying to rebuild a community, to make life better for people who lost everything."

I grip my tea more tightly. "What about you, Mrs. T? Why do you do it?"

"For similar reasons," she says, sighing. "What we lost . . . what *I* lost . . ." She touches a silver ring on a necklace she never takes off. "There is a reason I still go by my married name, even though he's long gone. And nobody else should know that pain."

I swallow. "What happened to the Roof of the World, Mrs. T?"

She shudders, and a look of nausea passes over her face. "Shadows," she says softly. "Shadows and cold." She looks at me, and for the first time I can remember she sounds afraid. "I will tell you the whole story soon, Nadya *rybka*. But you must give me a little more time to figure out how." I start to protest, but she stands up and I know the conversation's done. "You did wonderfully today," she says, and she plants a kiss on my forehead. "With the garden, with the ship, and with the Panpathia. You're a remarkable child, and you surprise me more and more every day."

Part of me's frustrated that she won't tell me more. I want to know what she lost. I want to know who my parents were and what happened to them. I want to know why I was alone in a cloud balloon in the desert, and what she and Nic talk with their old crewmates about. Part of me feels like kicking and screaming and throwing a tantrum until she gives in, but I used to try that, back in Vash Abandi, and it never worked. I was pretty wild when she and Nic first found me. I had a big temper. Used to flinch at loud sounds and have trouble

71

sleeping 'cause I was afraid of the dark. She helped me calm down. She still does.

I take a deep breath. "Thanks, Mrs. T," I say.

Mrs. T reaches down and hugs me, and I focus on what she feels like. The warmth of her body. The wiry strength of her arms. The incenselike sandalwood smell of her neck.

She squeezes my back and kisses my cheek. "I'm terribly proud of you, Nadya *rybka*," she says. "Sleep tight, my dear." She straightens up and takes my tea from me, and I slide under the covers while she snuffs the lamp. My frustration fades away. The routine makes me feel warm and safe, like nothing can touch me. Like no matter how high a place I fall from, Mrs. T will always be there to catch me.

She kisses my forehead again, and then she disappears into the darkness, closing my door silently behind her. I drift off into the Sea of Dreams, thoughts of my doorknob and shadows at the Roof of the World melting into better ones of constellations of glowing dots out on the Panpathia and of Mrs. T trusting and believing in me. I get the best sleep I've had in a long, long time.

CHAPTER 6

IN WHICH A LARGE BANK OF FOG FEATURES PROMINENTLY, AND NADYA FACES SEVERAL UNEXPECTED EMOTIONS.

When I wake up, cold fog wraps around my toes like . . .

I wriggle my toes. I have on two pairs of socks and my work boots. The vent under my desk that leads to the heating system is all the way open. And still, my toes are cold.

. . . like the icy tentacles of an octopus, crawling across the frozen mud at the Roof of the World.

There. That's a good line to quit journaling on.

I pull out my pocket watch. Ten minutes left to morning-dove. All I can see outside my window is dense gray fog. My breath mists inside my cabin. I throw on a frizzy green sweater on top of my overalls, wrap a scarf around my neck, bunch my hair up under a wool cap, and pull a pair of fingerless mittens on before I head out to the deck.

It's still awfully cold outside.

The fog sits around the *Orion* like a big, wet blanket, and I grumble as I sling my lobster claws over my shoulder and walk off down the deck. We were supposed to be sailing into a bunch of brightcloud today, and this seems more like what we call crudcloud. Nothing but cold water. I stick my tongue out to be sure, because the different kinds of clouds have different tastes. Brightcloud tastes salty and a little bitter. Crudcloud just tastes like water.

The cloud we're in doesn't taste like either.

It's cold and wet, definitely more like crudcloud than brightcloud, but it tastes wrong—like the difference between fresh bacon and bacon gone bad at the end of a long trip. It's twisted and cold, and it reminds me of engine oil or the shadows at the back of a closet at midnight, congealed into liquid and then spritzed out through a nozzle.

I jerk my scarf up over my mouth and nose and wipe my tongue off on it to get the taste to go away. I wish I could finish the job with breakfast, but it's too early for that, and since Nic will be working on the engines with us, there won't be much to eat anyway. A pot of porridge and brown sugar and raisins down in the kitchen, maybe. If I had more time, I'd stop by for a bowl, but I still have to feed the gormling, and I don't want to be late.

I like fog, usually. Thom always leaves the fire creatures in the deck lamps, and they sleep through the day, but still glow brightly enough to outline the edge of the ship in soft orange light. They make the *Orion* look like something out of a kinetoscope reel—all orange and white and fuzzy.

It's like that today. With the engines shut down so we can work on them, it's as quiet as the middle of the night. It would be a great day to sit in bed with a cup of tea and write or read or play an instrument, or maybe get Mrs. T to show me more about the Panpathia. But we can't afford to take a break, like Nic said. We've got to get the gormling to Far Agondy before we run out of food for it.

The stairs down to the cargo hold are dark. We don't use many fire spirits inside the ship, just in case something goes wrong. The *Orion* has a couple of electric lights, but we try to use them only in emergencies. They burn out quick, and Salyeh says they cost a lot to replace.

The gormling's asleep when I get to the cargo hold, but its ears twitch as I approach, and it wakes up fast, swirling over and around itself in that same figure eight, flashing patterns at me with the glowing spots below its spines. I bet if I watched it long enough, I could learn what they mean. It seems pretty smart.

But that'll have to wait. I toss its morning bucket of food over the top of the tank and then head back up to the iron-room. I work slowly through the gloom, keeping my hands on the walls and moving by touch, until I get to the big metal door that leads to the engines. It's cracked open, and I hear voices on the other side.

"I tell you, Nic, it worries me. Tian Li didn't say a thing about fog. This is supposed to be brightcloud."

"She could have misjudged the stars. She's still just a child, Thom."

Thom snorts. "And how about what Carla was saying? Skylung kids missing in the ports? People asking questions about Nadya? What about this guy Darkpatch and his ship that strikes in the mist?"

I pause outside the door, my heart pounding. I shouldn't spy on them. They wouldn't be saying all this if they knew I was out here. But why would people be asking questions about me? What kind of pirates attack in the fog? And when did skylung kids start going missing?

I hear a *thump* and the sound of Nic cursing softly. "Whether Carla's rumors are true or not, we need to get that engine fixed, Thom. I'll ask Tian Li for another reading once everyone's up and moving, and I'll help her interpret it."

"A reading? In the middle of this fog?"

"We'll just have to raise the ship."

"In a bunch of crudcloud, with the balloon as sick as Zelda says it is?"

"Nadya can do it."

My stomach takes a little tumble. I stop breathing and listen to my heart thump.

"You put too much faith in that girl, Nic. I don't care what Zelda says, or where you found—"

A hand bumps into mine on the wall. Then someone's chest hits my back and knocks me forward. My right foot catches on my left ankle, and all of a sudden I'm spinning and falling toward the iron door.

The hand on the wall grabs my arm and keeps me from falling all the way. The door swings open and Thom's scowling face peers out, lit up in orange by the fire creatures inside the boilers.

"What in Goshend's name are you two doing out here?" he snaps.

I'm all ready to come up with a good lie to keep from getting into trouble, but Tam speaks first. "Nadya was listening to you through the door," he says flatly.

I snatch my arm back and glare at him. "And you bumped into me and nearly killed me!"

Thom rolls his eyes and gives us a look that says *Grow up already, will you?*

My gills burn. "What were you talking about, anyway?" I mumble.

Behind Thom, Nic frowns. The pipes and pistons and gears of the engines hover over him on the roof of the ironroom like the limbs of a mechanical insect. The orange light sets his face glowing. I've never seen him look like that before.

"Things you shouldn't have overheard," he says.

There's another metal door behind him. It's got a huge wheel in the center of it. Nic takes a key off his belt and inserts it into the wheel, then leans against it and turns it to the left. The arms of the locking mechanism, which spring out from the center of the wheel, compress. There's an audible *chunk*.

Nic swings the door inward. White-gray light and fog pour into the ironroom from outside.

There's no more talking about me, or skylungs going missing, or the things Carla warned them about.

Two guide wires run around the *Orion's* hull to help us make repairs. Ten minutes after Nic opens the door, I'm standing on one and I've got my hands on the other. I'm trying not to shake as I pull myself along, and the fear of falling has chased all my worries about skylungs going missing and people asking questions about me into a little corner in the back of my head.

Still, there's no way I'm letting Tam do this repair without me. This could be my last chance to get back on track to be first mate. I won't let him beat me.

I'm about three feet below the door to the ironroom. Nic's standing in the door itself, his lobster claws clipped into two brackets in the doorjamb. He's got me on belay, which means there's a rope tied to my safety belt running up through a mechanism on his belt, then into the ship. He's slowly feeding more rope out as I move away from him, and if I slip, he'll yank on the rope, and the mechanism will stop it from running through and break my fall.

I've got my lobster claws clipped around the guide wires too, but Nic's my backup. We always use two systems to keep us safe if it might be dangerous outside the ship.

Unless one of us is dumb enough to charge into a storm alone, that is.

I try not to think about falling. Instead I try to think about how I felt last night with Mrs. Trachia tucking me in, like nothing bad could ever happen to me.

To my right, the metal housing of the *Orion*'s starboard engine curves out from the hull like a dark, silent beak. To my left is the misshapen shadow of the port engine's housing.

Two of the bolts that anchor it to the ship are gone, and the whole thing's hanging down and to the right by about a foot and a half.

Beyond it, there's only the gray.

"You're doing great, Nadya," I hear from above. "We're sending Tam down after you now."

I look back up and to the right. Tam, all clipped in, is climbing down the ladder that leads to the guide wires, carrying a load of gear and a tarp on his back. Show-off. He settles his feet on the lower wire and his hands on the upper wire. Then he pulls himself along after me. I swallow and tug myself toward the broken housing.

When I get to it, I stop. To go forward, I'll have to unclip my lobster claws from the guide wires, climb over the housing, then clip back in on the other side. Below me, the fog swirls hungrily.

I unclip the first of my lobster claws and throw it over my shoulder. Tam's weight on the guide wires sets them bouncing and moves me up and down a little. He's getting closer.

Don't let him see that you're afraid, I tell myself. *You can do this!*

My hand starts shaking when I go to unclip my second lobster claw. I have to grab the guide wire again to steady myself.

You're fine, I tell myself. *Nic's never lost anyone. And you've never fallen. Not once.*

Until yesterday.

All of a sudden I'm back in that moment, plunging toward

the sea with the sky and the lightning above me. The cloud balloon's metal catwalk drifts away. The *Orion*'s not there to catch me. I'm falling and falling and falling . . .

Tam's voice floats over my shoulder. "Hey," he says. "You okay?"

I take a deep, shuddery breath. My eyes swim with tears. "I'm fine!" I try to shout at him, but it comes out as a squeak and my voice shakes.

Tam gets up close to me and stops moving. The guide wires bounce slowly under my feet and hands. "Nic's got you," he says. "We double-checked the knots, right? You're safe."

I nod. The mist swirls around us. I feel like I've swallowed a rock, and it's just sitting in my stomach, getting bigger and heavier like a pearl.

Tam clears his throat. "You can do this. Nothing bad's gonna happen," he says.

My stomach twists. I don't trust him. I don't want his help until he apologizes. He doesn't understand anything, even when he's trying to be nice. And I'm sure Nic and Thom can hear him talking me through this, and that just means I'm getting farther and farther away from being first mate.

But I'm not giving up, either. I unclip my second lobster claw, scramble over the housing as fast as I can, and clip back in again.

My feet don't slip a bit.

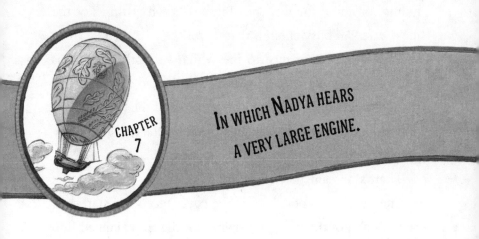

CHAPTER 7

IN WHICH NADYA HEARS A VERY LARGE ENGINE.

Repairing the engine takes a while.

First, Tam and I set up a big canvas tarp below and to the side of the housing so we can walk and store parts on it. Once that's done, we have to remove the engine cover. That's harder than it sounds, since we're trying not to drop anything off the back of the *Orion*. The canvas is slippery and hard to walk on, our lobster claws are constantly getting in our way, and the housing is bent and hanging at a weird angle.

Tam does most of the work. I'm pretty good with a wrench and crowbar, but he does this kind of stuff all day long. He moves from bolt to bolt on top of the housing, leaning on a foot-long wrench until the fastenings on the cover pop free. I do the same thing on the bottom, except that I have to use a breaker bar to extend the wrench because Tam's bigger than I am.

I try not to think about the clouds around us, or about

81

falling, or about the fact that Tam's so good at this. For the most part, I'm busy enough that it works.

Tam keeps being nice to me while we work. It's not as good as an apology, though, and I'm still mad at him. Eventually we get all the bolts on the port side of the engine cover undone and squirreled away. I scramble up the housing to pry the cover off.

There's a seam that runs right down the middle of the engine, where the port half of the cover meets the starboard half. Tam's got the biggest crowbar on the ship jammed into it. The bar's high end is so far from the guide wires that one of us will have to unclip our lobster claws to get out to it. Tam starts to do it, but I stop him.

"I want to do it," I say.

He raises an eyebrow, then shrugs and nods.

I reach over, unclip my lobster claws, and slide onto the housing.

This will probably be the most dangerous part of the whole operation. We're both going to be hopping up and down and yanking on the crowbar, trying to pop this thing off on top of an engine housing that's already dangling from the ship. At some point the cover's probably going to move all at once. Hopefully it'll just ease free and drop onto the canvas we've set up, but if it sticks, or it jams, or it wrenches more bolts loose from the *Orion*, just about anything could happen.

I wrap my chilly fingers around the far end of the crowbar and take a cold, damp breath. It feels good. My stomach stops doing flips.

I guess Nic knew what he was doing, sending me out here.

"You've got me, right, Nic?" I call into the fog.

"Safe as a penguin in winter," his voice says from above and to starboard.

I look at Tam and nod. "On the count of three. One . . ."

I square my feet and tighten my hands around the crowbar. Tam puts his fingers just in front of mine. The muscles bunch in his arms as he gets ready to push.

"Two . . ."

I stand up on tiptoe.

At the very edge of my hearing, I catch a sound. It's a constant, droning hum, real quiet but getting louder. It's coming from the far side of the *Orion*.

Tam looks at me expectantly.

I ease onto my heels and strain my ears. The drone isn't all one sound. There are two or three separate *thrum*s inside it.

It sounds like propellers. Big ones. A whole bank of them.

"Nadya?" Tam asks.

"Shh."

The noise keeps getting louder.

The door to the ironroom bangs open inside the ship. Thom swears. Pepper's voice says something very fast and very nervous.

"Nadya! Tam!" Nic barks. "Up here on the double! Leave the tools and canvas behind!"

"The housing's half apart!" Tam shouts back.

"Up! *Now,*" Nic says.

There's a cast-iron tone in his voice I've only heard a few

83

times before, like when we were inching through heavy fog and got caught on a spire of rock, or when the engines broke down and we drifted for a week before another ship found us.

My heart thuds. Tam swallows and takes his hands off the crowbar.

We share a worried glance, but we don't argue anymore.

A few minutes later, Tam and I are untying the ropes from our safety belts. The door to the outside has been closed and locked again, and the *Orion*'s horn has blasted our code twice with no response. Pepper's standing next to the door to the rest of the ship looking miserable. She's got one hand over her stomach, like she's got the flu or something.

I feel a little ill myself. Nic and Thom took off like rabbits after Tam and I got inside.

"What's going on, Pep?"

I'm having a miserable time untying the knot through my front belt loop. It's all tight after taking my weight when we tested it, and my fingers are pretty cold and not all that responsive.

"I don't know," Pepper says. She frowns at the door next to her. "We heard the engines coming, and then Mrs. T shivered and sent me to go get Nic and Thom."

My stomach starts to squirm. Mrs. T doesn't rattle easily.

I finally get my fingers into the knot and start working it loose. Tam's fully untied, but he's still got his safety belt on. He looks uneasy.

"I heard them talking, last night," he says. He stares at Pepper and me like he's not sure whether he should continue.

I try not to let him see how scared that makes me. I remember how serious they sounded, and what Thom and Nic said this morning. "And?"

"Carla said there's more pirates than usual out in this part of the Cloud Sea. She was worried about one especially—a guy named Darkpatch who's vicious as a shark. His gang's got a big old liner they stole called the *Remora*, and they've got cloud plants on its catwalks that make fog." He starts fiddling with the machines on one of the walls nervously, and when he talks again, it's in a whisper. "People are calling them the Darkmist Pirates. They were in Vash Abandi the same time we were, looking for a ship to hit. Carla said they were asking questions about the *Orion*, and about the kids on board, whether any of us were skylungs." He looks up at me, and his eyes look afraid. I don't think he's pulling my leg.

But I want him to be, real bad, because I don't want to think about pirates kidnapping skylung kids, so I act like he is. "No way," I say. "She never said that, and that's impossible anyway. You'd need a zillion plants, and I've never heard of any that make fog." As I say it, I remember how weird the fog tasted, but I pretend I didn't. It's probably just pollution from some big passing liner or something.

Tam stops fiddling and glares at me. "She did so. She changed course just to come warn us. And Nic and Thom didn't think it was impossible. They sounded worried."

I work the rest of the rope free and drop it on the floor, then wiggle out of my belt. "Well, maybe you heard them wrong. Maybe they were talking about something else."

The door to the hall bursts open.

Mrs. T, Salyeh, and Tian Li are standing in the hallway. Sal and Tian Li are wearing safety belts.

"Back into that belt," Mrs. T says, and I look at the belt on the floor and grit my teeth. "You're all going under the ship."

My jaw falls open far enough to catch a rhino fly.

Tam gulps. "It's pirates, isn't it?" he asks.

Mrs. T nods. Behind her, Tian Li and Salyeh look terri-fied. Pirates are scary enough on their own, but neither of them likes being outside the ship's hull, either. Next to Tam, Pepper looks even worse. The last time Nic had her help with hull repairs, she didn't come out of her cabin for three days afterward.

I feel pretty scared myself, actually. Part of me wants to ask if they're really after me, but I keep my mouth shut because I don't want to hear the answer if it's yes.

Instead I tug my safety belt back on, trying to keep my hands from shaking. Tam pulls another out of a chest near his feet and helps Pepper shiver into it. Mrs. T takes the ship's longest rope down from the wall and threads it through the belts, then goes to work on Tian Li's safety knots.

"We can't be *absolutely* sure they're pirates," Mrs. T says, "but whoever they are, they're very big, and they're not responding to our signals or to me reaching out through the Panpathia. And we're far from the normal liner routes."

Tam starts helping Pepper with her knots while I try to convince my fingers to do theirs again.

"What do you think will happen?" Tian Li asks.

"Hopefully nothing," Mrs. T says. "But if they're pirates, they'll want something. They'll board us and take whatever it is. If we're lucky, they'll then sail off and leave us alone." Mrs. T finishes Tian Li's knots and moves on to Salyeh's.

My mouth goes completely dry, because what if the thing they want is me? But I'm still too scared to speak up. Nobody asks what'll happen if we're not lucky. We all know: The pirates will kidnap us. The worst of them are known for selling kids into slavery on the warm shores of the sugar islands, or in the coal mines outside Deepwater. Or anywhere they can, for that matter. There's slavery in all the Six Cities, even though it's illegal. The police can't be everywhere at once, and you don't have to put a chain around someone's neck to make them obey you.

Sometimes I think some of us might've seen that already.

Once everyone gets tied in, Mrs. T looks at Tam and me. Her face is smooth and serious. When she speaks, her voice is steady as a level. "Tam, you'll lead the way. Nadya, you'll be anchor."

I swallow. I'm still mad at Tam. I don't trust him. I don't

want to put my life in his hands. What if he decides to make me dangle out there until I admit he's right?

Focus, Nadya, I tell myself. Mrs. T told us to work together, and I do trust her.

We drill for pirates every few months. There's a little nook on the bottom of the ship where the keel's hollowed out. You can fit eight people in it, if they huddle close together. To get there, we'll have to climb down a ladder, clip our lobster claws on to the guide wire along the ship's keel, and pull ourselves hand over hand to the hollow. For Tam, it'll mean going first and setting up a belay point inside the nook, anchoring himself to the ship so that he can safely brake the rope if one of us falls. For me, it'll mean belaying everyone else while they climb down, then going after them, alone.

Mrs. T pulls a key from a pocket in her dress and unlocks the door to the outside, then swings it open. I take hold of the rope we're all tied in to, run it through a belay device, and short-clip my lobster claws to an iron bracket near the door.

Tam steps up next to me and takes a deep breath. His eyes flick toward mine.

"On belay?" he asks.

"Belay's on." I brace myself for his weight and get ready to feed rope through the belay device.

"Climbing," he whispers. He puts his back to the sky.

"Climb away."

Tam steps onto the first rung of the ladder and starts to climb down. There's fifteen feet of rope between him and

Salyeh, fifteen more between Sal and Tian Li, fifteen more between her and Pepper, and then the whole rest of the rope between Pep and me. If the guide wire gives out or they fall before they get to it, somehow me, my belt, and the bracket I'm clipped to are supposed to hold up all of them.

Mrs. T's hand lands on my shoulder. "Everything will be fine, Nadya," she says.

I nod. I don't take my eyes from the rope or from Salyeh stepping out the door. His jaw's locked tight. His hands are holding the doorframe like if he loosens his grip even a little he'll fall.

I don't ask why Mrs. T and Thom and Nic have to stay. I know the pirates will never believe a ship this small has a flying lifeboat and that we're in it. Nic will be on deck, waiting for the pirates. Thom will be running through the ship, getting rid of the signs that anyone other than the three adults crews it.

We all know what to do. Everybody knows that pirates sometimes attack out on the Cloud Sea. Everybody plans for it.

But nobody thinks it'll happen to them.

Everything goes fine for the first part of the climb down. Tam gets under the keel without any problems. He's able to help the others clip their lobster claws to the guide wire. They head out along the bottom of the ship.

From there, things get a little more difficult.

I'm supposed to keep everyone on belay until Tam gets set

up in the hiding place. But once he disappears, we've got no way to contact each other except tugging on the rope. We don't want to yell because the whole point of us being out here is to keep whoever's running the engines thundering in my ears from finding us. And besides—those engines have gotten as loud as a hundred-car steam train. We'd have a heck of a time hearing each other anyway.

So I stand in the door and let the rope out while the others work their way beneath the *Orion*. The guide wire's one-and-a-half-inch braided steel, so it ought to hold them. But I still find myself grinding my teeth, wondering about the storm and what it might have broken that we don't know about yet.

Tam's with them, I tell myself. *He may be a jerk, but he knows what he's doing.*

Mrs. T stands next to me and looks anxiously at her pocket watch. The longer we take, the more likely it is for whoever's approaching the *Orion* to see us. But we can only go so fast.

After a few minutes, the rope goes limp and stays that way awhile. Then it starts to twitch, and I figure Tam's setting up in the keel.

I look nervously at Mrs. T, but she just nods and keeps her eyes on the swirling fog.

The line stops flying around so crazily a second later. Tam gives three sharp tugs.

Shivering, I unclip from the wall, take the rope out of the belay device, and step into the doorway. The fog wisps around my ankles and trickles down my shirt. I swallow and turn my back to the open air.

Mrs. T follows me and smiles. "You'll be fine, Nadya," she says. "It's just like the drills."

The gills around her neck flutter when she speaks. Mine are trying to do the same thing.

Settle down, you, I tell them. *You can be afraid after we're safe.*

I keep a very, very tight grip on the ladder as I start down.

"Good luck," Mrs. T says. She's got one hand on the door. I realize she's going to close it after I go.

Come on, Nadya, I think. *Of course she is. Leaving it open would be like hanging a big sign that says* Look Here!

The engine drone has gotten so loud I can barely hear anything else. Mrs. T looks up. So do I.

Above us, descending slowly, is one of the largest cloudships I've ever seen.

It's seven or eight times as long as the *Orion* and four times as tall. Room for twelve decks, at least, depending on how it's configured. It's got extra engine pods running all along the side of it. I can't see the main engines behind it through the fog, but I can just make out the shadowy outline of their housings. They're enormous—big enough to hide a good-sized house in.

Sketched out in paint on the side of the ship is a massive white skull. Below, the word *Remora* is written in sloppy letters.

My throat goes dry, and my gills flap harder. The big ship drops lower and lower. Its cloud balloon, big as a pod of galaxy whales, floats into view above it. Its design is a single, enormous whale shark with an open mouth, surrounded by a bunch of littler fish with sharp teeth. The cables running from the balloon to the ship look as big around as an oil drum, or maybe bigger.

A black object flies out from the ship's rail and sails toward the *Orion*'s deck. Something long and spindly trails behind it.

Rope. They'll be boarding any second.

I scramble down the ladder as fast as I can, hoping I won't miss a step. Above me, Mrs. T yells something, but I can't make it out.

"What?" I shout back.

More objects fly out from the pirate ship. The wash from its engines starts blowing over me. Drops of cold water from the fog skitter down my neck.

Mrs. T yells again. There's real, solid fear on her face.

I still can't make out what she's saying. It sounds like "Nickle leaf a rainbow hoping."

Mrs. T looks up again. I follow her eyes. There are people sliding down the ropes from the pirate ship to the *Orion*.

The door to the ironroom slams shut above me, and I start down the ladder again as fast as I can.

I'm moving so quick that my foot misses the last rung.

My other foot catches the weight, and my fingers clamp tight around the ladder. For a second, my leg dangles over the fog. My head tries to send me soaring through the clouds again, but I grit my teeth and tell it firmly that I will *not* think about falling right now. Instead, I get my foot back on the ladder, grab the first of my lobster claws, and start feeling around beneath the hull for the guide wire.

I can't find it.

It's okay, it's okay, it's okay, I tell myself. My fingers fumble over cold, hard wood. I try to remember the last pirate drill we had and where the wire was. I try to remember where I saw Tam and Tian Li and the others disappear under the hull.

Other side, Nadya, try the other side.

I skitter over to the other side of the ladder.

Come on, come on—

My fingers are starting to sweat, and it's making it harder to hold on to the ladder. I still can't find the guide wire.

I lean way out, as far as I can, and my fingers touch the wire. I slide open the catch on the lobster claw in my hand. I slip the claw over the wire. I close the catch again.

And then I fall.

I'm leaning so far over that I can't hold the ladder anymore. When my grip gives out, I swing down and left and bang into the side of the *Orion*. My face slides along it, and then I'm under the ship, dangling by one lobster claw with the other twisting below me. There's nothing between me and the sea but a mile of gray, grasping fog.

My stomach slides into my throat. I remember the storm, and the cloud balloon, and falling, falling, falling . . .

The line around my waist goes taut.

Tam.

He must've felt the rope go slack and known that I slipped. He must've hauled it in just in case he had to break my fall.

My one claw holds. I spin slowly around with the black, chipped underside of the *Orion* above me. I'm clenching my teeth around one of my hands, because when I fell my hand realized I'd scream if I didn't stuff something in my mouth. And if I screamed, I might've been discovered. Sometimes, my body thinks faster than my brain.

It's a good thing too, because the ironroom door crashes open above me.

Two men start shouting.

"Yeah—see it," one of them says. I can't catch all the words over the humming of the pirates' engines, but I can pick out a few.

I take my hand out of my mouth and focus on breathing.

"Looks—just bent—fix it?"

"—doing—morning—" a third voice says. It's Thom, and he sounds grumpy. He must be explaining our engine trouble to the pirates.

Why're they asking about the engines? Shouldn't they just take the valuable stuff and go? Isn't that what pirates do?

The rope around my waist tugs violently. Tian Li pokes her neck out of a hole in the keel about twenty yards away. She pantomimes clipping a lobster claw on to something above her head.

I grab my second claw and snap it around the guide wire. Tian Li gives me a thumbs-up and ducks back into the hiding place.

I tell my arms that they can shake later, and I start pulling myself along the guide wire. To keep from thinking about the thousands of feet of nothing below my toes, I wonder why the pirates were asking about our engines.

It's not all that comforting. But at least they weren't asking about me.

Salyeh grabs my safety belt when I get to the hiding place. His lips are almost colorless, but he hangs on to me until I can squirm through the entrance hole and settle my feet on the worn, wet wood inside the hollow. I unclip my lobster claws from the guide wire and attach them to a bolt near my feet.

As soon as I'm in and safe, Sal lets go of me and dives to the back wall, as far as he can get from the open sky.

The hiding place is about as long as my room, but it's only six feet wide. It's just a few feet high too, so we have to walk around all stooped—especially Salyeh. The entrance hole is big enough to let plenty of light in—or to fall through if you're not careful or have real bad luck. So I double-check my knots and tug on the bolt I'm clipped to, just to be sure it's not loose. The air only feels a little warmer inside the hollow than outside. We've got no blankets with us. No food. No water.

Pepper and Tian Li are huddled against the far wall, looking miserable, when Salyeh joins them. Tam's a little closer to me. He's got most of the rope coiled in front of him. Between us, it runs through loops on everybody's safety belts, then a bolt, then a belay device.

His face is covered in sweat. "I thought you fell," he says.

It's easier to have a conversation down here, with the bulk of the *Orion* blocking so much of the noise from the pirates' engines.

"I did." I look down at my lobster claws. "I had a claw on the wire, and it caught me."

Salyeh coughs, presses a finger to his lips, and points up. Tam and I stop talking.

Somebody stomps loudly into the *Orion*'s hold above our heads. Tam winces. I swallow hard. Salyeh shuts his eyes and grimaces.

"Where are the *children*?" a voice shouts up in the hold. It's loud as a shipwreck and harsh as desert sun. "What do you take me for? I know they're here somewhere!"

There's a loud *thump*, then a crash.

Tian Li starts shaking. She's got tears running down her cheeks, and Salyeh puts an arm around her. Pepper, looking pale as a ghost in winter, does the same. I creep over as quietly as I can and put my arms around all three of them. Tam follows and completes the huddle.

There's another crash above us, and more shouting.

Nobody says anything for a long, long time.

CHAPTER 9

IN WHICH NADYA OVERHEARS SOMETHING AND MAKES A PLAN.

Eventually, it gets quiet up in the hold. Whoever was doing all the shouting and throwing things around leaves, and there's just the drone of the *Remora*'s engines and the occasional moan of a gust of wind blowing over the opening to our hideout. The others drift off to sleep, one by one, but I can't do it. I keep thinking about Nic, Thom, and Mrs. T facing whoever was doing all that shouting. I keep thinking about what he said, about the children.

As I'm thinking, I hear footsteps above me again.

I breathe as silently as I can. The footsteps are slower this time, and quieter. There's two sets of them, and they stop just above my head.

"Old Darkpatch is really starting to lose it, isn't he," someone says. A woman's voice, and not Mrs. T's. I start to sweat, even though it's freezing down here.

"He hasn't been the same since Vash Abandi," says the

other voice, a man's. "We shouldn'ta let him go in the desert, or kept those plants he brought back. I don' like this fog they make. Tastes like nightmares."

I have to stick my hand in my mouth again to keep from making a noise. When I lived with Mrs. T in Vash Abandi, the desert outside the city was the scariest place I knew. Everybody always talked about it. There were bad things out there, they said. Dark things. Shadows that would steal your soul. Ancient ruins. A bottomless hole in the ground at the heart of a crater a mile wide. I used to have nightmares of being out in the desert, alone, running away from some faceless darkness into the teeth of a sandstorm.

"You think there were ever any kids on this boat to begin with?"

"Mighta been, but if there were, they're gone. Jus' a buncha junk and that baby leviathan now."

"Why're we searching for kids anyway? It's not like they're worth that much."

"Skylungs and cloudlings are. Darkpatch has a buyer for 'em, one who pays big."

My stomach flips and flops and tries to jump out of my body. I grab the bolt I'm clipped to and clench my fist around it, just to give myself something to do. The voices move away into the cargo hold, getting quieter. Then they come back.

"At least this tub had a skylung on it," the woman says.

"Yeah. Oughta make the captain a little less angry we didn' find any kids. Darkpatch seemed in a hurry to get her and the others back to the *Remora*."

There's some scuffling and shuffling, and the voices move away. When they come back, they're moving faster, and I catch just one sentence: "You think we should listen to Robles? Make a move soon?"

Then the door to the hold clicks shut behind them, and everything's silent again.

I stare at the wet wood of the hideout, thinking, breathing hard, trying to put the puzzle together. I want to know why they're after skylungs and cloudlings. Why they're after *me*.

You ever get chosen for something, and you're not sure whether it's a good thing or not? Like your teacher singles you out special, and you stand up and your guts are boiling and everybody's staring at you and you think if you play whatever's coming right, then maybe it'll be the best thing that ever happened to you, but if you get it wrong it might be the worst?

It's kinda like that, but a hundred times worse.

My mind takes me back to Vash Abandi. Tall palm trees. Little rivers and bayous all feeding toward the big one at the heart of the city. Bright sun. The calls of seagulls down by the turquoise water and the red howl of sandstorms when they blow in from the desert. Endless warrens of boxy buildings made from adobe or sandstone, crammed next to and on top of one another like the city was built by a god out of giant blocks instead of by a group of merchant families around a river and a good harbor. Rumors about the desert, the crater, the ruins.

The desert's where Mrs. T and Nic found me. Vash Abandi's where Mrs. T chose to raise me.

There's a clue there. Has to be.

I shudder. Mrs. T never felt comfortable in Vash Abandi, and I never did either. We lived on the western rim of the city, where the desert met the walls, and there was something dark in that place. People were nice on the surface and we had a few friends, but nobody went out after sundown, and when the wind blew in from the desert, the whole neighborhood got jumpy, like it was waiting for something terrible to happen.

So why'd we stay?

I can't figure it out. I'm too tired. My arms are sore from climbing. My legs hurt from being crammed in this little hiding place. It's cold and I'm hungry.

I pull the little leather coin Amber gave me out of my shirt and stare at the sketch of the *Dream* in the light from the entrance for a while, trying to think of something else, hoping everything will be all right like Mrs. T said. Eventually, I fall asleep. I dream of my doorknob and the silver tree on the front of it, reaching its arms desperately toward the sky.

"Nadya."

My eyes flicker open. I'm squatting over damp wood. Pepper's curled up next to me, shivering. Salyeh and Tian Li lean on each other across from us.

Tam kneels at my side. His hand's on my shoulder.

"Nadya," he whispers again. He shakes me gently.

"I'm awake," I say, but I don't really feel that way. My hands and feet are freezing. The tip of my nose is numb. My brain feels like it's floating in a bath of oatmeal, like the one they gave Pepper when she got a bad rash in Deepwater.

It's almost completely dark inside the hiding place. Outside there's a faint gray glow. Probably moonlight trickling through the mist.

"We started moving," Tam says.

I look over at him. If we *have* started moving, I can't tell.

"You sure?" I whisper.

He nods. "The engine sounds changed direction. They're coming from in front now. And there was a real gentle tug just a second ago."

I squint at him in the dimness. "I didn't feel it."

He shrugs. "You were asleep," he says.

I try to roll onto my knees as quietly as possible. I haven't heard anyone in the hold for hours—that's why I'm willing to talk at all—but better safe than sorry.

"So what next?" I whisper.

"I dunno." Tam settles his back against the wall and looks up at the darkened ceiling. "They shut the ironroom door after you, right?"

I nod.

"And I bet they locked it when they did."

"Probably."

"And if we're moving forward and the engine sounds are in front of us, and nobody's come to get us, then the pirates are probably stealing the *Orion*."

The others open their eyes. Pepper purses her lips and

starts tugging at one of her curls. Tian Li stares into the gray sky outside the hiding place. Salyeh frowns.

My stomach twists. "Mrs. T, Nic, and Thom are on the other ship," I say, remembering what I overheard. "We have to find them. We have to save them."

The others look at me in horror. That's not what we're supposed to do.

Part of our pirate drill is that if the ship ever gets captured, we do everything we can to cut her free, then run like the screaming north wind until we're safe and find one of Nic's old crew members to help us in port.

"They saved us," I say as calmly as I can. "Every one of us."

Tam from Far Agondy's shadows and silver and smoke. Pep from the madness and music of the Free City of Myrrh. Tian Li from T'an Gaban and its steep hills and deep fog and sandstone monoliths. Me from a crashed ship. And Salyeh from the dusty labyrinths of Vash Abandi.

"That's not the plan they gave us, Nadya," Tian Li says. Her hands are curled up tight in the coarse, baggy fabric of her pants.

Salyeh nods.

I don't bother arguing. "Pep?" I ask instead. "What do you think we should do?"

She stares into the shadows. The clouds twist by slowly outside. We're not being towed that fast.

"I'm scared, Nadya," she whispers.

I clench my teeth. "Tam?"

He looks at me for a long time. The drone of the pirate ship's engines fills the night. Pepper shivers against my leg.

Finally, Tam shakes his head. "I'm sorry, Nadya. There's no way we could do it."

I let out a long, deep sigh. Truth be told, a part of me's glad. Somewhere in the back of my head, I know there's no way we could do it. I'm happy that I don't have to try.

But that part of me is a purple coward, and I don't like it one bit.

"How do we get free?" Tian Li asks.

Tam leans his head against the wall and closes his eyes.

"They'll be towing us with some kinda cable system. If I set it up, I'd do it with one line to port and one to starboard near the bow, to distribute the load. If you joined the lines partway between our ship and theirs, it'd be pretty stable."

He tucks his hands into his armpits. "We must be pretty far back from their ship to avoid the wash from those huge propellers they've got. That's good. It'll take them a long time to turn that liner around and come after us once we cut ourselves free."

"How will we do that?" Pepper asks.

I think she knows, but she's afraid of the answer. "We'll need you and your fire creatures, Pep," I say.

Tam nods. "There's a cutting torch in the hold—or there was this morning, anyway—but we used up the fuel for it repairing the ship yesterday."

Pep swallows. "So I just cut the cables free near the ship, right?" she asks. Her voice trembles a little.

Tam shakes his head. "Cutting one side free before the other would put too much strain on the hull. If there are two cables, you'll need to crawl out to the point where the cables join, then get them both at once."

Pepper's voice gets real quiet. "I've never tried to cut anything that big before."

I squeeze her thigh. I can't think of much that would be scarier for her than being on a cable in the dark, dangling over the ocean, trying to cut the ship loose. "You can do it, Pep. I'll go out there with you if you want."

Tam's eyes flash up when I say that. He opens his mouth, then closes it. Sometimes he's smarter than he looks.

"You're assuming we can get to the deck, and that it's not guarded," Salyeh says. There's a worried, faraway look in his eyes, like he knows something we don't.

Tam shifts a little and glances at his feet. "We can get to the deck," he says. "We'll have to climb up the back of the ship, but Nadya and I can do it, and we can pull the rest—"

"No," Salyeh says. "I need to come with you."

It's my turn to open my mouth and close it again.

"The pirates will be in Nic's cabin," he continues. "You'll need me to handle them."

He's started shivering. His voice is flat and cold, like he doesn't want to do this but he's trying to convince himself to go anyway.

Nic's cabin.

That jogs something in my memory.

Nickle leaf a rainbow hoping.

Nic will leave a window open.

"Mrs. T said Nic would leave a window open," I whisper.

Everyone looks at me.

"I hope, anyway," I mutter. "It was hard to hear."

"How do we get up there?" Tian Li asks. Her eyes glimmer. I think she's got better night vision than the rest of us, or maybe she's trying to read the stars somehow, even though we can't see anything through the fog.

Tam frowns. "*We* don't. Sal and I will go alone."

I roll my eyes. "Tam, that's not gonna happen and you know it."

Pepper straightens up. Tian Li looks angry too.

Tam sighs. "Look," he says. "There's no ladder above the ironroom door. There's nothing to climb on but the places the wood has warped and chipped. There's an overhang where Nic's cabin sticks out over the rest of the hull. It won't be easy climbing, and the only anchor we'll have for the rope is the bolt to the left of the door. If we fall, we fall twice as far as we've climbed—all the way down to the door, then the same distance again before the rope finally catches us."

He looks like he's started sweating. He wipes his hands on his knees.

"That's assuming that the rope doesn't snap or the bolt doesn't pull out. We've only got one rope, so we all have to climb together, which means if one person falls, everyone falls. And all that weight goes fifty or sixty feet before the rope and the bolt try to catch it."

He licks his lips and looks at the rest of us. "So can you honestly tell me," he says, "that you won't fall?"

Nobody says anything.

He's definitely sweating. I can see the beads forming on his temples. His hands are trembling. He's terrified.

"Can you?" I ask softly.

Tam just looks away.

"We need to find another way," I say.

"There *is* no other—"

Pepper stands up.

She sways a little bit when she does. I don't think she's been on her feet since she got to the hiding place this morning. She's short enough that she only has to duck her head and shoulders to keep from bumping them on the bottom of the hull. She closes her eyes and puts her hands on the keel.

No one else moves.

Pepper's lips start moving silently, like she's having a conversation. She smiles, then frowns. For a second, she looks frustrated. The smile comes back.

"There's another way," she says. She traces a circle on the bottom of the hull with her fingers. "We can burn our way through."

"Is that safe?" Tam asks.

He's tucked his hands into his armpits again, and his shoulders are hunched so much his coverall looks like it's about to burst a seam.

Pep nods. "I made a deal with Ettingott. She owes me a favor because I let her eat some eggs at breakfast. She'll keep her end of the bargain."

Tam stays hunched. He doesn't like fire spirits, and he doesn't really trust Pepper to keep control of them. She once let one get loose, and it burned his arm pretty bad before she could suck it back into the World Beyond. He lay in his bed and moaned for days.

That was years ago. Still, I can't help but feel a little nervous too.

"Don't you usually call fire inside some kind of container?" I ask.

Pepper nods.

"What happens if you don't?"

Tam starts rubbing his left arm.

"Nothing out of the ordinary," Pepper says. "Unless a spirit breaks a contract. They get in trouble for doing that, back in their world, but sometimes they think it's worth it. Fire always wants to burn free." She lowers her head. "That's what Thom used to tell me, anyway."

I put a hand on Pepper's arm. "What'll happen if Ettingott breaks her contract here?"

Pep looks around. "In a space this small?" She sucks her bottom lip and frowns. "I try to drag her back into the World Beyond. She tries to keep me from doing it and burn up everything around her."

"Including us?"

Pepper nods.

Tam stands up and starts checking the rope behind him. "We're not doing that," he says. Nobody moves. He points at Pepper and Tian Li. "Untie your ropes. Sal and I will climb up to the cabin, and Nadya will belay."

Still, nobody moves.

Tam's eyes come up from the rope angry and afraid. "What in Goshend's name is wrong with you?" he shouts. "Move it!"

I slide over and put my hand on top of his mouth. "Tam," I say.

He stops fiddling with the rope and tries to move my hand away. I catch his wrist with my other hand and keep him from doing it.

"Calm down."

Tam's fingers tighten around my wrist. His eyes narrow. Then he takes a deep breath, and I feel the air run through my fingers. "I'm calm," he mumbles, and I take my hand off his mouth.

"We're not going to let you and Salyeh get yourselves killed." I glance back at Pepper and the others. The look in Salyeh's eyes has turned into something frightened and hard, like a cross between a cornered cat and one of the soldier statues in the walls of Vash Abandi. Next to him, Tian Li's jiggling her legs nervously.

"If Pepper says she can control the fire, I believe her," I say. "What about the rest of you?"

Tian Li looks at Pepper. "Are you sure you won't burn the gormling?"

Pepper bites her lip, but I've fed the gormling enough times that I know it's not going to be a problem. "The gormling tank's at the other end of the hold," I say. "We're right in the middle, where the aisle is. It'll be fine."

Tian Li thinks for a second, then gives a thumbs-up. Salyeh's chin dips down and up as he stares at the fog.

Tam scoots as far away from Pepper as he can. "Do it over there," he says, pointing at the entrance to the hiding place.

Pep shuffles there, into the moonlight.

And then she begins.

Watching a fireminder call a spirit from the World Beyond is a thing of beauty. Or at least I've always thought so. Pep

112

fishes in her pocket and pulls out a piece of charcoal. She pauses for a second, squeezing it between her fingers and chewing her lip. Then she starts to draw.

She moves fast once she's started, like a street artist making a sketch for a handful of coins. She traces a wide circle on the ceiling, one that's more than big enough for us to climb through, and then she starts making little marks inside it that I don't understand. They sort of look like letters, but there's a harshness to them that normal writing doesn't have—like each mark is a slash across the throat of a sacrificial chicken. They come together to form a picture of a house by a stream of fire, with a towering volcano in the background and clouds of smoke boiling across the sky.

After she finishes, she slips the charcoal back into her pocket and closes her eyes.

When she opens them again, they're full of flames.

They paint the dark wood of the hiding place with flickering orange light. Tam shrinks back against the far wall. Tian Li looks like she wants to join him, but Salyeh's in her way, and he's still staring into the fog and breathing hard, as if he hasn't even noticed that Pepper's calling fire.

"*Ettingott*," Pepper says. Her voice isn't her own. It's a lot lower, and it knocks against itself when she speaks, like it's a rock striking a flint. "*Ettingott, I call your name. Ettingott, come here.*"

She stretches her right hand toward the circle inscribed on the ceiling, spreads her fingers out, and then curls them in and moves her arm downward slowly, like she's pulling taffy.

"*Ettingott, come here,*" she repeats. "*Ettingott, come here.*"

She's not bothering to whisper. I worry about that for a second, but in the end I figure it's not such a big deal. We're about to burn a hole in the bottom of the hold. If anyone's in there, it's not like they won't notice.

As Pepper's hand comes down, flames emerge from the center of the circle. They spread quickly, in two armlike tongues that fork out at their ends like fingers. As the fingers reach the edge of the circle, they grow blue and dark. The arms bulge like they're pushing.

The fire in the center grows. A skullish face forms in the flames.

It's hard to tell that's what it is at first, but I've seen Pepper call fire before, so I know what to expect from a fire spirit. A flattened oval of white flame appears in the center of the blaze. Two chunks of yellow shine where a human's eyes would be. A slash of blue opens up in the oval's center like a nose. Ettingott's mouth, when she opens it to speak, is jagged and orange, like the ones people carve into pumpkins on Goshend's Funeral every year.

"*Pepperrrrrr,*" Ettingott says. Her voice is as deep and rocky as Pepper's was before. "*You promised me a feeeassst . . .*"

"I promised you a *meal,*" Pepper says. Her voice is back to normal, but her eyes still spark and burn. "And you've got one. Eat."

"*Feassst wasss implied . . .*"

"It was *not,* Ettingott. Will you eat what's here, or will you

114

break your contract and make me send you back to the World Beyond?"

Pepper's hand goes into her pocket again. I'm not sure what else she's got in there, but Ettingott's head snaps toward it. The fire hisses and pops.

"*Nnnooo, Pepperrrr! I willl fulfilll the contrrract . . .*"

Pepper's hand comes back out of her pocket.

"*But the nexxxt willl not be sssooo generousss . . .*"

Pepper crosses her arms over her chest. "We can talk about that when the time comes."

Ettingott grins. Her smile isn't a pleasant thing to see. The crooked orange crease of her mouth dances up at the edges, so wide it reaches almost beyond the white oval of her head. She laughs. It sounds like boulders falling down a mountainside.

"*Yesss,*" she says. "*We shhhalll . . .*"

Her face turns toward the wood and disappears.

The ceiling's well and truly on fire now, but only inside the circle Pepper made with charcoal. The characters she drew are completely gone. Where it's burning, the ceiling starts to flake.

Pepper whips out her charcoal and draws a square on the floor, then jumps over the lines and out from under the burning circle on the ceiling. A moment later, a flaming chunk of wood falls and lands in the center of the square Pep drew. The flames there spread faster than ever, pushing against the charcoal lines like they're trying to break free.

Ettingott squeals. *"WICKEDDD, WICKEDDD GIRRRLLL!"* she cries. *"YOU DENY ME EVVVERRRYTHINNNGGG!"*

Pepper says nothing.

The floor burns through completely inside Pep's square and crumbles away with a loud *crack.* I worry for a second that the whole hiding place will go with it, but the rest of the floor stays steady as a rock. More chunks of burning wood fall from the ceiling and drop into the sky through the new hole. Soon the circle's nearly gone, and only tiny flickers of flame remain at its edges.

One of them flares bright white. *"IT ISSS DONNNE, PEPPERRR— HOLLLDDD YOU THE CONTRRRACT FULLLFILLLED?"*

"I'll hold it fulfilled when you go back to the World Beyond, Ettingott," Pepper says.

Ettingott's laughter fills the hiding place again. *"WICKEDDD, WICKEDDD PEPPERRR,"* she says. *"THERRRE WILL COME A TIME WHEN YOU WISHHH YOU HADDD BEENNN KINNNDDDERRR TO ME."*

"We'll see," says Pepper.

She raises her left hand, open palmed like she did before, and makes a motion of pushing something up. The flames soak back into the wood.

Ettingott laughs harder and harder, until the flames disappear completely.

Pepper blinks. The fire winks out in her eyes.

I realize I'm standing rigid as a board. Tam lets out a long, slow breath behind me. Tian Li's holding Salyeh's hand, and Salyeh looks freaked out too—the stony stare has slipped from his eyes.

Pepper's face is covered in sweat. She licks her lips and takes a long, shaky breath. No one says anything, so I fill the silence.

"Thanks, Pep," I say. "That hole looks perfect."

It really does. It's about three feet wide, and it goes all the way through the *Orion*'s hull and into the darkness of the hold above.

Pep wipes her sleeve across her face.

"Thanks," she says. "Watch out for the second one." The hole that burned up near her feet is big enough that someone could fall through it, if they weren't careful.

"Why did you need it?" Tian Li asks. She's released her hold on Salyeh, but she still looks scared.

"The fire has to stay inside the charcoal," Tam says. He's rubbing his left arm again. "If it gets on anything outside it, it gets to eat whatever that is, unless the summoner can force it back into the World Beyond."

Pepper looks down at the hole. "I should've drawn it in the first place, but I didn't think about what'd happen when the circle started burning." She sighs and puffs a frizzy curl out of her face.

"And if you hadn't drawn it fast enough, that fire spirit woulda eaten the hiding place, and we'd have all either burned up with it or had a nice long fall to our deaths." Tam looks at Salyeh and Tian Li. "Still think that was a good idea?"

"We're all here, aren't we?" I say, glaring at Tam. "Think that'd be true if we'd done things your way?"

Tam glares back at me. Pepper looks at the hole in the floor. Salyeh and Tian Li just stare at us.

Eventually, Tam unclips his lobster claws and heads toward the hole. His shoulder brushes past mine when he does. His arm's cold as ice.

"Come on," he mutters. "We've got a ship to take back."

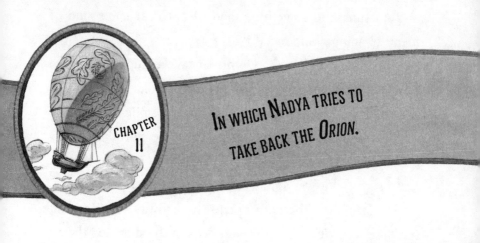

CHAPTER 11

IN WHICH NADYA TRIES TO TAKE BACK THE *ORION*.

Inside the hold it's dark and gloomy. There's only a tiny bit of light leaking in from the hole that Ettingott burned in the keel, and a little more from the gormling near the door. But this is our home, and we know our way around it even in the dark.

Pretty well, at least.

My shin crashes into something hard and round, and I have to grit my teeth to stifle a shout. As I rub my leg and squeeze carefully past the thing I bumped into, I figure out it's the leg of the big pedal-powered flying machine made of pipes and sheet metal that Tam likes to work on when we're in port. He calls it the Flightwing. I hear the others bumping into things as well, and I worry about the noise we're making. None of us knows where the pirates are, and we don't want *them* to find *us*. If we're going to have a chance against them, we'll need the element of surprise.

Tam runs into something, and then I hear the sound of metal scraping along metal.

"What're you doing?" I whisper. We're supposed to be heading for the door at the aft end of the hold.

"You'll see," he whispers back. There's a smile in his voice.

We reach the door not long after. The gormling looks quiet, its spots pulsing slowly and steadily. I figure that's a good sign—if it was agitated, I'd be more worried.

Salyeh nudges the door open. The hallway outside is lit, but deserted. We're on the lowest deck of the ship, and there's not much down here but cargo and ballast and the water supply. The light in the hall comes from a lamp near a set of stairs at its aft end.

In it, I see what Tam was smiling about.

He's carrying the biggest wrench on the ship. It's three feet long, with an adjustable head almost a foot wide. We use it to loosen or tighten the enormous bolts around the bases of the capstans—big mechanical winches on the deck that look like wheels with rods sticking out of them—that stretch out the cables to the cloud balloon.

Well, we used it for that once, anyway. Other than that, I've never seen it outside the hold.

Tam looks ridiculous holding it. He's not much over five feet tall. Strong as I know he is, I'm surprised he can even carry the thing by himself.

"What're you going to do with that?" I whisper.

He pantomimes knocking me over the head with it and grins.

"Really, Tam?"

Tam's grin melts into a scowl. "What did you wanna do?" he whispers back. "Brain them with your stupid doorknob?"

I stop walking. I straighten my back and raise my shoulders, like I've seen Mrs. T do when she has to stand up for herself in port. My heart thunders, my gills burn, and all the fighting I've been doing with Tam rushes back over me. Tam notices. His face goes a little gray.

"Take it back," I whisper.

"What?" he says, but his eyes dart toward the hold, where Thom will have stashed the doorknob and everything else that was in my room. He knows what I'm talking about.

"Everything you've said about me and my doorknob. Take it back."

"Nadya, this isn't—"

I hear two footsteps and then Salyeh's there, staring down at me and Tam. "Shh," he whispers. He glances meaningfully at the stairway up to the rest of the ship.

My heart keeps pounding. I stare at Tam until he looks away.

Salyeh turns around. "We should check the bedrooms," he says, shivering. They're on the second deck, along with the galley and the ironroom.

He starts to creep forward. Tam, after a nervous glance at me, follows him.

"Maybe . . . ," Salyeh mumbles, swallowing, "maybe the pirates will have drunk themselves to sleep."

Tian Li and Pepper are staring at me and Tam. I ignore

them and keep glaring at Tam's back. I'll get my apology, sooner or later.

Whether he wants to give it or not.

We check Tam's bedroom first.

Salyeh and Tam and I go in ahead of everyone else. We don't want to risk a light, so we listen. Luckily, Tam keeps everything on the ship in good order. The hinges on the doors don't squeak. Neither do the boards.

We don't find anyone in Tam's room.

Next we check Thom's, a real big one across the hallway, then Pepper's, then Tian Li's.

Empty. Every last one of them. Nothing but bare closets and vacant drawers and perfectly made beds.

Pepper looks distraught to see her room abandoned.

"It's okay," I whisper. "It's all in the hold."

This is part of the plan for pirates. Thom empties the rooms, so that it looks like the *Orion* just couldn't find any passengers for its voyage. Pepper nods, but she still looks like someone kicked her in the stomach.

When I think of my room, with its haphazard piles of clothes, its desk jammed full of sheets of paper and pens and ink and books, and its wardrobe always open and messy, I think I can understand why. If I saw it empty and clean, it would feel like it belonged to someone else. I don't know how well I could take that. It's my *home*.

We check Mrs. T's room, at the end of the hallway, next. It

still has most of her belongings. Her desk's untouched, with its books and potted plants all exactly where I last saw them. But her wardrobe's been ransacked. Her dresses and long skirts and trousers and blouses, normally folded perfectly away on hangers, are scattered over her bed and the floor. A lot of them are missing.

That turns my stomach too.

It's in Salyeh's room, next to the stairway to the main deck, that we find our first pirate.

We hear him the second we open the door. His snores fill the hallway like a steam train rumbling down a track. I wonder, briefly, if that's why his friends made him sleep down here. Sal's room's the quietest one on the ship. The stairs block the noise from it.

Tam hoists the wrench off his shoulder. Salyeh takes a deep, shaky breath and stalks into the darkness. My heart leaps into my throat.

Until now, I hadn't really thought about what we'd do when we found the pirates. Somewhere in the back of my head, I knew we'd have to hurt them. But seeing Tam with that huge wrench and Salyeh flexing his hands—

Knowing you have to do something and watching it being done can be two very different things.

When they strike, I'm glad for the darkness.

They do it in silence. I hear scuffling sounds, grunting, a loud *thump*—

And then nothing.

Salyeh walks back into the light. Tam follows him, shaking a little.

"It's done," Salyeh says. Tian Li glances away, and Sal's face twitches. For a second he looks like he wants to sit down and cry, but he clenches his jaw so fast I'm not sure what he's feeling, and then he pushes past us and heads for the stairway.

"What happened?" I whisper to Tam as we follow.

Tam just shakes his head.

We find no one in the galley or the ironroom, so we head out onto the deck.

The lamps on the railing are still lit. We leave the stairwell slowly, one by one. Salyeh watches the foredeck. Tam turns around and looks aft. I watch the egg-shaped shadow of the cloud balloon. There's no movement.

It's cold and misty out on deck. The fog streams past us like the grasping fingers of long-dead giants. The *Remora*'s engines drone in the darkness off the bow. They're quieter than they were when she was boarding us. The pirates must be towing us on a long line, just like Tam thought.

We check my room next. I don't want to see it empty of everything that makes it mine, so I don't look in. Tam comes back out and shakes his head. No pirates. I think Salyeh was right back in the hiding place, and the rest of them will probably all be in Nic's cabin. It's got the softest bed and the nicest couch.

Not to mention that's where he keeps the wine and liquor he breaks out on holidays and special occasions.

The moon has set, and there's no light other than the glow of the fire spirits dancing in the lamps. They turn and glare at Pepper as she passes, like they've heard about what happened with Ettingott, and they're mad on their friend's behalf.

Pep walks past them with her head held high. She doesn't even look at them.

We head toward Nic's cabin slowly. We've worked out the basic plan already—Salyeh and Tam will go in first, then I'll follow, and Pepper and Tian Li will come last. All of us know a thing or two about scrapping. We used to live in places that could be rough. You don't do that without picking up a few things. Mrs. T tried to protect me in Vash Abandi, but I'm kinda hard to protect. I still snuck out on my own. I still saw a lot of things. I still got into trouble and back out again.

I think about Tam telling me I'm just dumb and lucky, and I stick my tongue out at his back. He doesn't know me half as well as he thinks.

There's soft, flickering light licking the bottom of Nic's door. Salyeh puts one hand on the handle and holds up the other to count down.

Three.

Two.

One.

He opens the door and sneaks in. Tam follows.

Then it's my turn.

Inside, the room doesn't look much different than it would on a normal night, except that the gas candles in the chandelier are lit. The table's in its usual place. A book sits on top of it. The little statue of Goshend, with its big belly and long seaweed beard, stands in its shrine with a green candle behind it and a little prayer rug on the floor in front of it. The cabinets closest to me are closed and latched, although some of the ones in Nic's desk are busted open. One of the back windows is open too, and a stream of mist is pouring through it.

The first big difference other than the chandelier and the desk sits on the table next to the book: three bottles of wine, all empty. Next to them there's one bottle of rum, mostly empty, and a bottle of whiskey, half empty. Nic's liquor cabinet is open too.

The next big difference is lying on the couch.

He's a tall, lanky man, dressed in oversized leather boots and baggy trousers. A black peacoat with huge buttons down the front hangs open on his chest on top of a white tunic with some red wine spilled on it. There's a wide-brimmed hat over his face.

He looks very human, lying asleep like that. He doesn't look dangerous. He doesn't look like

he'd sell me into slavery if he woke up and got the jump on us. But he would.

I don't see any weapons on him. That scares me—it means they must be hidden someplace I can't see, like inside the hat, or the coat, or the boots, or the trousers. Pirates always carry weapons. We all know that.

Tam eases the wrench from his shoulder. Salyeh creeps forward. Tam looks back at me, swallows, and slinks after him.

Halfway to the pirate, Salyeh freezes. I follow his eyes as they turn to the right.

There's another pirate sitting upright against the head-board of Nic's bed. She's a woman with flowing brown hair and a bright red, ankle-length overcoat with yellow trim.

And she's awake.

Or at least I think she's awake. Her eyes are closed, but her lips are moving, like she's having a conversation with someone in her mind.

Pepper sucks in a sharp breath behind me.

Fireminder, I think.

The pirate's eyes open, then widen.

Salyeh takes a step forward and stops. Tam can't get around him.

"Harry!" the woman shrieks. She reaches inside her coat for something.

My feet start moving. I pick up one of the empty wine bottles from Nic's table.

"Wake up! There's—"

I vault over the table and swing the bottle like a giant fly-swatter.

It hits the pirate square in the side of her head with a heavy *crack.* The impact travels up my arm and jars my teeth. I feel like *I've* been punched in the head.

The bottle doesn't break. It's made of stronger stuff than that. But it falls out of my suddenly numb fingers.

The pirate's eyes roll back and she keels over. A tiny one-shooter flintlock pistol drops from her fingers to the bed.

I hear more scuffling behind me. Someone shouts. There's a heavy *thump.*

But I can't take my eyes off the pistol.

She would've shot it, I think. *She would've shot Salyeh, or Tam, or me. She would have—*

Pepper screams.

I whip around and see Tam and Salyeh struggling with the other pirate. Salyeh's on the man's back, and he's got one arm hooked underneath the pirate's chin and the other around the back of his head. His legs are trapping one of the pirate's arms and his biceps are squeezing, and the pirate's face is turning red.

The pirate's got an arm free though, and in it is a much bigger pistol than the one the woman was carrying.

Tam drops his wrench and gets both hands around the pirate's wrist, trying to control it. But the gun's still waving in the general direction of Pepper and Tian Li.

"Duck!" I shout.

The pirate's face turns redder. Pepper dives under the table.

Tian Li runs forward instead.

There's a deafening *crack* and a bright spark of light. The sharp stink of burnt gunpowder fills the room. A shower of glass and splinters rains over the table, and Pepper screams again.

Tian Li reaches the pirate and kicks him between the legs. Then she does it again, and again. They're big kicks too. Full pull-your-leg-back-all-the-way and lunge-forward and put-all-your-weight-into-it kicks.

The man's eyes bulge and he groans. Tam rips the pistol out of his hands.

A second later, the pirate falls to the floor, and Salyeh pulls him flat with his legs. The pirate claws at Salyeh's arms for a few seconds, and then he goes limp.

Salyeh doesn't let go.

Tian Li stands in front of him and stares. Tam, panting, opens the flash pan of the double-barreled pistol's other side and pours out the gunpowder there. Pepper crawls out from under the table.

Still, Salyeh doesn't loosen his grip. The pirate's face turns purple.

"Sal?" I ask.

His eyes are wide. He's breathing harder than ever. His arms are shaking.

"Sal?" I ask again.

Another few seconds pass.

And then, finally, Salyeh loosens his arms and crawls off the pirate.

There are white marks where Salyeh's arms went around the pirate's neck, like all the blood's been squeezed out of those places. But they fade. The pirate's face turns a normal color again. He's still breathing.

Salyeh brushes past me, shivering like he's standing in a midwinter blizzard. He walks to the female pirate, flips her over, and pulls her hands behind her back. Then he takes a length of rope out of his pocket and binds her wrists. He fumbles more rope around her ankles. He ties them together and anchors the whole mess to one of Nic's bedposts, and then he tears a long strip from her trouser cuffs and wraps it tightly around her mouth.

"Somebody search her, please," he whispers. His voice cracks, but he goes to truss up the other pirate.

As I rifle through the woman's coat, I find a long knife and another tiny pistol. I pull her boots off and search them, and I find a knife in there too. I run my hands up and down her trousers and discover another long knife in a pocket on her thigh.

It's all much easier than I expected it to be.

Don't look at her face, I tell myself. I heard a bouncer outside a pub say that once, when he was telling a boy on his first day how to turn away beggars. *It's easier if you don't see a face.*

Her chest juts unusually far out and moves as one piece when she breathes. I run my fingers over it and discover she's wearing a kind of wire-filled brassiere.

I find a razor hidden in there.

When all's said and done, I have two pistols, three long knives, one short knife, and two tiny razors laid out in a pile on the end of Nic's bed. Tam has a pile just as big going on the table. The male pirate's trussed up like the woman.

Salyeh's hunched over at the table, clenching and un-clenching his fists.

Tian Li's over by the cabinets, looking nauseous.

Pepper's sitting with her knees tucked to her chest by Tian Li's feet. There are tears on her cheeks.

I smell something smoky and sweet and look up.

The pirate's shot shattered the glass bulb around one of the gas candles. Its flame is almost two feet tall, and it's licking the ceiling.

"Pep," I say.

She raises her head and wipes her nose with her sleeve.

"We've got a fire problem—do you know where the switch for the chandelier is?"

She looks at the chandelier, then unwinds herself and stands. She reaches behind one of the cabinets and cranks something.

The flames in the chandelier shrink, then flicker, then die. And then we're lit only by the lamps out on deck, shining weakly through Nic's open door.

I scoop up my pile of weaponry and lay it next to Tam's on the table.

"I . . . I should go search the other guy," Tam mutters. He rubs a red spot on his wrist—probably a burn from the pistol shot.

"I'll go with you," Pepper says.

"Be careful!" I call after them. "We still haven't checked the cloud balloon!"

But I know there won't be anyone in it. The pirates' sky-lung will be back on the *Remora*, watching over *its* cloud balloon. It's got a much bigger ship to support.

When Pep and Tam have gone, I pull up a chair across the table from Salyeh. He's staring at the wall now, still making fists.

"Sal, are you okay?" I ask.

"You have to hold it," he mutters. His fists squeeze, then relax. "You have to hold it, if you want them to stay out for a while. Even once they go limp, you have to hold it. But if you hold it too long, you'll kill them."

I put my hand over his, but he pulls it away and turns to look anywhere but at me.

"I froze," he says. His eyes look wide and ghostly. "You can't freeze. If you freeze, you die. That's the first thing they teach you. If you *freeze*, you *die*."

He squeezes his fingers into his palms. "And I froze," he whispers.

There are underground fighting rings in Vash Abandi, down by the river in a bad part of town. I tried to sneak off to see them once, but I couldn't get in. The closest I got was the back door near the water, where I saw a kid bruised and bloodied and crying his eyes out.

I've never asked Sal where Nic found him, but with how big he is and how he keeps quiet about where he came from, I've always wondered.

I put my hand over his again. This time when he tries to move away, I hold it there. His fingers are ice cold.

"You didn't die," I say.

His whole body shivers. "I should have," he whispers.

"No," says Tian Li. She puts an arm around his neck. Tears wind shining streams down her face.

Salyeh's shoulders rise and fall in big, broken judders. When he turns and the lamplight hits his face, I see he's crying too.

Footsteps echo in the doorway. "We got all the stuff off him," Tam says. "I—"

He stops halfway through the door and stares at Tian Li and Salyeh. Pepper pokes her head in behind him. Her eyes widen.

I get up from the table, shoo Pepper and Tam out into the fog, and close the door to Nic's cabin behind me.

Tam and Pep look like they want an explanation, but I don't give them one. Sal can talk to them later if he wants.

"Come on," I say instead. I walk toward the stairs. "Let's get the other guy stashed someplace safe before he wakes up."

We've got a lot to do, and it's gonna take us all to do it. But Sal deserves to rest, and I bet Tian Li can help him better than anybody else.

I just hope they'll be ready again before Pepper has to cut us free.

Since one of the pirates is a fireminder, we stash all three in the boiler of engine two. It's the only place we can think of where the fireminder won't cause trouble if she works her gag free and calls a fire spirit. There won't be anything in there for her to burn but herself, a bit of air, and the other pirates. The boiler's a little small for the three of them, but we figure that'll just make it harder for them to get loose and cause problems.

It still feels wrong to be stuffing three people into a space so small.

Don't look at their faces, I remind myself. They came for us first. They would've killed us if we'd let them.

The woman, smushed so close between the others she can barely move, stares daggers at me and mutters into her gag.

I close the door of the boiler and turn the wheel that

latches it. Tam pulls one of Nic's keys off the ring we took from the female pirate and locks it.

He looks scared.

I feel the same way.

After a quick vote on deck, we decide to pitch the pirates' weapons overboard, just in case.

We don't want to use them, so there's no sense hanging on to them. If the pirates do get free somehow, the last thing we need is for them to be able to get their weapons.

As the guns and knives and razors tumble into the darkness, I tell myself again that they would've killed us if we'd let them, and that they still will if we let our guard down.

Still, my mouth tastes ashy. I wish we hadn't had to lock them up. I wish they'd never come here in the first place.

After the weapons are gone, we stand in a circle on the deck, listening to the drone of the pirate ship's engines. With the moon set, the only light in the mist comes from the lanterns along the sides of the *Orion*. It feels like we're sailing off the edge of the world and into the jaws of Goshend's judgment.

It's also cold. The fog leaves lines of water in my hair. I rub my arms for warmth. My skin feels rubbery.

For a few seconds, we all just stare at each other. Salyeh looks tired and ashamed. Tian Li looks completely exhausted. Tam looks nervous. Pepper's staring anywhere but at the two cables that stretch from the *Orion*'s sides into the darkness off its bow.

"Last chance," I say. I look toward the sound of propellers. Somewhere out there, in the middle of this big bank of gross-tasting crudcloud, there's a giant metal ship. And somewhere in that ship, the pirates have Mrs. T, Nic, and Thom. If we cut loose from them now, we might never see them again. "We could still try to save them."

Tam frowns. "We've been over this, Nadya. How do you wanna rescue them? We'd all have to climb out on the cables and get over to their ship. Then we'd have to get inside from wherever they attached the cables. Then we'd have to *find* Thom, Nic, and Mrs. T. Then we'd have to get them out. Then we'd have to climb back, cut ourselves free, and outrun the pirates before they notice what happened. It's impossible!"

"I want a vote," I say. I cross my arms. It's the least they can do. Nic's from Myrrh, where they're big on voting, and anytime he leaves a decision up to us, he tells us to vote on it.

Tam rolls his eyes. "Fine," he says. "You're for rescuing them. I'm opposed. Sal?"

Salyeh shakes his head. "Opposed."

"Tian Li?"

"Opposed."

"Pepper?"

Pep stares at her feet. "I—"

"Never mind," Tam says. "That's three to two at best. We're going to do what they *told* us to do. We're going to cut ourselves free and run."

"Every vote matters," I say quietly.

Tam snorts, but he also shuts up.

"Pep?" I ask.

She looks toward the sound of the *Remora*'s engines, then at the dancing flames on the *Orion*'s rails. *Thom's flames,* I think. Still bound to the contract he made with them, even though he's not here.

"I'm for saving them," Pep whispers, and my heart soars because at least Pep's with me now.

"Three to two then," Tam says. "We cut the cables and we run."

I put my hand on Pepper's shoulder and glare at Tam. "You mean *she* cuts the cables and we run."

The *Orion* sways gently from left to right as the wind pushes her. The cloud balloon floats over us like a huge black spider's bloated egg sac.

Pepper takes a deep breath and looks at the cables. "I can do it," she says, wiping some fog drops from her face with her sleeve. "Not with Ettingott, but there's another fire spirit—one of the big ones that runs the engines. His name's Rottfeuer."

She shivers, and her eyes flick nervously toward Tam. "I'll have to offer him something big, though. And unusual. He's already got a contract to gobble coal in the engines. He'll want something else, like fuel oil or dry wood or—"

"Garden air," I say.

Pep looks up at me with wide eyes.

The air in the cloud balloons burns crazy easy. We hear about accidents out on the Cloud Sea every once in a while—some fireminder gets careless, and a spark gets onto a balloon's skin and catches. The balloon burns. Everything in it burns. The ship crashes into the sea, and some watership finds the pieces, or they wash up on an island months later if the leviathans and giant squid don't get them first.

"I'll get him a jar," I say quietly. "We can throw it off the back of the ship, or lower it on a rope."

Pepper bites her lip and rubs her hands on her coveralls. The light of the fire spirits dances and sparkles on the mist in her hair.

"That might work," she says. She takes a deep breath. "I'll ask Rottfeuer."

Her eyes close. Her lips start moving again, forming words that don't even look human to me. Tam walks away and starts checking the cables attaching us to the *Remora*. Tian Li stares into the fog. Salyeh looks at his feet and whispers something to himself.

Pepper opens her eyes. "He wants the jar first," she says. A bead of sweat rolls down the side of her head. "He doesn't believe we can get it for him."

I nod. "Easy enough."

Tam comes back over and frowns. "And what if the pirates notice the big lamp we're dangling out in the fog?"

Pep looks at her feet. "It was the only way he'd do it, Tam. He doesn't trust me. Says I lied to Ettingott."

Tam crosses his arms. "Did you?"

"No!" Pep stamps her feet. Her eyes glisten. "But she's been spreading rumors about me in the World Beyond! All kinds of things—that I went back on my contract, that I tried to bind her against her will—horrible things! Things I'd never do!"

I grind my teeth and mouth *dead man* at Tam. His nostrils flare, but he shuts up.

"It's okay, Pep." I give her arm a squeeze. "Rottfeuer's willing to do it, right? And then he'll go back to the World Beyond and tell the other spirits they can trust you."

Pep storms away and slumps against the rail. Her eyes are red and watery. She's exhausted, I realize. We all are. Tired and cold and hungry.

"I'll go get a canning jar and fill it," I say. "Can you guys make some sandwiches or something?"

They look at me like I just asked them to hold a square dance. But after a second, Tian Li nods, like she gets it. Salyeh heads toward the kitchen. Pep sits against the rail looking miserable.

Tam just stares at me.

So I turn my back on him and go get my jar.

The inside of the cloud balloon's a wreck.

The plants have turned awful shades of orange and yellow and purple and red. The birds' nests are in shambles. The birds themselves look upset and dirty. The frogs sit nervously on lily pads in little clusters, like the old men in Vash Abandi who talk about the desert at cafés.

Their voices hit me like a tidal wave.

Nadya, what's going on? I thought—

Nadya, where's Zelda? She was supposed—

Nadya, are we safe? I heard shouts—

Nadya—

Nadya—

Nadya—

Quiet! I shout, as loud as I can get. The tidal wave recedes into quiet, whispery shallows.

You're all safe, I tell them. My gills suck in the warm, moist air of the garden. It calms me. And my calmness will calm them. That's what Mrs. T always told me.

There's a problem on the ship, I say. *Mrs. Trachia's dealing with it.*

The voices start in again right away.

What kind of problem?

Will it hurt us?

What about the children, Nadya?

I close my eyes and let their chatter wash over me. I don't bother trying to pick out words or voices. I just focus on the tone. They're scared. They want to know I'm looking out for them, and that all they have to do is carry on as usual.

So that's what I tell them.

They calm down then. The birds cock their heads and blink at me. The frogs look up at me with wide yellow eyes. The minnows in the pond stop schooling and drift. The plants exhale.

I have to go back down now, I tell them. My jar's full of garden air, and I've sealed it tight. *But I'll be back soon. Just pretend that everything's normal.*

I swallow. *Mrs. Trachia will be back before long.*

The birds stare at me. The frogs bob on the lilies. Even the insects stop buzzing.

It's not a lie.

I won't let it turn into one.

The voices of the garden follow me into the waiting house with good-byes and good-lucks and thank-yous. They're only drowned out when I seal the door behind me and the pumps start to work.

I slump against the metal walls and wait for the rush of outside air. For the first time in my life, I'm glad to leave the garden.

• • •

The others are waiting for me when I get back down. They've got salami-and-sharp-cheddar sandwiches on yesterday's brown bread, spread with mustard and mayonnaise and topped with cloud lettuce and sky tomatoes. We sit cross-legged on the deck and pass around a thermos of lemonade as we eat.

I'm glad I asked for food. I'm absolutely starving. I tear through one sandwich and half of another before I realize there are eight sandwiches in all, and I ought to only eat my share.

Salyeh notices me stop. He waves at one of the sandwiches that's left.

"Go ahead," he says. His eyes look deep and sad, like sink-holes full of brown water. "I'm not hungry."

I frown. He should be eating more than any of us. He's bigger, and he used all that energy wrestling with the pirates.

But my stomach's happy about the promise of more food, so I grab another half sandwich and tear into it.

"What's the plan after we cut free?" I ask around a mouthful of cheese and mustard and bread. "How do we run away?"

Tam looks at Tian Li.

"We talked about that," she says. She sets her sandwich down and nods at the cloud balloon. "We think the best way will be to drop as low as we can—almost all the way to the sea, maybe."

"That'll get us out of the fog," Tam continues. "Plus the pirates' cloud balloon has got to be massive to support that

143

ship. Refilling it with garden air could take days. They probably won't want to go that low to come get us."

I nod. He's right, and it's a good plan. It would take our garden most of a day to get us this high again if we dropped down to around a thousand feet. Longer without good clouds or if the plants and animals were unhappy. The pirates would take a lot longer to pull the same trick.

I slurp down a loose tomato slice and wipe my mouth with the back of my hand.

"And then what?" I ask.

Tam frowns. "Then we have a problem. We've got to figure out what to do with the pirates we caught, and we've got to avoid the other pirates. We only have the one engine, and I don't want to start it for a while anyway, so the other pirates won't hear it if they *do* decide to come after us."

I crunch through some lettuce. "We can fix engine number two, Tam." We were almost finished with repairs before the pirates showed up.

"But we can't run it." He raises an eyebrow at me. "Did you forget where we stashed the pirates? We can't run whichever engine has them in the boiler."

I remember turning the wheel and locking them in the darkness. I remember the woman staring at me.

I lower my head.

"Okay," I say. "So we sit for a little while and wait until we're sure the pirates are gone, and then we go somewhere on one engine. Where?"

Tam shrugs. "Vash Abandi's still closest."

I raise my eyebrows. "You think we'll get a good welcome in Vash Abandi? Five kids alone on a cloudship, with three captured pirates? They'll seize the *Orion* for sure, auction it off to some slimy merchant and throw us all on the streets. Besides, that's where those goons found us in the first place!"

Tian Li looks up. "There's the gormling to think of too," she says. "We only have a few days of food left for it."

Tam rolls his eyes. "If we go back to Vash Abandi, we can just return it to whoever gave us the contract in the first place."

Salyeh leans back and shakes his head. "Far Agondy," he says quietly. "It's got to be. Nic said we should get help from his old crewmates if we were ever on our own. More of them run in and out of Far Agondy than anywhere else. That's where *Dream* was headed too."

I nod. So do Pepper and Tian Li.

"Fine," Tam grumbles. "Have it your way."

I look at Thom's lanterns and the old, scarred wood of the *Orion*'s deck. The thought of taking it away from Nic, even if it's really the pirates who did the taking and we're just stealing it back, feels horribly wrong to me.

I take a deep breath. If we sit down by the waves while we make sure the pirates are gone, maybe I'll be able to change someone's mind about rescuing Nic and Thom and Mrs. T. Tian Li can be pretty brave. So can Salyeh. I bet they're just rattled from our fight with the pirates. I bet I can talk them into it.

The drone of the *Remora*'s engines fills the night. Thom's fire spirits flicker and dance in their little glass prisons.

145

"What's going to happen when I cut the cables?" Pepper asks. She's finished her sandwich, but she looks sick to her stomach and she's hugging her knees.

Everyone stays quiet. I try to imagine it. Pep, dangling out on the cables, will summon Rottfeuer to cut them. He'll bite his way through. The cables will fall.

With Pepper still clinging to them.

Tam's eyes glitter in the lamplight. He swallows. He's known. The whole time we've been ready to act out this plan, he's known Pepper will fall.

"We'll have you roped up," he explains. "You'll be totally safe. Once it's over, we'll just pull you back on deck."

Pepper squeezes her eyes shut. The veins in her neck flutter. She clutches her knees so tightly her fingers turn white.

"Okay," she whispers.

Tam looks like he's swallowed a fish bone. A few seconds go by.

"You're not coming out there with me, are you, Nadya?" Pepper asks.

In my mind, the clouds rush up to swallow me. "I will if you want me to."

Pep shakes her head. "That's okay."

I reach out and hold her hand. "You'll be fine," I tell her. "I promise." She doesn't even open her eyes.

Tam's mouth twists to one side, like he's suddenly having doubts about his plan. *You better be sure about this,* I mouth to him.

I am, he mouths back.

You don't look it, I retort inside my head. But I can't come up with another way to cut the ship free. And if we don't cut the ship free, this ends in disaster.

Still, in my mind Pepper falls, over and over again. The cables snap. The mist rushes up to meet her. The rope tied to her safety belt stretches . . .

It won't break, I tell myself. *We have good ropes. Nic buys the best.*

I sit for a long time holding Pepper's hand. The last of the sandwiches lies untouched.

I don't much feel like eating anymore.

CHAPTER 13

In which Nadya makes a big mistake.

We hang the garden air off the back of the ship. With Rottfeuer eating it, it looks like a giant will-o'-the-wisp on a chain.

Once it's gone, Tam ties Pepper into an elaborate safety system. He winds a belt around her waist and legs, then a second belt over her chest and shoulders, and he ties them together and to a rope we'll use to belay her from the deck. Having two harnesses, he says, will distribute the shock of her fall. Then he gives Pep a set of short-roped lobster claws and clips them to the cable she's about to climb out on so she won't fall far if she slips before she cuts us loose.

Tam ran deliveries on the zip lines between skyscrapers in Far Agondy before he joined the *Orion*'s crew. I ought to trust him with ropes and harnesses. But I'm nervous anyway.

Once she's all tied in, Pep turns and looks at us. Tian Li gives her a hug. So do I. Her heart's pounding when I do it. Her fingers dig into my shirt. I want to say something, but my throat's all clogged up, and I can't make the words come out.

Pep lets go of me, takes a deep breath, and starts out into the mist.

She has to scrunch down on her belly and crawl onto the cable. I wish I had good advice to give her about how to get out there, but I don't. I look over at Tam, but his focus is on the rope and the belay device between him and Pep.

The cable bounces and jiggles under Pep's weight. She only gets about six feet before she falls.

My heart jumps into my throat, but her lobster claws catch her. Tam brakes the rope in the belay device just in case. He takes a deep breath.

For a second, Pep's hanging upside down above the mist. She's still close enough that I can see her face in the dancing orange glow of the lanterns. Her eyes are closed tight. She's covered in sweat.

"Be brave, Pep," I whisper.

And she is.

Tam keeps feeding rope through the belay device as she gets back onto the cable and crawls farther out. Salyeh's tied to Tam, and they're both clipped to the safety lines on the *Orion*'s deck. Everything should go fine. But when Pep gets past the little halo of light around the *Orion*, my throat closes up again anyway.

She's my best friend, but the darkness doesn't care about that. The sky doesn't care about that. The cables don't care, and Rottfeuer sure as spit isn't going to care either.

Dumb and lucky, Tam called me, and ever since I feel like I'm just waiting for something terrible to happen to prove him right.

"What if Rottfeuer burns through the rope, Tam?"

Tam's sweating now too. He's got leather gloves on to help him keep a good grip on the rope. "That's on her," he says, and then his mouth twists, like he wishes he hadn't said that. Maybe he's trying to be nicer but hasn't figured out how. "I mean, 'He won't,'" he says. "She knows what she's doing, Nadya."

I tap my hands on my forearms and bounce on my toes, trying to get some of the nerves dancing through me like hyperactive fire spirits to settle down. For a second, I start thinking about whether him or me is in charge and who's gonna be first mate, and then I realize that the contest is kinda over. None of that matters anymore. We're already running the ship now, all of us together, and it's not about who's in charge but about making sure we're all safe and get what we need.

Huh.

Salyeh lets out a deep, heavy breath. He's standing just behind Tam with his fingers hooked through the rear loop of Tam's safety belt, ready to help anchor him if something goes wrong. Tian Li's somewhere behind me. Her feet tap on the deck, like she's got fire spirits in her nerves too.

I take deep breaths. We can do this.

A breeze kicks mist over the ship. We watch Pepper's rope sway. A bright, red-orange light flares in the darkness.

"Get ready," Tam whispers. He tightens his grip on the rope and leans back.

The red-orange light stays lit a long time. Long enough for me to get nervous. Long enough for Tam to ask Tian Li to wipe the sweat from his forehead twice.

Like he doesn't want to take his hands off the rope that's going to keep Pepper alive.

There's a loud groan, then a nauseating, wrenching *crunk-SPANG*. The *Orion* lurches. The cables fall.

So does the red light.

Tam brakes the rope and braces his feet against the deck. Salyeh tightens his grip on Tam's belt and leans back. The rope goes slack over the *Orion*'s rail, and the red light disappears. Tam barks out a string of cuss words I've never heard him use before. So does Tian Li.

I have curses too, but I don't use them. *She'll be fine she'll be fine she'll be fine,* I tell myself.

The rope stretches and goes taut. Tam skids across the deck, dragging Salyeh with him. His curses get louder. I snatch at Salyeh's belt as he slips by and try to dig my heels in. Tian Li's arms wrap around my waist, and then all four of us are sliding toward the ship's rail. I pray that we'll stop soon. Because if we don't, the ropes tying Tam and Salyeh to the ship will do the stopping for us, and Pepper's rope and harnesses will be a lot more likely to snap.

Tam thumps into the rail. Salyeh plows into him. The ropes tying them to the deck stretch as far as they can go.

And then everything stops.

Tam's bent over the rail, staring into the darkness. His head's next to one of the lanterns, and the fire spirit inside is leaping up and down and throwing itself at the glass, trying to get to his hair.

My throat's got a lump the size of an apple in it. "Is she . . ."

"She's still there," he says. "I can feel her weight."

Bring her back, I want to say. *Pull her back up, right now!* But the world goes all fuzzy, and my legs feel weak.

No, I tell my body. *You won't do that. Look at what Pepper just did. You're going to be* strong.

By the time I've gotten my head under control again, Tam and Salyeh are starting the long, careful process of hauling Pepper up.

First, they back toward one of the ship's capstans. Then Salyeh pulls Pepper up a foot or so, and Tam takes the slack out of the rope and tugs it through his belay device. I feed the other end of the rope through the capstan and turn the winch to coil it up once it's pulled in.

An awful lot of rope comes up over the side. I look down at the coil I'm making around the capstan. We picked a three-hundred-foot rope to anchor Pepper with. It looks like maybe twenty feet of it didn't go over the side with her.

Tian Li's standing by the rail, staring down into the night. "I hear feet on the hull!" she calls. "Pepper, is that you?"

There's no response. I want to run over and help, but Sal and Tam need me to coil the rope while they pull.

It's okay, I tell myself. *Feet on the hull. She's trying to climb up it. She's okay. Maybe she just hasn't caught her breath yet.*

A pale hand materializes out of the mists and grasps the top of the rail. Tian Li grabs it and pulls, and I leave the rope and run over and take hold of Pep's fingers as her other hand appears. They're cold as a midnight river in winter.

I can hear her now. She's sobbing and hyperventilating, and I look over the rail and understand why she didn't call back to Tian Li.

Pepper's hair is singed. There are tiny, shallow cuts all over her face and arms. Half of her upper-body harness is snapped and flapping in the breeze, and she's shaking as she cries.

Tian Li and I grab her under the armpits and haul her back on board.

"It's okay, Pep," I whisper, stroking her hair. "You're safe. We've got you."

Gently, Tian Li and I set her down against the rail. She shakes her head viciously. Her breath jerks in and out of her chest. I cup my hand over her cheek. It's as cold as her fingers.

"It's okay, Pep," I say again. "Everything's fine."

I hear the boys rushing over. Pepper's got a death grip on my arm.

"Nadya," Tam says.

I squeeze my eyes shut. I know what he's going to say.

"Nadya, you have to let the air out of the balloon. We have to dive now, before the pirates can get their ship turned around and come after us."

Pep's fingernails dig into my skin.

Tam's right.

And I hate him for it.

I scramble up to the cloud balloon as fast as I can. It feels like hours before the waiting house pumps out all the outside air and floods with the sweet, dense scents of the garden.

The voices hit me as soon as I'm inside.

Nadya, what's happening?

Where's Zelda, Nadya?

Nadya, the children—

I ignore them, even though I know that'll just make them more upset. I sprint over paths through the leafy ferns, around the glassy eye of the pond, past the girders with the birds' nests and through the shade of the trees. The sun-in-a-jar has gone into its night cycle now, and it's letting off a soft white replica of moonlight.

The controls for letting air out of the balloon are nestled near the very front of the garden. There's another set outside, in case emergency maneuvers need to be made without a sky-lung aboard, but it's much better to use the ones on the inside. You need more than an altimeter to know how much garden air you can let out safely. You have to keep track of how thin the air's getting inside and how hard it will be for the plants and animals that live there to breathe.

The only way to do that is by keeping track of how dizzy you get and how hard your gills are working.

The controls are simple. There's a metal seat in front of a console with dials showing altitude, outside air pressure, outside air temperature, inside air pressure, and inside air temperature. There are two levers: one to let garden air out and a second to take outside air in.

When I slide into the seat, the voices in my head grow into a shrieking symphony. I've never done this on my own before, and everything in the garden knows it.

Nadya, what are you doing?

Where's Zelda, Nadya?

I'm afraid!

What's happening? What's happening? What's happening?

I close my eyes and concentrate. The last time we had a crisis, Mrs. T showed me a trick for quieting the voices in the cloud garden when they get too shrill.

I imagine a whistle. A loud, harsh whistle, like a train coming into the station if your ear's right next to it. The whistle rises up to meet the voices. The voices get louder, but they can't match it. It swallows them. It swallows everything.

And then I stop it, and for a second there's perfect, crystal silence.

I have to let air out of the balloon, I say into the void. *I have to let out a lot of it. It'll make you sleepy. Just sleep. I'll take care of you. I'll keep you safe. You just have to sleep, and everything will be fine.*

The balloon stays silent.

I reach for the lever that'll vent the garden air and pull it toward my body. There's a loud *thunk* and *whirr* as the machinery

155

clunks into place and the vents outside the balloon open up. Then there's a thin hiss as the garden air starts to leak out. A little breeze strokes my cheeks. The top of the balloon shrinks toward the girders. My stomach jumps as we start to descend.

I watch the altimeter.

6,000 feet. 5,750. 5,500.

Nadya, a voice says in my mind. It sounds like pebbles clacking in the throat of a very old man, and it's close by.

I look down and see a wart-covered brown frog with one eye gone completely cloudy. His name is Mudwumple. He's the oldest of the frogs.

4,750. 4,500.

I don't have time to talk, Mudwumple. This is important.

My gills start to struggle a little, as if I've been climbing the supports in the balloon or transplanting a tree.

Nadya, look at the garden.

4,000. 3,750.

I look around. The trees are sagging and wilted. The leafy ferns have grown a bright, sickly shade of yellow. The birds are huddling together in their nests, shivering, too afraid to even speak.

Nadya, the garden is sick. Zelda is gone. We feel your fear, and it grows inside us like a cancer. We must know what is wrong, or the shadows of what it might be will swallow us.

I imagine Pepper's face, covered in cuts. I see her eyes staring blankly into the mist. I see her harness half broken.

My friend, I say quietly. The images seep over the words

and leak onto the Panpathia. *My friend is hurt, and I can't be with her because I have to be here, doing this.*

Breathing gets harder again, and I'm not sure whether it's because of the air leaving the balloon or the lump in my throat getting as big as a melon.

Everything will be fine, I say. *I just want to know that Pep—that Pep—*

The words stick in my mind. My head sways. The world gets far away and tilts up on its side. My lips and tongue go numb.

The world spins, and all of a sudden I realize I'm on the ground.

The voices around me have gone silent.

What was I going to say? I think. *Pep—Pepper—*

My hand's touching something cold and hard.

The lever.

I lurch to my feet and crank it back to the shut position. My gills flap unhappily on my neck. The world looks blurry. My head starts to feel like there's a tiny person drumming on it with a hammer.

There's more, I think. *Something else—*

I stumble, and my leg knocks into the second lever. I grab it and jerk it down. There's a gentle hiss, and misty outside air flows into the top of the balloon.

The outside air sinks fast. Soon the mist is swirling around my calves, and I crank the lever shut again.

I bend down so that my head's buried in the mist, and I

take deep breaths through my nose. My gills shut. The outside air fills my lungs.

Before the mist scatters all the way, my head's clear again.

I straighten up, and my gills twitch to life and start drinking in the garden air. It doesn't feel as refreshing, watered down with outside air like this, but it's better than the thin stuff I was breathing in before.

I look down at the altimeter. It's fogged up, so I wipe my fingers over it.

180.

And it's still dropping.

My heart dives into my stomach. We've never taken the ship this low this fast before. I spin around to ask for help, but everyone's gone—even Mudwumple. They must be asleep. There isn't enough garden air left for them to do much else. There's barely enough for me to breathe, and I need less of it than they do.

My head starts pounding again. The cloud balloon sags around the girders above me. I look back at the altimeter.

120.

90.

75.

It finally levels out around sixty. Way, way lower than I meant to go. Barely far enough off the waves that we'll be safe if there's a storm. My head's thundering, and my body feels like I've got the flu.

The garden's silent as a tomb.

It's my fault, I think. *It's all my fault.* I got distracted. I could've killed us all.

The thought bounces around in my head. There aren't any other voices left to contradict it. I stagger to the waiting house with tears in my eyes.

When the door shuts behind me, the tears start to fall.

"Nadya, what happened up there? We fell like a stone! Aren't you supposed—"

I shut Pepper's door in Tam's face and lock it behind me.

Pep's lying in bed, staring up at the ceiling. Her room's a small one, but I've always liked it. Her bed nestles against the *Orion*'s hull, and she's got two portholes to look through. Thom cleaned everything out of here, but it looks like Tam and the gang have moved it all back in for her. A little oil painting of the beach in the Free City of Myrrh hangs over her wardrobe, turquoise water and bright blue sky and swirling, shady buildings kissing white sand. A hand-sized statue of Goshend's Daughter, a smiling goddess with seaweed hair that reaches down to her ankles that some people from Myrrh ask for favors, is back on her desk. Her seashell box sits on the shelf beneath one of the portholes, and the other shelf's got her storybooks and engine manuals, all mixed up together.

The big mirror she spent a month's wages on is back in the corner. They even set up the old cargo net she hangs from her ceiling and put her collection of toy seals, dogs, and rats back in it. The room looks like it's hers again. Maybe that'll help.

The sky is starting to turn gray outside, so it must be close to sunrise. I pull out my pocket watch to check the time, but it's not running. I can't even remember when I wound it last.

My head's still pounding and my vision's blurry, but I'm not sure whether it's from the lack of air in the cloud balloon or just exhaustion. Probably both. It seems like a month ago I got up to fix engine number two.

I sit on the edge of Pep's bed and hold her hand. Her fingers are a bit warmer than they were right after we pulled her up, but they're still cold. I touch the back of my hand to her forehead. It feels a little chilly too.

"Pep?" I say.

Her fingers twine themselves in mine.

"It broke," she whispers. Her voice is smooth but fragile, like the wet wings of a newborn butterfly.

I squeeze her hand. The cuts on her face and arms were too small for bandages, but Tian Li told me she cleaned them with alcohol in the sickroom before putting Pepper to bed. Salyeh heated up some soup using an oil stove, and Tam made Pepper drink a cup of it.

They're good friends, every one of them. Even Tam, I guess.

"What broke?" I ask.

Pep's eyes drift down from the ceiling and settle on me.

They're bloodshot, like she got a bunch of smoke in them. "The cable. Rottfeuer was chewing through it, telling me if I ever wanted him to do this again, he'd need a whole barrel of garden air. Then the cable started to pull apart. There was this horrible twang, and then it just snapped, and my face and arms hurt and I was falling."

I nod. Tian Li was able to get that much out of her, and the others pieced together that the cable must've shredded after they found slivers of steel in Pep's clothing, hair, and skin.

Pepper turns to face the wall. "He got *on* me, Nadya."

She squeezes my hand so hard it hurts.

Rottfeuer.

Pep shuts her eyes. Tears drip down her cheeks. "He was on my arm and in my hair, and he was laughing and roaring and I was burning and falling at the same time."

"You sucked him back into the World Beyond."

Pepper nods. Her fingers loosen, and I run my hand through her hair.

"Where did he burn you?"

She shudders. "Nowhere bad. Just my scalp and my forearm. But he was so *close*—" Her breath goes in and out in little puffs. "I panicked. I don't know what would've happened if I didn't suck him back in when I did. I wasn't even thinking. And Rottfeuer's *strong*. That's why we use him to power the engines."

Now that I know what happened, I can see the parts of her hair that burned.

"You're strong too," I say.

Pep stares out her porthole windows at the growing light. "I guess," she says.

The *Orion* creaks and swings gently to the side. Nobody's at the wheel. We're below the fog around the pirates, down so far they won't be able to reach us, and we're just letting her drift in the wind while we rest. We don't have much of a choice without running the engines, but we could rig up a sail if we had to. Nic bought a big one and stowed it down in the hold after that time we got stranded.

"The harness snapped too," Pep says.

I run my hand over the side of her head, where she's not burned. "I know. I saw it. But only part of it broke."

"I thought I was going to die. The cable, the fire, the falling, and then the harness . . ." She swallows.

I can imagine.

"Will you stay with me?" Pepper asks. "Like you used to?"

Pep used to have these awful night terrors, right after we found her. She'd wake up screaming bloody murder, or sometimes she wouldn't wake up at all, and she'd just be sitting in her bed and shrieking, lost in a nightmare that wouldn't end.

I was the only one who could snap her out of it back then. Mrs. T would send someone running to fetch me, and I'd look Pep in the eyes and say her name and rub the back of her hand with my thumb, and eventually she'd wake up. She always asked me to stay so that the nightmares wouldn't come back for her.

I rub the back of her hand with my thumb.

"Sure," I say. I take my boots off, clamber over her, and slip under the covers beside her.

She curls into a ball against my chest, and I shut my eyes and realize just how tired I really am.

I leave the door locked.

We both deserve the sleep.

I wake up with the sun on my face.

It takes me a second to realize where I am, but the feeling of Pepper snuggled up against my chest reminds me. The red beams of her cabin walk the ceiling over my head beneath the crisscrossed ropes of her cargo net. The mirror in the corner stares back at me, near her wardrobe and desk.

I let out a long, deep breath. My body feels like I ran it through a clothes wringer, and my eyes keep wanting to shut again.

But sore as I am, I drag myself upright. Someone must be awake and keeping watch, and there's a chance whoever it is hasn't slept yet. It wouldn't be right for me to just go on snoozing.

Pepper's breathing changes beside me.

"You awake, Pep?" I whisper.

The blankets rustle around her. "Yeah," she mumbles. She pulls a pillow over her head, then flops it onto my lap and sits up.

She looks a lot better than she did when we went to bed. Her skin's not so pale, and her cheeks are less saggy. Even her cuts look smaller, but that might just be my eyes.

"I dreamed about when we found Tam," she says. "You remember?"

I nod. Tam used to work for this inventor named Gossner in Far Agondy, making deliveries and doing repairs for her clients all over the city. Nic didn't find him. We did. Pep and I were running around on the docks by the ship, stretching our legs a bit and kicking a ball, when we caught sight of this little boy watching us. Tam was a lot smaller then, way littler than normal for his age. I invited him to play with us, but he shook his head. He just sat there and watched. I pointed him out when Thom came to bring us back onto the ship, and Thom went and talked to him. I don't know what all they said, but by the time they finished, Tam was on the crew.

"Yeah," I say. "What about it?"

Pepper shrugs. "I'm just glad we did, that's all." She grins. "Thanks for staying." She slides off the bed and winces, then looks down her shirt.

"Man," she says. "You don't even want to *see* the bruises I've got."

And I get up feeling amazed she's back, more or less, to her old self again.

As I leave Pepper's room, I see Salyeh's door wide-open down the hall. I want to make sure he's all right after fighting the pirates last night, so I knock on it and stick my head in.

Sal's sitting at his desk, his head in his hands, reading a book with a beam of sunlight pouring over it through one of his portholes. He's moved some of his stuff back in from the hold too. His wardrobe's open, and I can see the edge of the dark suit that's his prized possession peeking out of it, along with the mess of shirts and trousers he wears around the ship.

He's also got a lot more stuff from Vash Abandi in his room than I do. I think he feels more attached to the city. There's no statue of Goshend by his prayer rug, which some people from Vash Abandi prefer, and he usually has some dried palm leaves on the wall and a miniature cactus on one of his shelves too.

"Hey, Sal," I say. "You okay?"

He looks up and blinks at me. His eyes are watery, and the muscles in his face look really tight. "I can't sleep," he says quietly.

I yawn, thinking I could use a little more sleep myself. "What're you reading?"

Slowly, he leans back in his chair. He focuses on the wall and grimaces, like he does when he's wrestling with difficult math. "I don't know," he says after a second. "I found something the pirates took out of a locked cabinet in Nic's desk. Come see."

I head in and peek over his shoulder. The book he's reading looks like a ledger, the kind Nic keeps track of money and cargo in. It's covered in columns full of numbers and descriptions written in Nic's chicken-scratch handwriting, but they don't look any different from the others I've seen. "What's the big deal?" I ask. "They're just numbers."

Sal huffs. "I've never seen them before," he says, and he looks at me as though I should pick up why that's important.

I try to fake it, but my face must show I don't get it, because he frowns.

"Nic shows me everything, Nadya," he says. "I know the accounts for the ship like I know my own hands. But he's never shown me these. Look." He flips through a few pages and points to a number. It's a big one. "That's as much as he has deposited at Farsky and Sons in Far Agondy, sitting in a bank I've never heard of in Myrrh. What's it for?" He flips another few pages. "And this. A withdrawal this big could pay half the deposit on a cloudship. And he just has the note here: *Compensation and repairs. ED.*" He points to the top line of the book, repeated on every page. "It's just labeled *Diaspora.* Maybe that's the name of another ship?" He rubs the sides of his scalp. "The normal ledger says *Orion Accounts,* real big and clear at the top."

I frown. "Well, maybe it's just his private bank account or something. Nic keeps some money for himself, right? I mean, he's captain of the ship." When I dream about being captain, sometimes I think I'll have a nice apartment in port at the Free City of Myrrh, full of comfortable chairs and a big bed and books and a writing desk the size of a breakfast table.

Sal shakes his head. "He keeps a little, but not this much. All this money going in and out, no records of where it came from or where it's going." He leans back and stares at the ceiling. "I should understand this, Nadya. Nic doesn't do anything without a good reason, but he's never kept secrets like this from me, and nothing in here makes sense. And then there's this." He reaches under the ledger and pulls out a brass badge about the size of my palm, all shined up with a picture of a skyscraper city in the middle of a river and a rat with a sword perched on the top.

I stare. I've seen something like it before, but it takes me a second to remember where. It's the badge of the Far Agondy customs inspectors, who search every ship that enters the city and make them pay their taxes. "What's Nic doing with that?" I ask.

"It wasn't Nic's," Sal says. "I found it in my room when I was cleaning up. Next to the bed." I raise an eyebrow, and Sal shakes his head at me. "Where the *pirate* was sleeping."

My stomach twists a bit. Anything to do with the pirates makes it do that. But I'm having trouble putting together why my stomach, and Sal, are so worried about this badge. "So . . ."

"So the pirates have an in with the customs inspectors in Far Agondy," Sal says, frustrated. He flips the badge over. "Look, it's got a real serial number and name engraved in it and everything. This is legit. And if they've got one, they might have more. And it might not just be in Far Agondy. They could have spies in the customs inspectors everywhere."

My brain starts to catch up. "And if a crooked inspector boards the ship and finds the pirates we tied up . . ."

Sal nods. "Bad news for us. Real bad news." He puts his head in his hands again. "Far Agondy's not safe, Nadya. There might not be any port that's safe."

I lean against his desk for a second and try to think. But every port we could reach before the gormling starves has customs inspectors. There's some smaller towns around the coasts we could try to get to in an emergency, but even there we'd make a big splash and news would get around to the customs people eventually.

All I can think of is a hundred million ways this goes wrong and we end up in jail, or lose the *Orion*, or get captured by the pirates. I'm groggy and hungry, and I miss Nic and Mrs. T and Thom. They'd know what to do.

"Sal, we're not gonna solve this on our own," I say. "We need Nic and the others. We have to go back for them. Maybe it's not too late."

Sal picks up his head. He turns away from me and looks at the corner he prays in. His face goes cold, like his mind's just walked into someplace icy and miserable. "No," he says quietly.

"Come on, Sal! We—"

"I made a promise, last night," he says, still looking at the corner. "To Goshend. I said I'd never lift a finger against another human being in violence, ever again. And I'm gonna keep it."

My mouth flaps. "But—I—You—"

"You don't know what it's like, Nadya," he says, and my gills burn because I hit that pirate with a bottle and it hurt my hand and my heart and I locked them up and I know *exactly* what he's talking about. I think. Maybe.

"I see you watching me sometimes. And the others. Everybody's heard about the pits. But you don't know what it's *like* down there," he says. He squeezes his fist, then looks down at it, shudders, and slowly unsqueezes it and lays his palm flat

171

on his desk. "Hurting people. Being hurt. But that's just the half of it. It's the way people look at you. The way they *expect* you to hurt people. Like that's all you're capable of. Like it's all you'll ever be able to do. They look at you and they see how big and mean you are and they think that's all there can be to you, and if you let yourself, you can become that person. You can lose all that's bright and good about yourself and just be what they want you to be. I've seen it happen, but it's not gonna happen to me."

He squeezes his fist again, and closes his eyes, and there's tears in the corners of them. "I made a promise to Goshend," he says again. "He got me out of there, Nadya. He brought me Nic. I made him a promise, and I'm not gonna break it. Not for anybody."

I just stand there, not knowing what to say for a second. I think over his story. I think over the soldier stare in his eyes, the way he cried last night, the way Tian Li looked at him. I think about right and wrong, and the way Nic and Mrs. T and Thom never made us do things that would hurt us.

"Okay," I say.

He looks up at me like he's surprised. "You're not gonna argue?"

I shrug, and I let my shoulders slump. "I still think we need them back, Sal. And I bet we could figure out a way to do it without you having to break your promise. But I'm not gonna try and make you."

Something flits across his face. A look of relief, like he's feeling the warm breeze of Goshend's breath. "Thank you," he says, but I don't think he's saying it to me. I think he's saying it to the corner, and what it represents to him. He opens his eyes again. "I'll think about it, Nadya. Maybe we can crack this on our own. Or maybe we can't and we need their help, and maybe it won't break my promise to go back and get them." He closes the ledger on his desk and twists to crack his back, then lets out a long, deep breath. "I think I need some sleep though." He smiles a little. "Maybe I can get it now."

I nod. I'm glad he's feeling better. But there are more butterflies than ever flying around in my stomach. I don't like that Nic's been keeping a secret ledger. I *really* don't like that the pirates have some kind of in with the Far Agondy customs people. And I don't think Sal's going to change his vote, which means it all comes down to Tian Li.

CHAPTER 15

IN WHICH NADYA TALKS TO THE GORMLING, AND HEARS AN UNEXPECTED PROPOSAL.

The rest of the day passes in a blur. I can't find a good time to talk to Tian Li alone, and even though I try to concentrate on how I'm going to get her to change her vote, I keep forgetting and thinking instead about what secrets the ledger's hiding, and how we can rescue the adults without making Salyeh break his promise not to hurt anybody.

It doesn't go very well. I'm still tired and worried and sore and hungry, and there's a lot of chores to be done to get the *Orion* back in shipshape.

Pepper keeps a lookout for pirates most of the day while Tian Li, who did it while we slept, gets some rest. Tam, apparently, is watching the pirates in the boiler. He and Salyeh give them food and water too. At lunchtime Pepper looks sick to her stomach when Tam asks her to call a fire spirit so we can cook, and after Pep tells the story about Rottfeuer, we make do with lemonade and cold sandwiches again.

Partway through the afternoon I realize nobody's checked on the gormling, and I slip down to the cargo hold to feed it. I get a little worried when I see how low our stash of its food's getting. Four days' worth might not be enough to last us all the way to Far Agondy on one engine.

I decide to start giving the gormling smaller meals, just in case it takes a while. It seems to notice—its flashes look a little grumpy after it finishes eating, and it nudges against its tank near me, as if to say, *Aren't you forgetting something?*

"Sorry," I tell it. "It's just to be careful." I put my hand on the tank, and it stares at it for a second, then rubs up against the other side, and I figure that means it still trusts me.

I'm still chewing on the problem of Sal and his promise, and I just stand there for a few minutes, thinking. Sometimes when I'm working real hard on a problem, my thoughts start to wander off on their own. Usually I think about breakfast or something me and Pep were talking about or how I'm going to describe the day in my journal, but this time feels different. I realize after a little while that I've closed my eyes and I can feel something, sort of like I did when I saw Opal on the Panpathia.

There's no voice, but I see the hazy outline of a creature, something bright and smart, like a Deepwater sheepdog made of sunlight. It turns to face me, and I figure out it's the gormling. It sets its eyes on me, and I shiver. They're deep green like the seawater in the tropics, and endless. I get the feeling it's a lot older than I thought it was.

Hi, I say, but it doesn't respond except to swish its glowing body back and forth. It feels weird to be talking to something outside the garden, but Mrs. T said I'd be able to do that someday. Maybe that day just came sooner rather than later.

I try reassuring it. That's what the things in the garden usually want. *You'll be okay,* I say. *If we have to, we'll set you free in the ocean.* Its body swirls around more quickly, like it's getting agitated, a cat twitching its tail. There's something big bubbling in its emotions, but I can't tell what. *Is that what you need?* I ask. *Do you want to be in the wild?*

I feel a rush of movement next to me, like an owl buzzing past in the middle of the night. A second later there's a loud splash and the wet smack of water on my head, and I open my eyes, confused. The water in the tank's surging back and forth, and the gormling gathers itself at the bottom, then jumps out of the tank and three feet in the air before splashing back down and soaking me again.

"Hey!" I yelp. "Quit it!"

The gormling jets down to the farthest corner of its tank and curls up there in a ball, spines out, staring at me. The sense of its mind floats slowly out of my head, but as it goes, I feel fear like an anchor plunging into the depths of the ocean. It's afraid of the open water. There's something out there, hunting creatures like it with bright, smart minds.

Something made of shadows and cold.

I shiver, and I wipe the water from my arms and wring it out of my hair, and then I walk away.

●●●

Life feels quiet for a few hours. I change into dry clothes, scrub the gormling's fear and Sal's promise out of my head the best I can, and take a nap. When I get up, I feel a little better. The world's brighter. The shadows and cold seem far away, and my friends and the ship are right here with me. We can't even see the edge of the pirates' fog anymore, so they must be pretty distant, and the setting sun shines gently on us while the *Orion* twists in the wind. Everybody in the cloud garden's still sleeping, and I'm glad. They can use the rest after the last couple of days.

A little before dinner I go into the cloud balloon to clean things up, check on everybody, and apologize to anyone awake to hear me. Mudwumple sleepily accepts on behalf of the frogs. Butterbeak does the same for the birds. The plants don't even bother to respond. They just sigh in their sleep, and I figure it means they're not too mad at me. I test a couple soil samples at the chemistry bench near the wall and scatter some fertilizer by the moonferns and some lime under the hydra plant, whose flowering heads are turning a little blue. Then I spend a few minutes dipping my toes in the pond, thinking and relaxing. It's the best I've felt in days, like if the cloud garden's okay, then I'm okay too.

I keep right on feeling that way until after dinner, when Tian Li calls everyone together on the aft deck near the ship's wheel.

We sit in a circle and wait for her to talk. The sun's long

gone, and the sea is black and glassy. The stars are out in bunches, so bright you can see their reflection on the water if you look hard enough.

"I want to call a vote," Tian Li says. Her voice rings clearly in the evening air. It's warmer down here than it is up high, and the air feels sticky after the mist's disappearance.

Tam squeezes his eyes shut. "On what?" he asks. His teeth grind like gears in an engine that's lost its oil.

"On going back to rescue Mrs. T, Nic, and Thom."

I smile. My heart thumps. She must have changed her mind, without me even trying to convince her. Good ol' Tian Li.

Tam places a thumb and finger on the bridge of his nose and pinches it. It's a gesture he picked up from Tall Thom. Drama king. "So you changed your mind?" he asks.

Tian Li nods.

"Wanna tell me why?"

"I read the stars tonight," Tian Li says. "To see where we are and plot a course." Her eyes drift up to the schools of white dots swimming across the sky like pilot fish above us. "But I saw our future too, and I didn't like it. I think we need to change our fates."

Tam groans. Like Pepper said a few days ago, he doesn't believe in starwinding any more than he trusts fireminding or the cloud balloon itself.

"What'd you see?" Pepper asks.

Tian Li shudders. "Shadows and cold, sweeping down from the sky to swallow us."

I feel like there's ice forming at the back of my skull, and

I hunch my shoulders and roll my neck to try to get it to go away. People keep talking about shadows and cold. Mrs. T. Nic and Thom. Even the gormling.

"That's it?" Tam snorts.

Tian Li hesitates. Her eyes look far away. Her hands clutch each other in her lap, like kids clinging together in the face of a thunderstorm or a grown-up's anger. Then she nods.

"You saw shadows, so now you want—"

"Tam," I interrupt.

He glares at me.

I swallow. My throat's dry. I'm still thinking about shadows and cold, and suddenly I'm a lot more scared of what I think we're about to do. "She asked for a vote," I croak.

Tam growls. "I'm trying to keep us safe, Nadya, no thanks to you. You saw how many weapons those pirates had. We got the jump on them, they were drunk and sleepy, and we still barely managed to take down three of them!" He stares at the rest of us. "How do you wanna find them, or get onto their ship and get Nic and the others back without getting caught or killed? Huh?"

I take a deep breath. The stars wink at us overhead. The *Orion* creaks in the wind. The cloud balloon moves from side to side against its cables. He's got a point, but we need the adults back or we might never be safe again. And anyway, all that's just another problem to solve. I bet we can do it.

"First things first, Tam," I say, getting my voice back. "We decide to go; then we make a plan. I'm for rescuing."

The vote moves counterclockwise around our circle.

"Me too," Pepper says.

"And me," says Tian Li.

Salyeh stays quiet for a while. He sits cross-legged, with his arms splayed out behind him to prop him up. He's staring at the horizon, where a ragged band of clouds is blocking the starlight.

"I am too," he sighs.

"Unbelievable," Tam says. He claps a hand to his forehead. "You're all unbelievable. I'm still against."

I smile. So do Pep and Tian Li. Even Sal cracks a grin for a second.

We've got all this scary stuff around us. Shadows and secrets and cold and fog and pirates. We're just five kids on a beat-up old cloudship. But when we work together, I feel like we can do anything.

We are *unbelievable,* I think.

My heart soars. I look up at the stars, and at the cloud balloon floating between me and them, and I feel like I could fly.

And we're going to do the unbelievable too.

Before bed, I figure I ought to thank Tian Li. She's not in her room, or the galley, or at the wheel, but Pep tells me she saw her climbing up into the catwalks around the cloud balloon, so I look for her there and sure enough she's sitting on a platform at the aft end of the balloon, all clipped in, dangling her feet through two gaps at the bottom of the railing. When I settle in next to her, I notice she's breathing fast.

"Hey," I say.

She swallows. Her eyes are fixed on the stars over the horizon, a great big swirl of them sort of like a fishhook, with the Fruitstream crossing over it. "Hey," she says. Her voice sounds far away, like she's concentrating.

"I came up here to thank you," I start, "but I don't want to interrupt whatever, ah . . ."

"I'm trying to be brave," she says. "I'm sick of being afraid." She lets out a shaky puff of breath. "I wanted to start with heights."

I look down at the jet-black ocean, dotted with bright froth where the waves crest and their bubbles catch the starlight, and I remember falling and falling. I stick my feet out next to hers and let them hang. "Lean forward," I say.

She turns and looks at me like I told her to light her hair on fire, so I show her. "You've gotta trust your lobster claws to keep you safe. See?" I lean into them, heart pounding like the wheels of a steam train, until my whole torso's sticking out over the water.

I look back over my shoulder. Tian Li's still staring at me. But then she closes her eyes and leans forward too, slowly, until she's hanging over the ocean like I am, looking straight down. "Open your eyes," I say. "You won't fall just because you can see it."

She does. Her whole body shudders.

"You're safe," I say. "I promise. Try moving around." I shift from side to side to show her, and she follows, just a little wiggle, then some bigger movements. She still looks pretty freaked out. "If it's not working, we can—"

"No," she interrupts, and she takes a deep breath. "Let's talk like this. Right here."

I nod, looking down, thinking about falling and waiting for my heart to slow down. I remember the first time I ever did this, when Mrs. T wasn't around to stop me, and how thrilling and terrifying it was. I remember showing Pep the next day.

"Right. So, thanks." I grin at her. "For changing your mind, and calling the vote."

Tian Li nods, still staring down at the ocean. "I didn't do it for you, Nadya," she says. She smiles a little. "But you're welcome anyway."

The wind gusts up from below us, hard enough to push our feet and send our hair puffing up. Tian Li whimpers, and she grabs the platform like a spooked squirrel jumping onto a tree trunk, but she doesn't stop leaning forward. "I wish we didn't have to do it," she says when she can talk again. "I wish we were doing it because we *wanted* to. Because it's the right thing to do, and nothing else."

I know what she means. "It still counts," I say. "Even if we're doing it because we're afraid."

She looks up at me, and a little finger of surprise crosses her face. I smile. Sometimes I'm smarter than I sound. Sometimes I figure out what's really bothering somebody without them having to come right out and say it. It always seems to catch Tian Li by surprise when I do.

"What'd you see, Tian Li?" I ask. "Up in the stars?"

She shivers. "Just what I told you. Shadows and cold.

But the stars were afraid, Nadya. I've never seen that before. They're so old, and they've seen so much. Nothing spooks them. But this . . . it was like they didn't want to show me anything to do with it."

My stomach swirls and crashes against itself like the sea in a storm. I think about how scared the gormling was, about what Mrs. T said.

"I wish I was brave like you," Tian Li says after a second, and she looks at me and I can't understand what's in her eyes. The colors are the same as always, but the feelings behind them are all muddled. "I feel like I'm scared of everything, sometimes. I know what's right but I don't always do it." She's still holding the edge of the platform with a grip that could punch holes in a steel sheet.

"Let go," I say. She squints at me in confusion, and I take my hands off the platform and let my safety belt take my whole weight. My heart pounds again, like my body's fighting me, and I stare down at the starlit waves and remember when I thought they were going to swallow me. "I get scared too," I say. "Being brave's not about never getting scared. It's about doing things anyway."

Tian Li stares at me, and then, slowly, she pries her fingers off the platform and leans out next to me. I reach for her hand, and she grabs it and squeezes it so hard her arm shakes.

"You're brave when it counts," I tell her, and I mean it.

She hangs there a minute, holding my hand and shaking, and then she takes a deep breath and lets go. She turns away from me and looks at the horizon again, all those stars hanging above it like a wall full of diamonds. "Can I tell you a secret?" she asks.

"Sure," I say. "Anything."

"Sometimes I wish I wasn't a starwinder."

My jaw drops. I think starwinding looks like the coolest thing on the planet. "How come?" I ask. "You can tell the future, and see the past, and I wish I could see what you see when you look at the stars because it's probably the most beautiful—"

"Why'd Nic rescue me?" she interrupts.

I blink, and then I remember him looking into her eyes back in that market in T'an Gaban. "Because . . . you're a starwinder?"

She nods. "Not because I earned it. I just got born with a talent that's useful." She shifts against her lobster claws. "I lived on the streets in T'an Gaban for a while, Nadya. I met a lot of people. Some of them saved my life, and they're probably still there digging for scraps in the trash behind restaurants and hoping some rich person tosses them a coin so they can buy a coat to sleep in at night."

She looks at me, hard, the night sky behind her and the ocean below and the wind tossing her hair around like the breath of a ghost. I lick my lips, trying to come up with something to say that feels right, but I can't. I never had to do that in Vash Abandi. I never knew anybody else who did, either. I didn't even know Tian Li lived that way.

Tian Li snorts, but it's not at me. She turns to the horizon, southwest, where T'an Gaban's a few hundred miles away over the ocean. "I used to sit and stare at the big houses on the hill," she says.

I remember those houses. T'an Gaban's built around a huge bay, and hills dotted with giant sandstone monoliths jut up around the water. The scientists and engineers the city's famous for live on those hills in mansions they keep lit with electricity all night long. Everybody else lives down below, crammed in with the fog and the smoke by the water. You can see the mansions from everywhere, floating above the city like cloudships.

"I told myself if I ever could, I'd change all that," Tian Li says. "Make sure nobody lived that rich while people went hungry below them." She shakes her head. "But here I am, not doing anything about it. Some days I don't even remember anymore."

I watch the waves. I think about my parents, how bad I want to find them, and how it would make me feel if I thought about it every day. "So?" I say. "You can't remember everything bad in the world all the time, or you'd just sit around moping and never do anything." She grunts, but then she sighs, like she thinks maybe I'm right. "You're gonna be a navigator, right? Once you're done learning you can take jobs on other ships, make a pile of money, and . . . I dunno, give it away or something."

Tian Li snorts again, but I don't think it's at me. Her nostrils flare like she's trying not to smile. "I've got bigger dreams than that," she says. "I want to go back and turn the whole system on its head, make things fair for everybody." She takes a deep breath and looks between her feet, straight down into the waves. "That's why I can't be afraid. Because if I let myself worry about how to do it, or who might try to stop me, I'll never get started." She looks back up, and her eyes twinkle. She jiggles her feet around and slides toward the edge of the platform, close enough that my heart jumps. I must let it show, because she grins at me.

"Thanks, Nadya," she says, and she scoots all the way back onto the platform and stands up. "Seeing the future's less fun than you think. You can see what you want, and you can see when something's messing it up, but you can't always see what to do about it."

She holds out her hand, and I wriggle back onto the platform, where she helps me up. We stand there for a few minutes more, watching the stars. I think about what she was saying about T'an Gaban, and her wishing she wasn't a starwinder. I've never wished I was anything but what I am, except maybe a little smarter or faster or taller or stronger. Maybe I am kinda lucky after all.

I'm still thinking when Tian Li bumps me with her hip. "You ready to head down yet?" She points toward the ladder and the ship, where my cabin's a comforting lump in the flickering light of the deck lamps. "I'm getting kinda cold." She smiles, and I realize she can't get around me on the catwalks. "Besides, shouldn't you get some sleep? You've got a lot to do tomorrow."

I swallow a lump. After the meeting, everybody assumed I'd come up with the plan for rescuing Nic, Mrs. T, and Thom.

I don't have a clue how I'm gonna do it, but I wanted them to trust me, so I agreed to anyway.

"Yeah," I say. "Sure." I start walking along the catwalks toward the ladder and what I really hope will be a good night's sleep. *Being brave's not about never getting scared,* I told Tian Li, and I hope it's true, because when I think about trying to get Nic, Thom, and Mrs. T back from those pirates, I'm downright terrified.

CHAPTER 16

In which Nadya forms a plan.

It's morning. The sea glimmers below us like a serpentine bath of shimmering sapphires . . .

. . . a shimmering, serpentine, sapphire bath . . .

. . . a bath of serpentine, sapphire shimmers . . .

I set my pen down and jam my knuckles into my eye sockets. I'm supposed to be figuring out a way to get us on board the pirates' ship. Tian Li's trying to find it again. Pepper's getting ready to fire up engine number one. Salyeh's watching the pirates, and Tam's making sure the ship's in order. I can hear the *shush-shush-rush-shushshush* of his brush against the deck outside my cabin.

"Aaagh!"

I flip over a new page and start scribbling and doodling and trying to figure out how in Goshend's name I'm going to get onto a pirate ship, rescue three adults who are probably in different places, and then get everyone off again without getting noticed.

So I make a list. Nic used to make lots of lists. They seemed to help him solve problems.

US	THEM
Surprise	Numbers
Small	Big
Few	Many
Quiet	Loud (?)
Nimble	Lumbering
Sober	Drunk (?)
Noble	Greedy
Good	Evil

The list doesn't do much good. We've got some advantages, but not a lot, and none we can really count on. They might be drunk like the pirates we surprised on the *Orion*, but then again, they might not. They might not be expecting us, but then again, they might. Nic, Thom, and Mrs. T probably didn't want to tell them how the *Orion* got free, but the pirates could've figured it out for themselves if they suspected there were kids on board in the first place. And if the pirates made threats, I bet Nic and the others fessed up. No sense risking your life if you think we're just going to cut and run like you told us to.

So the pirates will know who we are, then. Five kids.

I write down *Overconfident* in the pirates' column and stare at it for a second.

That's something we can count on. They won't expect much from us. They'll think we only got the drop on the pirates on the *Orion* because they were drunk and we had the element of surprise. And if we take away the element of surprise, or we make them think we've taken away the element of surprise, then they'll be even more overconfident.

"Knock, knock!"

Pepper nudges my door open with her hip and carries in a tray with a salad with oil and vinegar and a couple big slices of cheese. She sets it on my dresser and comes over to my desk.

"Got anything?" she asks. She peers over my shoulder at the list I'm making.

"Sorta," I say. "I think we can trick them."

"How?" She nicks some cheese from the tray and pops it in her mouth.

I grin. I'm starting to feel like maybe we can do this. "You'll like it. It's wild."

She waggles her eyebrows. "Ooh—so tell me, tell me!"

Shush-shush-rush-shushshush.

Tam, stripped to the waist in the low-altitude sun, moves across the doorway. He's scrubbing like the deck is responsible for everything that's happened over the last few days, and he's gonna make it pay.

"Later," I say. "I want to figure out all the details first."

Pep shrugs. "Suit yourself. I'll be in the galley cleaning up and prepping for dinner with Tian Li for the next couple hours. After that, I've got pirate duty."

My stomach flips when she says that. "Pirate duty." Like it's nothing.

There are three people crammed into our boiler, I think. *And they've been there for a day and a half.*

I wish there was something better we could do with them. But it's just not worth the risk. They're bigger than us, and stronger, and if we give them a chance they'll overpower us and take the ship back.

Don't look at their faces. Don't even let them have *faces, Nadya. You can't afford to.*

Pepper sashays away, whistling a quiet ditty. The night before last, she was so scared she couldn't talk. I think about how much I've been bothered by falling off the ship and fighting with Tam, and I wish I could bounce back from things that easy.

I turn to the list again and stare at it. I think I've got a good distraction in mind. Something that will put them off their guard—keep their attention forward while someone slips in from behind. I'm just not sure how to do the slipping.

Shush-shush-rush-shushshush.

And then it hits me.

I peek my head out of my cabin. Tam's moving away from me down the starboard rail, still scrubbing like a demon.

"Tam?" I ask.

Shush-shush-rush-shushshush.

"Tam?"

He doesn't even look at me.

"Tam!" I shout, and I stomp the deck.

Finally, he turns around. "Having trouble with your plan to kill us all, Skyqueen?" he asks. His chest heaves. He's covered in sweat. His bangs stick together and hang over his eyes.

My gills burn, and I consider picking up his bucket of mop water and dumping it over his head.

But I need his help.

"Yes," I say. "Can I ask you a couple questions?"

He leans on his brush handle and squints. "Why should I help you? Seeing as I don't share the death wish you've infected everybody else with and all."

I take a deep breath and remind myself I should be nice to him if I want his help with my plan.

It doesn't work.

"Because you owe me, Tam. You owe Pep. You owe all of us, for acting like a Grade A, gold-plated jerk!"

Tam falls silent. The sun goes behind a cloud. A little breeze picks up a few strands of hair on the top of his head. He scratches his scalp, and his skin pricks up in goose bumps.

"I saved your life, Nadya," he says eventually. "I don't think I owe you anything."

I swallow. He did save my life. But I still want my apology, and I'm gonna get it, and then he'll have to help me because he'll know he was wrong.

"Why'd you say I was dumb and lucky after you rescued me?" I ask. "And that I'm Nic and Mrs. T's favorite?"

Tam's face twitches. He fiddles with his brush. "I was mad," he says after a second. "I shouldn't have said you were dumb, or everybody's favorite. But you *are* lucky, Nadya. What's the worst thing that ever happened to you?"

My temper burns, because he'd know the answer if he stopped to think about it for half a second. But I started this conversation to get Tam's help, so I don't let it loose. "I lost my parents," I growl.

"We all lost our parents," he says. He looks up and shrugs. "I don't even remember mine. What's the worst thing that ever happened to you since then?"

I blink, trying to think. I've been sick a few times. I got in a fight with Pepper once and she wouldn't talk to me for three whole days and I bawled like a baby about it. Thom scolds me every once in a while.

That's really it, until the last couple days.

"It's not a contest, Tam," I say, even though I think I'm starting to see where he's coming from, and maybe it makes more sense than I thought. "We're all in the same boat here. You and me and Sal and Pep and Tian Li."

Tam frowns. "I know, but everybody else, we all went through a lot before we got on the ship. Get Salyeh to talk about Vash Abandi sometime. Ask Tian Li about T'an Gaban. You gotta realize we know stuff you don't." I look up. He's staring at the horizon now, twisting the handle on the brush.

"Bad things can happen, Nadya, and I just want to make sure they don't happen on this ship. Sometimes when you don't listen to me, I think it means someone's gonna get hurt, and then I get mad at you." He shrugs. "I don't think that's wrong."

My gills burn. I didn't come out here to get lectured by Tam Ban. I came out here to get his help.

But then I think about Salyeh crying and talking about what it was like in the pits of Vash Abandi, and about his promise. I think about Tian Li staring down at the waves and talking about being homeless in T'an Gaban. There *is* stuff they know that I don't. Same with Pep. Even Tam, I guess. He was a jerk after he rescued me. But maybe he wasn't as wrong as I thought, either.

"What'd you go through, before you came on the ship?" I ask while I'm trying to figure it out.

He grimaces, like just thinking about it makes him feel sick to his stomach. "I hurt somebody," he says. Every word sounds like he's whacking it out of his lungs with a hammer because it doesn't want to go. "In Far Agondy. I hurt them and I ran away."

I breathe deep, watching him grimace and thinking about him on the dock in Far Agondy back before I knew him, when I thought he was just a sad little kid. "Is that when we found you?"

He nearly drops his brush. Carefully, he sets it down instead, then leans against the gunwale. "Yeah," he says. "It was." He slides down until he's sitting on the deck, then looks up at me. The sun waddles partway out from behind its cloud and sends streaks of light scattering shadows along the wood in front of him. Pepper's laughter, like a tinkling bell, echoes inside the ship. "I thought you forgot about that," he says. "Or you wished you never did it. I thought you hated me."

I grit my teeth. I don't want to admit what I'm about to say, but it's true. "I don't *hate* you, Tam. I just . . . I love being on this ship, and I don't want to spend all my time terrified something bad's gonna happen. Plus I really wanted that first mate spot, okay? And sometimes you do things that hurt me, or the others, and then I get mad."

Tam looks up. "What?" he says. "When have I ever hurt anybody?"

I take a deep breath. "The doorknob, Tam. Remember?"

He stares at me blankly. "That hurt you?"

"It hurt my heart, Tam! My mother gave it to me. It's not a piece of junk. It's not worthless. It matters to me, and if I lost it I'd feel like I lost a part of myself. And you know what? I know stuff you don't too. Stuff about the cloud balloon and the ship and the crew. I have good ideas, and if you really wanna keep everybody safe, maybe you oughta listen to me more often."

Tam stares at me for a few seconds. A gull flies alongside us, calling. The sea twinkles sapphire-green below, and the sun comes all the way out from behind its cloud. Slowly, it dries the parts of the deck Tam was scrubbing, brightening the darkened wood.

Tam looks down at his feet for a long time, like he's thinking hard, going back over all our fights, trying to understand them better. "I'm sorry, Nadya," he says eventually. "I didn't know. Heck. I wouldn't have said all that stuff if I had." He looks real green, like he feels it in his gut.

The apology loosens something in my chest, like somebody dumped a bucket of water on my anger and then cleared out the ashes. Part of me still doesn't want to let him off the hook. Part of me wants him to suffer a little. But I don't think he really deserves it.

So I forgive. "That's okay," I say. "I'm sorry too. For not listening, and stuff." I'm about to remind him to trust me more, and tell him that sometimes he also hurts Pep and the others, but judging by the look on his face I bet I don't need to. "Tam," I ask instead, "will you help me?"

He looks up at me again. There's sadness in his eyes. Deep green sadness, flecked with crisp little dots of blue.

"Yeah," he mutters. "I will."

His shirt's hanging on one of the capstans. He puts it on and follows me inside my cabin.

We talk. He helps me. I leave the door open so I can hear the wind and Pepper's laughter. By the time Tam leaves again, the sun has sunk a lot closer to the horizon.

And I feel like I have a pretty solid plan.

I share my plan with the others at dinner.

We're sitting around the table in the dining room, eating

an old loaf of brown bread that's still buttery and tender, drinking sweet tea brewed in the afternoon sun, and picking at a couple of oranges and some salty strips of spice-cured beef. The pirates have been given food and water, and Sal, Tam, and Pepper moved them from one boiler into the other so that they could clean out the first. They'll have to move them back again before we can start engine number one, but still, I'm glad they did it. It matters that we treat the pirates like people, as best we can.

Tam stares glumly at the wall when I stand up to speak.

"So," I begin, and everybody turns to look at me. "I have a plan." Pep grins and picks a bit of orange out of her teeth.

"The pirates won't be expecting us to come back," I say. "And if we do, they'll assume we're just dumb kids and don't know what we're getting into. That will make them overconfident, which will give us our biggest advantage. Using that, plus our second-biggest advantage—the *Orion*'s quickness—and one of their disadvantages—that they're greedy—I think we can create a big enough distraction to get on board, free the others, and get back again."

Everybody stares at me. Pepper raises an eyebrow. Salyeh looks a little queasy. Tian Li blinks expectantly.

"Isn't anybody going to ask me how?" I grin.

The answer comes in chorus.

"Nadya—"

"Just get on with it!"

"Come on, Nadya . . ."

"We do the plan in three stages," I explain. "First, we buzz the pirates. Swing the *Orion* right over them, close enough to make them duck if we can. Get their attention and make them think we're being stupid."

Tam's frown deepens. Pepper smiles. Salyeh
looks uncomfortable, and Tian Li takes
a deep breath.

"We know they've got guns. Someone'll probably be dumb enough to shoot one at us before whoever's in charge realizes they could take our ship back and orders them not to."

The scenario starts playing itself out in my mind, just like it did all afternoon—the *Orion* sailing through the fog and that metal behemoth shrieking after it like an iron banshee.

"We act like the shooting panics us. We turn the *Orion* around, and we crank our engine up to full speed, and we start dropping altitude." I hold my hands out to demonstrate. "With only one propeller running, we won't be able to outrun them, but we'll still be able to outdrop them. Except we'll choose not to. We'll drop just slow enough that they can follow us—just slow enough that they *want* to follow us. We bait them into thinking they can catch us if they just keep going—just drop a little lower."

Pepper presses her lips together. "How does that help us free Nic, Thom, and Mrs. T?"

Tam's grip on the table tightens. His face flushes.

"Because," I say, "before we start shedding altitude, we drop off a little package for the pirates in the clouds."

Everyone's still staring at me. Nobody says a word.

Tam bangs his hand on the table. "Will you just get to the point, Nadya?"

I glare at him and cross my arms over my chest. "Tam and I will jump ship, fly onto the *Remora* with the Flightwing, and find Mrs. T, Nic, and Thom while the pirates are worried about chasing the *Orion*. Once we've rescued everybody, we'll fly back to the *Orion*, drop as much altitude as we can as quick as we can, turn around, and make our getaway."

More stares. Salyeh lets out a long, slow breath. Tian Li frowns. Even Pepper shakes her head.

"The *Flightwing*?" she asks. "Does that thing even—"

"It works," Tam mutters. He fiddles with the silverware in front of him. "Or it will anyway, by the time we're done with it."

More silence.

Then Pepper laughs, breaks off another chunk of bread, and crams it into her mouth.

"You know, Nadj," she says with a lopsided, bready grin, "you were right. It's wild." She swallows. "And I love it."

CHAPTER 17

IN WHICH NADYA AND TAM REPAIR THE FLIGHTWING.

Tam wants to do some thinking after dinner, so we don't get started on the Flightwing until after breakfast the next day. When I meet him in the cargo hold, the contraption's sitting under its usual tarp, between two shelves full of spare parts at the very end of the hold. I remember bumping my shin against it when we were blundering around in the dark earlier.

It's Thom's, technically, but everybody thinks of it as Tam's now. Thom built it when he was around Tam's age. After he left the ship, though, it just sat around in the hold until Tam noticed it a year ago. It's been Tam's pet project ever since. When we get to it, he whips the canvas off eagerly.

Underneath is a skeletal frame of pipes, gears, chains, pedals, seats, wheels, and propellers, welded together in the general shape of a rowboat with a pair of legs jutting off from each side. Each pair of legs is joined together by a skid. The whole thing's maybe twelve feet long, six feet wide, and nine feet tall.

Apparently, Thom's original Flightwing had wings. But it sure doesn't anymore.

It always takes me a second to remember how the thing's supposed to work. There are two seats facing forward and two facing rear. In front of each seat is a pair of pedals. The pedals rotate an axle that turns a gear. The gear spins a chain that turns another gear that links up with another gear to rotate a vertical shaft in the center of the Flightwing. At the top of the shaft is a huge propeller made of four thin blades of sheet metal. They droop down over the machine like the petals of a wilting flower.

It really shouldn't work.

But Tam's done something to it, and the last time he tested it out when we were in port, it got a solid fifteen feet off the ground before it crashed.

The key's some kind of lubricant or something, I think, that he's greased the central shaft with. Once it starts spinning, it just doesn't want to stop. I think if nothing got in its way, it would just keep on spinning forever. Every time you pedal, it spins a little faster, until eventually the blades are rotating fast enough to get the thing off the ground.

Tam's got a brake on it too so he can control the speed once it gets going. A lever and cable clamp some felt-covered vise grips over the shaft and make enough friction to slow it down.

Controlling it's the trouble.

The last time Tam flew it, he got it into the air and more or less stable. But then it started spinning counterclockwise, and then a gust of wind came along and tilted it to the side, and that was all she wrote. All of a sudden the Flightwing was flying sideways and everyone was diving for cover. Tam had to grab the brake to stop it. It hit the ground so hard that his shoulder was in a sling for a week.

"I've got an idea," he says. On a shelf behind the Flightwing there's a bunch of tools and drawings, and he rifles through the sheets of paper until he finds the one he wants.

"And I've got a question," I say. "How do we get it out of here?"

About half of the main deck of the *Orion* opens up to allow access to the cargo hold. The planks can be removed and stacked on the rest of the deck. When we're in port, we use a crane to lift out heavy stuff like the Flightwing, but out here, we don't have one.

"We'll have to fly it out," Tam says. He's pulled a monocle over his eye and he's peering at the blueprint he's picked out.

"Tam, it doesn't work. That's why we're here, right?"

"It does work," Tam says. He looks at the machine's aluminum skeleton, which is scuffed up and bruised from its latest crash but otherwise unharmed, and pats one of its beams affectionately. "I just haven't figured out how to fly it yet. That's not its fault."

Tam turns back to his blueprint.

"We need two mechanisms, really—one to control the angle of the main rotor so I can react if the Flightwing's body gets tilted like it did last time, and another to keep it from spinning and control its orientation."

He looks up from his blueprint and eyeballs a line along the Flightwing with his thumb. "The orientation part should be easy. If I extend its tail a little bit and add a rotor that spins vertically, it should give me something to generate horizontal lift with."

I cross my arms over my chest and try to keep from getting frustrated. If he thinks he's got all this figured out already, then why am I even here?

He just keeps going. "But the first—I dunno. It's like I'd need to set the main rotor on some sort of platform that I could move up or down in any direction—"

He goes on for a while, mumbling about hydraulics and crosses versus hexagons or maybe a circle and completely ignoring me. I hear thumping around on the deck above us, and then some of the planks start to move. I guess Tam must've told Salyeh and Pepper to start pulling the deck off already.

After a minute or two of watching Tam crawl all over the Flightwing, I clear my throat. "Tam."

He looks at me. He's sitting on one of the upper struts of the Flightwing with its rotors hanging down above his head. He's got a tape measure in one hand, a sheet of paper in the other, and a pencil in his mouth.

"What did you want my help for?" I ask.

He flips the monocle up, sets the tape measure down, and plucks the pencil from between his teeth. "You need to understand the Flightwing if you're gonna help me fly it, Nadya. What if something happens while we're on the pirates' ship and you have to come back alone?"

He looks away real fast, like he's scared and didn't mean to show it.

"Tam," I say, "nothing's going to happen to you on the pirates' ship, okay?"

Tam shrugs and slides between a couple of the bars. "Sure. But still—just in case, you know?"

I walk forward and put my hand on the cool metal of the Flightwing's nose. Tam swallows. He wipes his palms on his trousers.

"Okay," I say. "Tell me how it works."

And he does. He doesn't act like I'm dumb. He doesn't roll his eyes or sneer at my ideas. He acts like we're equal. Partners. Maybe for the first time ever. I spend the next couple hours learning about friction and momentum and the First Principle of Flight, which says that if air is moving faster on one side of something than the other, the side where it's moving slowly generates lift, and that's how propellers work.

"Where did you learn all this?" I ask, wedged next to him underneath the Flightwing's body. He's pointing at the gears near the shaft that spins the Flightwing's rotor. He's just finished telling me how thick the air is over the Cloud Sea and how hard he thinks we'll have to pedal to lift ourselves and three adults.

"Gossner taught me a lot. She's the best engineer I know. But books, mostly. Thom gets them for me when we're in port and helps me understand them, and Carla always gives me some when we see her. She and Thom used to fight over who was better at my job, and I think they're still not done. A lot of books are full of junk, but sometimes one of them's got something that's just a hair off from right. I got the idea for the rotor from a drawing I saw in one. It was a squirrely looking thing with a giant canvas screw around the central shaft. Never woulda worked—wouldn't have generated enough lift because the shape of the screw woulda messed with the airflow. But I saw it and figured that if you took the basic design and stuck a propeller on top—"

He stops and looks at me. There's grease all over his face and hands. We're pretty close to each other—there's not much room under the Flightwing. I think it's the first time since we crawled under it twenty minutes ago that he's realized how much attention I've been paying.

"Am I—I mean—do you care about this stuff?" He gestures up at a bunch of little metal balls between two plates that set off the rotor shaft from the gears.

I look up. The afternoon sun winks at me through the open planks of the *Orion*'s deck and flickers across motes of dust in the hold.

I've never cared much about machines. I just let Pepper

and Tam handle them and concentrate on the cloud balloon. It works out pretty well.

But I'm starting to care now. I wanna know everything. I wanna understand the things Tam knows that I don't. I wanna know the ship and everything on it inside and out, like Thom and Nic do, or maybe even better.

I'm glad I'm here.

I think I'm starting to get Tam a little more too. He lives in a world of black and white, blueprints and textbooks, where there's a right and a wrong answer for everything. A thing works or it doesn't. And he's good at finding what works— real good. He's just not so good at dealing with it when people disagree with him. If he got better at that, he'd be a pretty great teammate, and I think he's trying to. Something he said yesterday stuck with me too, about trying to keep us all safe. I try to do that too. I just do it without making everybody mad at me . . . most of the time.

Besides, life is short, and I want to see as much of the world as I can before it's over, whether that means the tops of the Alinese mountains or the white sand beaches of the Pineapple Islands or the greasy innards of Tam Ban's impossible flying machine.

"Yeah," I say finally. "I do care. Thanks."

Tam smiles. It's not a normal smile, either. It's the kind you make when you realize someone you thought hated you kind of gets you, and maybe they think you're all right after all.

I punch him in the arm. "Knock it off," I say.

But he just keeps smiling, and in a second, I'm smiling too. Eventually, he starts talking again.

Neither of us stops smiling for a long time.

It's after dark before we get the modifications to the Flightwing finished, and I've stopped smiling. We're working by moonlight and the strobing of the sleeping gormling in the corner. We fed it in the afternoon, and it looked so hungry—it kept rubbing up against the tank in the direction of the buckets—that I gave in and fed it an extra half a serving, even though I'm still trying to save food. We're down to six buckets, which is only four or five days' worth of half rations. I'm scared we won't get to Far Agondy in time, but if we rescue Nic, Mrs. T, and Thom, maybe they'll know what to do. For a second I wonder again whether Tam or me is closer to winning first mate, just out of habit. But then I remember there's no contest at all until we get everybody back, and I focus on the plan again.

I'm so tired it's hard to think. My vision's getting blurry. My arms and legs and back all ache.

But Tam isn't ready to hang it up, so I'm sticking around to help.

"Try it again!" Tam calls.

He's standing by the elongated tail and the second rotor we rigged up. For the last hour, I've been sitting in the pilot's seat, pedaling and pulling levers when Tam tells me to.

He's made a second set of gears and chains that spins the

new rotor in the Flightwing's tail. He put in a new lever next to the pilot seat too. When you pull it, a little piece of metal kicks the chain connected to the pedals over to either the tail rotor or the main rotor. All we have to do is make sure the tail rotor works well enough to actually spin the Flightwing, and we'll be just about ready to fly.

I pull the lever. Behind me, I hear a *thunk*.

"Good!" Tam says. "Now pedal a bit and get the main rotor spinning."

I push the pedals around a few times. The rotor overhead starts to spin. I don't get it going fast enough for the blades to flatten out, so they just swing around uncomfortably close to my head, making loud whooshing noises.

"Okay! Now shift over to the tail rotor!"

I pull the lever again. There's another *clunk*.

"Great! Now pedal forward!"

I start pedaling. Little beads of sweat roll down my face and collect in the hollow under my throat. This is the first time we've gotten this far, and I'm not sure what's going to happen.

"Bit faster!"

I pedal harder.

"Bit faster!"

I keep pedaling.

The Flightwing starts to spin. Its tail skids to the left and bangs into one of the shelves. I stop pedaling.

Tam laughs. "Great! Perfect! Ha! Try the other way!"

I start pedaling backward. It takes a few seconds for the tail rotor to get up to speed, but once it does, the tail swings to the right until the shelves on its other side stop it.

"All right, you can stop! And brake the main rotor, would ya?" Tam calls.

I let my feet rest on the pedals and pull up on the mechanical brake for the main rotor. It slides to a stop pretty quickly.

Tam's feet clang over the metal frame of the Flightwing, and then his arms close around me from behind and pull me back against the seat. "We did it!" he shouts. "We did it! Haha!"

I let him hug for me for a second, and then I turn around and look at him.

He's sweaty and flushed, and there are streaks of soot and grease all over his clothes and body. His arms are red because he's too proud to wear a heavy jacket when he runs the welding torch. He's grinning like a puppy wagging its tail.

"It's gonna *fly*, Nadya! Really fly! Can you believe it?"

I nod and peel myself out of the deep bucket of the Flightwing's pilot seat. "Yeah," I say, leaning on one of the bars of its nose. "I sure can."

Tam hops down and spins in a circle with his hands on his head. "Thom's gonna lose his breakfast when we go get him in this! I mean—we've been working out the kinks all year, but I—and you—together—"

He puts his arms out and spins again, like a little kid.

I catch his hand and stop him before he falls over and

bangs his head or something, and he looks at me and grins. "We're a heckuva team, Nadya Skylung. You and me. We could fix anything."

"Thanks, Tam," I say. I squeeze his hand. "I know you didn't have to do this."

"Shoot, Nadya," he says. "You're the whole reason I'm here." He looks down, like he's embarrassed, and lets go of my hand. "I mean, 'cause you and Pepper found me and all."

"I'm glad we did. You're a good friend, Tam," I say.

He looks back up, smiling, and runs a hand through his hair. "So are you."

The shadowy bulk of the Flightwing sticks up behind him. Our sky chariot, the thing we're counting on to save the people who mean the most in the world to us. The thing that really shouldn't work but does.

Tam looks at it with me, beaming like a proud parent. "We should get some sleep," he says. "Tomorrow, we're gonna fly it."

I watch the moonlight glinting off the Flightwing's metal skeleton for a little longer, and then I give the gormling a bit of food and head up to my cabin.

It takes me a while to get to sleep, since I'm about to do the most dangerous thing I've ever tried. I keep thinking about Nic, Thom, and Mrs. T, wondering whether they're okay. I keep thinking about shadows and cold, and about Nic's ledger, and about Tam reminding me that bad stuff can happen. I try to remember what it felt like when Mrs. T tucked me in a few days ago, but I can't. I open my desk to get out my doorknob, but the drawer's empty—I haven't been able to find the knob since the pirates showed up.

It's funny. A week ago, if the doorknob had gone missing, I would've torn the ship apart until I found it. I still miss it, but I know I'll get it back eventually. It's down in the hold somewhere, wherever Thom stashed it, and once we rescue him I'll just ask where it is.

For a few minutes, I wonder why I don't worry about it as much as I used to. But then the long day catches up with me, and I fall asleep before I've figured it out.

CHAPTER 18

IN WHICH, BRIEFLY, NADYA FLIES.

The sun flickers through the candied glass of my cabin windows like the gossamer strands of an enormous spidery god, tugging at my eyelids . . .

. . . yanking at my heart . . .

. . . jerking at my soul . . .

"Maybe all three," I mutter, and I set my pen down. I smell bacon, which means Pep must have gotten the fire spirits that dance under the range working again.

But there's more than just bacon waiting in the dining room.

There's eggs, and cheese, and some of the spiced cider we picked up in the shady lakeside orchards of Nash Valour last fall. We have home fries with sky potatoes and cloud onions and crisp green peppers. Pepper's even whipped up a fresh batch of hot sauce to go over it. And when I've stuffed myself as full as I think I can get, Tian Li slips into the kitchen and comes out with a platter of sweet pancakes and a flask of maple syrup to drown them in.

After the meal's over, I loosen my belt and lean back and pat my stomach. "Wow," I say. "You guys are amazing—next time I cook, I'll have to do something special." I close my eyes and slump happily into my chair.

"It was Tam's idea," Salyeh says.

I open my eyes again. Sal's sucking maple syrup from his fingers. Pepper's just slurping hers right from her plate.

Tam, sitting in the corner, is pushing a couple of uneaten pieces of potato around and staring uncomfortably at the table. He looks a little off, like he's worried about something.

Pep sets her plate down and licks her lips. "He said that since you guys'll be taking the Flightwing out today, we should give you a good meal. Just, um—"

The table goes silent. Everybody glares at Pep.

"Well, just in case—"

She sighs and puts her head in her hands. "I wasn't supposed to talk about that."

Tam gets up and starts clearing dishes. Nobody else moves.

"It'll work," I say. "Tam and I got it fixed last night. You'll see."

Pep reaches over and squeezes my hand. Tian Li and Salyeh look at me sympathetically.

"It's going to work, really! I—Tam!"

He comes out from the kitchen and starts gathering up plates and cups.

"Tam, tell them it's going to work!"

"It's going to work," he says, but he still looks worried, and he turns around and takes his armload of dishes into the kitchen.

I scoot my chair back, grab the big frying pan that held the home fries, and follow him.

We don't talk until the dishes are cleared and we're standing next to each other, me washing and him drying. Everybody else is gone.

"Tam, what's your deal?" I ask.

He polishes a plate and sets it in the drying rack, then holds his hand out for another one. His fingers shake a little bit.

"Do you remember when I said I hurt someone, in Far Agondy?" he asks.

I nod. I've been wondering what he meant by it, but I didn't want to pry. He seemed like he didn't want to talk about it.

He looks up, blows out a long breath, and stops drying. "I built a machine. It was supposed to make cleaning up Gossner's workshop a little easier. You just stoked its boiler, pressed a switch, and then instead of mopping and scrubbing by hand you could push the machine around and it would do the mopping and scrubbing for you."

He stops talking for a bit. I still don't want to push him, so I start washing dishes again. He starts drying. A couple dishes pass between us before he opens up.

"It had a lot of moving parts, and they weren't all covered. There were long pistons that drove the brushes and the mop heads, and if you really got it up to full steam, they moved crazy fast. Gossner had other kids working for her, but I was the best with machines. I told everybody else that the cleaner was dangerous, that they shouldn't try to use it without me there."

He hands the home-fry pan to me, and I go to work. When it's clean, I hold it up, but he's not paying attention. He's gripping the edges of the sink so hard I worry he might bend them, and he's staring at the wall. His eyes are watering.

"One morning, I woke up and heard one of the other boys screaming. He'd been watching me work the machine and tried to start it up himself so it'd be easier to clean the kitchen before breakfast. I ran down to see what was wrong and saw him with his arm caught in the cleaner. He'd noticed the rag I used to polish the pistons still inside once he got it running and reached in to get it out. Stupid, but every kid makes mistakes like that. It's why you don't start them out with big, dangerous machines. You start them out with little ones so the worst that happens is maybe they get a bruise or lose a fingernail or something."

He shuts his eyes, and tears well at the edges of them. "His arm looked awful when we finally got the machine shut down and him out of it. It was chewed up like a dog had gone to work on it. Gossner took him to a surgeon right away, but it didn't matter. When they came back that night, his arm was gone."

Gently, I put my hand on his shoulder. He doesn't even seem to feel it.

217

"You should've seen the way the other kids looked at me, Nadya. Like I tore up his arm myself. I should've built the machine better. Put a lock on it so you couldn't start it without a key. Put panels on the outside so nobody could stick their arm in while it was running." He shrugs out from under my hand and wraps his arms around himself. "I ran away. I couldn't stand them looking at me like that. I felt like a monster." He wipes his eyes with his arm. "I found you guys the next morning, and when Thom offered me a chance to join the crew, I took it. I didn't even say good-bye."

He stays quiet for a second, then turns to look at me. "When I got back to my cabin last night, all that hit me like a sledgehammer. I don't want you to get hurt, Nadya. I don't want to lose all you guys too."

I lick my lips and clear my throat. It shouldn't be me talking to him like this. It should be Thom. Thom's the one who takes care of Tam, like Mrs. T takes care of me. They're thick as thieves.

But Thom's gone, and so's Mrs. T, and until we get them back, I guess we just have to take care of each other.

"It's gonna be fine, Tam," I say. "The Flightwing'll work. We tested it."

He nods, sniffs, wipes tears from his eyes again. "I know, but what if something goes wrong?"

I shrug. "Then we'll fix it. And Tam?" I pull him around so I can look him straight in the eye. "Nobody's gonna hate you, no matter what happens, okay?"

Tam takes a deep breath. "Promise?"

I let go of him and hold out my pinky, like I do with Pepper. "Swear it on a finger."

He looks at me for a second, then smiles and wraps his pinky around mine. We shake on it.

By the time we're done with the dishes, Tam seems back to normal. We're laughing and joking. But I feel like something's changed. I get him. He gets me. All this time I thought he didn't trust me or Pep or Tian Li, but it was really that he didn't trust himself, and that meant he couldn't trust anybody else either.

I think maybe he's getting over that though, and we can finally trust each other. And given what we're about to do, that's a huge relief.

We test the Flightwing that afternoon.

Tam digs a couple pairs of goggles out of storage, and we each put one on. Apparently, he made more modifications after I left last night. He's rigged the pedals up so that one of us can work the tail rotor while the other works the main rotor. He's also put a panel with six levers on it between the two front seats. Each one activates a hydraulic lift on a different side of a plate under the main rotor. We can adjust the rotor's tilt a little bit in any direction with them.

We try the new systems out when we sit down. Everything seems to be working fine.

"You wanna steer or work the elevation?" Tam asks. The goggles make his hair stick up in a big, flowing wave. He looks like a mad scientist or a motorcycle bandit.

"Elevation," I say. "It's kind of my thing."

He nods. "Put your lever forward then. I'll pull mine back."

We're still in the cargo hold, but the deck's open and the sky is crisp and blue above us. We were hovering at around 7,500 feet when I checked the cloud balloon this morning, and the air in the garden seemed fine. The birds chirped happily and asked when Mrs. T would be back, and the frogs croaked little jokes to each other in the mud. The plants presided over the whole thing like smiling, silent grandparents.

Tian Li says she read the stars last night and that we've drifted south a bit, toward the shipping lanes between Far Agondy and Deepwater. I wonder, briefly, what'll happen if we run into a ship of the Cloud Navy.

Tam puts his hand on another lever and grins. "You ready to do this?" he asks.

"Yeah," I say.

"Then start pedaling!"

I lean back and pump my feet. The first few spins take a lot of effort, but once the axle gets rotating, it's not too hard to speed it up. The rotor whizzes by above my head, faster and faster.

Tam pulls the lever that shifts the gears. It gets a little harder to pedal, but soon I'm going as fast as I can again, and the rotor's starting to make a *chuff-chuff-chuff* sound.

Tam pulls the gear shift again. And again. The rotor goes from *chuff-chuff-chuff* to *wubbawubbawubba*, and then the blade sounds blur into a loud, deep rumble. Tam starts the rear rotor spinning.

The Flightwing lifts off the floor.

Getting it out of the cargo hold will be the trickiest part of the whole operation, except maybe landing it. I try to keep a steady rate of pedaling going so that the rotor spins just fast enough to take us upward. Tam's got his feet poised on the steering pedals and his fingers on the hydraulic levers.

As the Flightwing lifts off, its nose dips down and we start to move forward.

"Tam—"

"I've got it," he says. He pushes up a little on one of the hydraulics, and our nose levels out. We stop moving forward and start moving straight up again.

We're hovering well above the shelves now, and the rotor's almost even with the deck. The gormling swirls around in its tank anxiously, watching us.

Tam pedals gently backward. The Flightwing's tail swings obediently to the left.

My heart's pounding, but it's not from the pedaling. It's surprisingly easy to keep the rotor spinning once it gets going, courtesy of Tam's magic oil, I guess. But I'm still scared because if something goes wrong now and we crash into the *Orion*'s deck on our way out, I'm not sure how it doesn't end in serious injury or worse for Tam and me.

The rotor clears the deck. A few seconds later, so do we. Salyeh, Tian Li, and Pepper are all on the aft deck, watching. They whoop and holler and cheer.

"Steady," Tam says.

We're still under the cloud balloon. If we go up much

higher, we risk running into it, and that might be the worst disaster we could cause. The ladder to the catwalks is right in front of us too, blocking our way out.

"I'm gonna try to back us out," Tam says.

I look behind us. There's nothing between the Flightwing and the blue sky off the *Orion*'s bow but my cabin.

Tam flicks up again on the same hydraulic he adjusted before. The Flightwing's nose tips up slightly, and we start to move backward.

"Bit higher, Nadya," Tam says. He's got his head craned over his shoulder. I do the same and see that we're not quite high enough to clear my cabin.

I give the pedals a little more juice, and we rise up another two or three feet. Then I let the Flightwing level out again.

"Good," Tam says. "Good . . ."

We get over my cabin and out of the shadow of the cloud balloon. The *Orion* sits a few feet in front of and below us. There's no wind. I've got a pleasant burn in my legs from pedaling, the sweat's starting to bead on my face and in my armpits, and the Flightwing bounces gently as it hovers.

I'm flying.

Tam stops our backward motion, looks over at me, and grins. "We could land now, I guess, but I want to go for a quick spin first. You up for it?"

I grin back. "Love to," I say. I look up.

There's nothing above us but clear sky.

• • •

Twenty minutes later, the Flightwing's settling down on the aft deck. Tam has the brake on. The main rotor's whining to a stop, and I'm feeling breathless and giddy.

I've lived in the air for years now, but I've never flown like *that*.

We soared high above the *Orion*, and when Tam set the hydraulics to full forward, we moved faster than the ship does even with a strong wind behind her and the engines maxed out. We took the Flightwing up a few thousand feet too, just to see how it did at the altitude we expect the pirates to be at. It went just fine.

When we were up that high, I spotted something out near the horizon. It looked just like the enormous bank of fog that swallowed us before the pirates captured the *Orion*.

"Tam," I say once we've got the rotors fully braked and Tian Li and Pepper are running up with chains to lock the Flightwing down. "Did you see it?"

He pulls his goggles off. His face looks grim. "Yeah," he says. "To the southeast, maybe a hundred miles?"

I nod.

"Nadya," he says, "are you still sure you want to do this?"

A memory flashes through my head. I'm starving. I'm thirsty. I'm alone in a rotting cloud garden, where the plants are so close to death they no longer speak and the birds and the frogs are long gone. A door hisses open. The balloon starts deflating. I breathe outside air for the first time in ages, and I panic and scream. A voice speaks, but it's not in my mind, and I don't understand it. I shriek until I pass out.

When I wake up, I'm in a soft bed with the sun on my face, and Nic and Mrs. T are sitting in chairs next to me. Nic's got a steaming bowl of soup in his hands. Mrs. T dips a spoon into it and holds it out for me.

There's so much wrapped up in my feelings for Nic and Thom and Mrs. T I can't keep track of it all. Love and tenderness and frustration and secrets and mystery. But I know this much. They're more than just my captain and teacher and first mate. They saved my life. And I want to do the same for them.

"Yeah," I say. "I'm sure. We owe them."

Tam stares down at the deck. Tian Li and Pepper do the same. They've all got memories like that, somewhere in their heads. I'm sure of it.

"I guess we do," Tam says.

A few minutes later, we're firing up engine number one and heading southeast as fast as the Orion will take us.

CHAPTER 19

IN WHICH THE ORION ENTERS THE FOG, AND NADYA ENCOUNTERS SOMETHING ON THE PANPATHIA.

We sail into the fog a little after lunch the next day.

The mist is as cold and damp as I remember, and it licks at my skin like the thousand icy tongues of a Valourian snow monster. Salyeh's at the wheel. He decided that steering the ship wouldn't break his promise to Goshend. I think he feels pretty good about it too.

"How're we going to find the pirate ship?" I ask. I tuck my hands into my armpits to warm them.

Salyeh turns the wheel a little to the left. Tian Li's at his side, and the starwinding haze hovers over her eyes.

"The pirates cause the mist," Tian Li says, "so they should be at the center of it." She swallows. Her eyes shine in the flat light. "I can't see through the mist. So we head where I can see the least. The deepest darkness."

I nod.

The deepest darkness.

Sounds like a true name to me.

Below us, Pepper's lighting the lanterns on the *Orion*'s rails. Whatever popularity she lost with the fire creatures after what happened with Rottfeuer and Ettingott doesn't seem to affect her status with the smaller ones much anymore. She was able to get the engine going yesterday too. I was a little worried about that.

"How will we know when we've found the pirates?" I ask.

"We'll hear them," Salyeh says.

Tian Li taps his shoulder and points a little to port, and he turns the ship's wheel and sends the *Orion* scooping through the fog in that direction.

I spend a minute or two standing with them, watching the ship move. The *Orion*'s bow cuts through the fog like a pair of scissors going through a thick gray curtain. The clouds part around her, lick her sides as she moves through, and then tumble and swirl behind us before closing up again.

I shiver. "I'm going up to the cloud balloon," I mutter. "I need to let the garden know what's going on."

Salyeh nods. Tian Li points to port again. The ship turns.

I swallow and head to my cabin to grab my safety belt and lobster claws.

The warm, damp air of the garden feels like a hug when the door to the waiting house shrugs shut. My gills flutter open, and I take my time walking to the center of the balloon, let the air fill my body with calmness and my heart with peace. I run my fingers over the leaves of the plants, and they sigh too.

For the first time in days, I leave the main path, take off my boots, and let the mud and grass reach up through my toes.

I lean against a *caru* tree, and its long, willowy fronds shiver in delight. I close my eyes. The voices of the garden surround me. They ask me what I'm doing and what's happening on the ship, and I answer them, but I don't feel like the one behind the voice. I feel part of something bigger, connected to a web of gardens and plants and animals that stretches all over the world.

The Panpathia, I realize. I wonder whether I'm always connected to it somehow. I must be, I guess, if other people can see my glow the same way I see theirs. I reach for the leather medallion I got from Amber and give it a squeeze. If I can find Amber and Amy again, maybe the *Dream* can help us. They're probably far away, but they might not be.

I close my eyes and start to reach out with my mind, then stop. Mrs. T told me not to venture onto the Panpathia without her. She said it could be dangerous.

For a few minutes, I stand quietly in the garden and mull it over. I've got time. I can think clearly. And the more I think about it, the more I think it's worth the risk. This is an emergency, and I'll be careful. If it works, maybe we can find a safer way to get everybody back.

I reach out to the Panpathia. I move cautiously, letting my mind slip along the familiar, shining pathways of the cloud garden around me first. I see the glittering flame of Butterbeak in her nest and the tiny flickers of her chicks beside her. I see Opal, languidly curled around the outside of the cloud balloon, sleeping as we pass through the crudcloud fog. I see Mudwumple awake at the bottom of the pond, puffing out bubbles like an old man with a pipe. And then, drifting farther, I start to see the tendrils that connect the balloon to other places in the world, little gauzy strands of light reaching out into the darkness.

One of them leads to a ship in the lanes to the south of us, a rich trader with a fabulous balloon full of enormous groves. It whispers messages of welcome, but I can't find its skylung so there's no one there to ask for help.

Then I'm off to the next garden, somewhere even farther south. It belongs to a smaller ship—even smaller than the *Orion*—and it's sick. Its skylung is young and inexperienced, and he's having trouble keeping the garden healthy while obeying his captain's commands to rise and fall in search of the best winds.

The garden cries out to me. I do my best to comfort it, and then I move on from there too. We'll get no help from that ship, not with how small it is and the trouble its cloud garden is in.

I move in wide, drifting circles, until eventually I reach a cloud garden bigger than the whole of the *Orion*. There are waterfalls and grottoes and cliffs and hills inside it, all out-lined in the glorious golden motes of rich, healthy plants. There's more life in its soil alone than in all my little patch.

There's a skylung inside. Her mind is calm and loving. She's holding the paw of a catlike creature as it dies of old age beneath the flowers and thorns of a rosebush. I reach out to her mind, to offer my sadness for her garden's loss and to see if she can help us.

I freeze.

It's Mrs. Trachia.

Her shock at seeing me snaps along the Panpathia, and I bounce off the web like a pebble from a slingshot. My eyes twitch. My heart pounds. I try to reach her again, but I can't figure out which strand to follow away from the *Orion*. I keep finding other ships or just getting lost in the darkness. I'm getting frustrated, and a sharp, painful headache builds up behind my eyes, but I slow down, try to go calmly. Eventually, I find the pirates' ship again, with the giant, glowing egg of its cloud garden.

Something's wrong, though. That feeling I got once before, of ice freezing the back of my skull, comes back. I try to ignore it, but I can't. The ice reaches forward, little iron-pinch fingers of freezing darkness crawling over my scalp toward my face. It gets harder to breathe. My vision dims. I feel something dark and vicious on the Panpathia, far away, a deep shadow in the frozen cold way off to the north. It's looking for me. It's where the ice comes from.

Desperately, I send my mind stumbling through the pirates' ship, but I can't find Mrs. T. She's not in the cloud garden anymore. The fingers of ice get closer to my face, and my body starts to wobble and move on its own, like I'm sleepwalking. Dimly, I'm aware of heading toward the controls to let garden air out of the balloon.

My mind's still on the pirates' ship. I know I need to get off the Panpathia, but I can't. I'm stuck. The little golden strands won't let me go. There's something indigo and cold on them, like spider silk, and I'm trapped. The shadowy thing up north trundles toward me, just over the horizon. I can almost see it in my mind—glistening beady black eyes, and long legs of crystal blue with sharp points at the ends. I panic and start trying to yank my mind free of the silk, but that just makes the thing speed up. I don't want it to catch me. I want to be free!

There's a bright flash. Somebody's mind jumps onto the Panpathia and shoves me. I get a glimpse of a kid with curly hair and chains around his arms and legs and neck. No gills. A cloudling, maybe? *Go!* he tells me. *Run away!* and I break free of the Panpathia's stickiness. His mind pushes mine again, and then I'm hurtling back toward the *Orion* at the speed of light.

I open my eyes. I've moved a lot. My hand's on the lever that lets the air out of the balloon, and I jerk it back like I've been stung. My heart's beating so fast I can feel it in my ears. My head feels like somebody stuck a bunch of spikes into it, and the back of my skull still feels cold.

"Nadya!" Tam shouts from a speaking tube near my ears. I grunt and hold my head. It's really pounding now, and the pain behind my eyes is starting to pulse, but at least the feeling of ice is melting away.

"Nadya!" Tam calls again. He must be standing on the catwalks outside the balloon, talking into the other end of the tube.

I get up and grip the tube's warm copper mouth to speak back into it. It swallows my voice like a living thing. "What?" I croak. My throat's dry.

"We can hear the pirate ship."

An icy slush slides into my guts. My eyes are watering, and I wipe them and take a deep breath. I wish my head didn't hurt so much. I wish I had time to think about what just happened. Who was that kid with the chains and no gills? What happened to Mrs. T? And what in the world was that monster on the Panpathia?

"It's above us," Tam says. "Salyeh's guessing maybe three or four hundred feet. Can you get us up that high?"

The question echoes in my mind, each echo hurting like someone's pressing on a bruise.

—up that high?

—up that high?

I take a deep breath. I have a job to do. No time to wonder about the Panpathia, or shadows and ice and freezing cold and why I was reaching for the lever to let air out of the cloud balloon. I can figure all that out once we get Nic and Thom and Mrs. T back.

The garden hears Tam's question in my head. The birds wake up in their nests. The frogs float to the edge of the pond. The plants seem to straighten.

The answer thunders back from a hundred voices, and I flinch at its loudness.

Yes.

My head's in agony, and I'm sweaty and scared and feeling kinda weak, but still, I smile. The sun-in-a-jar casts warm golden light over my trees, my grove, my pond.

My home.

I'm proud of it, and of the plants and animals inside it, and they can feel that pride. They puff up all around me.

You're all so brave, I tell them. *Thank you. You make me strong.*

I lean back down and speak into the tube again.

"We can do it," I tell Tam. "I'll stay here until it's time to fly. Just let me know what to do."

An hour later, I'm in my seat in the Flightwing. My headache's calmed down a bit and the ice at the back of my skull's gone, but my heart's skittering a rumba around the inside of my chest.

Tam sits next to me. We're both wearing our flight goggles. The sun has set, and outside our deck lamps the fog has taken on the blackness of Goshend's abyss, except for a hundred feet or so below us and a few hundred yards ahead, where there's an egg of cloud that's brighter than the rest.

The *Remora.*

The hundred-engine drone of the pirate ship's propellers fills the sky. Salyeh's got his hands on the steering wheel. His face is bathed in cool, focused shadows.

Tian Li's at his side, wrapped in a thick leather jacket that belongs to Thom. She's been starwinding all day, and she looks exhausted. Salyeh told her she could rest now, but she shook her head. She wants to be here for this, and I'm glad she is.

Pepper's up on the catwalks, ready to let garden air out of the cloud balloon when it's time for the *Orion* to dive and run.

"Are you ready?" Salyeh asks. There's a throttle next to him, which he can use to control how much air to give the fire spirit in the engine, and therefore how hot it burns and how fast the propeller spins.

He puts his hand on it. It's at half speed now. When he cranks it to full, we'll close on the pirates pretty quickly.

Honestly, I don't know if I'm ready or not, but I think I have to be. "Do they know we're here?" I ask.

Tian Li nods. "They knew where we were the first time. They'll know where we are again."

None of us is sure how they know this stuff, but I think about that thing on the Panpathia and I start to wonder whether it's all connected. Either way, it's better to plan on them knowing where we are.

"So why aren't they coming after us?" I ask.

Next to me, Tam shrugs. "Maybe they're surprised. Maybe they're waiting to see what we do."

I take a deep breath and look around me. Tian Li and Sal. Pep on the cloud balloon. Tam flexing his gloved fingers on the Flightwing's controls. *We can do this,* I tell myself. *We can do anything.*

"Ready," I say.

"Ready," Tam echoes.

"Ready!" Pepper shouts from the darkness above.

Salyeh throws the *Orion* into full forward. The high-pitched whine of our propeller gets louder. The ship doesn't lurch ahead—it's not as fast a change as that—but the acceleration pushes gently on my chest. The bright patch in the clouds gets bigger. I start to see a network of white lamps inside it.

I wrap my left hand around the Flightwing's bars next to me. Tam taps his toes on the pedals and squeezes the gear shift and brakes.

There are no lights on the Flightwing. In fog this thick, at night, the other two ships won't be able to see us. If we lose them, it'll mean a desperate struggle to keep the Flightwing aloft as long as we can, and then a long fall into the sea and a cold, wet death.

Don't think about that, I tell myself.

My mind starts thinking about ice on the back of my skull instead, and about Nic's secrets, and the pirates kidnapping cloudling and skylung kids.

I frown. My mind can be a jerk sometimes.

Don't think about that either! I tell it. *Think about how this is going to work!*

Tam and I aren't sure how we're going to land on the pirate ship. We're hoping to find someplace we can set down on the hull where we can't be seen. If the ship's engines are big enough, something as small as the Flightwing might be able to land on their housing. Then we'll just have to climb up the hull to get on board. We're counting on their engines being so loud that the pirates won't hear the Flightwing's rotor, either.

I swallow. *It'll work,* I tell myself. I think about Mrs. T in the pirates' garden. I think about what I told the plants in ours. *It has to work.*

"Coming up on them," Salyeh says.

The *Remora's* white lights get brighter. The grayness between them turns into the jawlike shape of a ship.

It's even bigger than I remember, and it's all made of metal. No wonder its cloud balloon, perched above it like an enormous, shadowy grub, has to be so big.

"I think they see us," Tian Li whispers.

"Take us lower, Pep!" Salyeh calls. "Thirty feet! I need to buzz them!"

The vents on the outside of the cloud balloon hiss as Pep opens them. We drop twenty or twenty-five feet. The hissing stops. We stabilize.

Closer up, I see that only the sides of the pirate ship are metal. The deck's made of wood, and so's the massive aft castle. The ship might be all wood on the inside, with metal plating around parts of it for armor.

Salyeh angles us for a gap between the tree-trunk-sized cables connecting the ship to its balloon. The gap looks just larger than the *Orion.*

"Sal . . ."

"We'll clear," he says.

The cables draw closer. So does the pirates' ship. There's shouting on its deck. The voices sound startled.

Our cloud balloon looks like it will barely fit under theirs, and our hull looks like it'll just clear the deck. Salyeh's hands tighten on the wheel.

"Sal . . . ," I say again.

We're moving fast enough that the mist streams over us, tugging at our clothes. A gunshot cracks out and crunches against the *Orion*'s hull. My heart beats faster. There's another shot, and another.

"Be ready to do your part as soon as we're past them," Salyeh says.

"Nadya, start her spinning," says Tam.

I start pedaling, but my eyes are glued to the quickly approaching shadow of the pirate ship. The shots chain together, until they sound like firecrackers snapping in the summer heat.

Please don't hit the balloon, please don't hit the balloon, please don't hit the balloon . . .

The *Orion*'s bow threads between the pirate ship's cables. The bulbous shadow of the *Remora*'s balloon passes over our heads. The popcorn sounds of shooting stop.

We swoop over the ship like an enormous eagle.

And then we're out in the darkness again, and Salyeh's turning the *Orion*'s wheel furiously. The ship swings to port. The shooting starts up again behind us.

"Now, Nadya! Now!" Tam shouts.

I put everything I have into pedaling. The shots break the windows to Nic's cabin below us. Tam shifts once, then a second time. The Flightwing rises off the *Orion*'s deck.

The fog curls underneath us like Mother Death's grasping fingers. The *Orion* scoots out from below us so fast we barely clear the back rail, and we keep rising.

Salyeh shouts out orders to Pepper. The *Orion* sails back toward the pirate ship. They thread the needle again and pass into the darkness beyond.

My heart's going a hundred miles an hour, but the shooting follows the *Orion*. Nobody seems to notice us.

"Okay," Tam breathes. His voice sounds hoarse and thin. He pedals a bit. The Flightwing spins to face the rear of the pirates' ship. "Time to go."

He flicks two switches on the Flightwing's panel. Her nose dips forward.

"A little less altitude."

My legs slow down automatically. My eyes scan the fog for another sign of the *Orion*.

"Focus, Nadya," Tam says. "They'll be fine."

I take a deep breath and turn to the massive shadow of the ship in front of us. He's right.

And we have a job to do.

CHAPTER 20

IN WHICH NADYA FINDS SOMETHING UNEXPECTED.

The Flightwing settles on the *Remora*'s engine housing with a muffled clank.

"Do you see a place to tie down?" I shout. The propellers below us are deafening. The turbulence they're kicking up washes over my shoulders, and I'm glad Tam and I were able to approach from above. If we'd tried to fly in behind the *Remora*, we would've been blown right out of the sky.

Tam nods. He's got a safety belt on, and he checks the knot in the rope tying it to the Flightwing's frame. "Stay here!" he shouts. "If you fall off, fly straight up and try to keep steady until I can pull myself back in!"

I give him a thumbs-up, and he jumps out of the Flightwing and onto the metal roof of the housing we've set down on. He's got two thick ropes over his back. Each of them is tied to the Flightwing's frame and has a massive metal barb at one end that he made special yesterday. Tam pulls a sledgehammer from a box behind his seat and walks, hunched over, toward the hull of the *Remora*.

The Flightwing's pretty close to the edges of the engine housing. We've got four or five feet of space on each side and maybe twenty feet between our nose and the aft of the ship. There's no armor plating there, which is a stroke of luck for us.

I keep the main rotor running until Tam has the barbs hammered into the *Remora*. He ties a knot in the rope attached to each barb and cranks the ropes down tight. Together, they ought to keep the Flightwing from slipping off the housing.

Tam slides his hand across his throat, and I brake the Flightwing's main rotor. Without the *chuff-chuff-chuff* of it over my head, all I hear is the drone of the *Remora's* engines and the occasional *crack* of a gunshot.

"I thought you said they wouldn't try to shoot her down!" I yell to Tam.

"I didn't think they would!" He works his way back toward the Flightwing. "I hope Sal keeps the *Orion* above them so they can't hit the balloon!"

If he doesn't, I think, *we'll find out soon.*

I grit my teeth. The sounds of gunfire continue above us. "Let's go! The sooner we're out of here, the sooner we can get back to the *Orion*!"

Tam nods. I slide out of the Flightwing and lower myself onto the engine housing. It's slippery with condensed mist, and I nearly lose my footing. I'm glad for the safety belt tying me to the Flightwing, and for the hooks holding her in place.

But we'll need to untie in order to climb.

I crane my neck to look up at the aft castle of the *Remora*. It's a huge black wall, nearly featureless. We're maybe seventy feet below the ship's deck and the lights on its rail, and I can't see a darn thing below them, it's so dark back here. I hug myself and shudder. I don't want to climb into that darkness. I can't get the memory of that shadowy thing on the Panpathia out of my mind. I feel like it's hiding in there, waiting for me.

Tam reaches under my seat and pulls out a few long climbing spikes. "You okay?" he asks.

I nod. I can't be afraid of shadows. Not now. "Do you see anything up there?"

"Hang on," he says. He pulls his flight goggles up and fishes out what looks like a pair of silver opera glasses from his pocket. He puts them to his eyes.

"There!" He points to a spot in the shadows about thirty feet up from us.

I freeze, afraid he's spotted some kind of monster, but he seems excited, not worried. "What is it?"

"See for yourself." He hands me the opera glasses. I look through them and the world brightens.

The colors look off—purple and green and amber and sky blue, swimming over and through each other whenever I move the glasses—but I can see pretty clearly in spite of that. And in the spot Tam pointed to, there's a bank of three windows. A safer way to get in than over the rail and onto the deck, where the gunfire's coming from.

I move the glasses away from my face, relieved. The aft castle looks dark as coal again without them. "How do we get in?"

Tam grins. A gust of turbulence kicks up and sends the Flightwing skittering a foot or so toward the edge of the housing. Tam and I slide with it. I grab the rope in panic while my stomach does jumping jacks in my throat.

But Tam's grin doesn't change. He holds up the sledge-hammer, and part of me relaxes. Seeing Tam in a good mood helps calm my thumping heart and pounding headache a little. The shadows seem less scary with him along.

Still, he doesn't have to *enjoy* it so much.

The window breaks on the first swing. I'm down on the engine housing, belaying Tam as he hangs from a spike he's driven in above the window so that he can get a good whack at it. I duck my head to protect myself from the glass, but it spills over me harmlessly. The pieces are pretty small.

Tam clears a few jagged shards from the window frame with the hammer, then drops it and a crowbar he grabbed from the Flightwing inside and climbs after them. A second later, I feel two sharp tugs on the rope and know I'm on belay.

I start climbing.

The wood on the *Remora* is newer than the *Orion's*, and it's a dark cherry oak I've never seen on a cloudship before. It feels damp but tacky beneath my fingers, and there are lots of little nicks and bumps in it. It's easy to climb.

There's no shadows. No ice fingers on my skull. Nothing

worse than the roughness of the wood and the chilly fog down the back of my neck. I breathe a little easier.

I reach the broken window pretty quickly, and Tam stretches a hand through it. He pulls me up and past the broken pane like I'm weightless.

I land in a richly furnished bedroom. A four-post bed takes up about half the suite. A mirror stretches from floor to ceiling opposite it, with a wardrobe nearby. An iron chandelier swings from the ceiling, empty and lifeless in the shadows.

My heart clenches when I look at the mirror. I don't like it. There's something off about it. It's cold and dark, and I feel like there's a presence in the shadows on the other side of it, watching me. I shiver.

Focus, Nadya, I tell myself. *You're okay. Get in, get out, get back home.*

The engines sound a little quieter inside, but I still have to talk pretty loud to hear myself over them. "Where do you think we are?" I ask.

Tam shrugs.

"Where do you think Thom and Nic and Mrs. T are?"

He shrugs again.

I swallow. We thought about asking the pirates on the *Orion* where they keep prisoners, but none of us really wanted to talk to them. And none of us really trusted them to tell the truth anyway. I just hope Mrs. T's not up in the cloud balloon again. I doubt we'll make it all the way up there without being noticed.

Tam grabs the sledgehammer from the floor and unties

the rope from his safety belt. I undo mine as well. While Tam coils up the rope and slings it over his shoulder, I creep to the door. A thin line of yellow light peeks under the bottom of it, and the keyhole has an orange glow.

I kneel and peer through the keyhole. I can't see much. Just the light and what looks like a hallway. Tam squats next to me.

"I can't tell if there's anyone out there," I whisper.

He nods, and then he motions for me to back away from the door. I do it. He tries the gold-filigreed handle, but it won't turn.

Locked. I frown.

Tam lifts the sledgehammer over his head and swings. The handle shears off. Sparks hiss toward the floor. The clang of metal on metal barks over the drone of the engines, and the tangy smell of smoke fills the room for a second.

I grab Tam by his collar. "What in *Goshend's* name are you doing?" I hiss.

"Getting us outta here," he says. He swings the hammer again, more softly.

The door pops open and swings outward. Tam picks up the crowbar and steps through, carrying both tools.

I follow him into a dimly lit, wood-paneled hallway lined with doors. An old, poorly-cared-for carpet squishes under my feet. Each doorway in the hall lies six or eight feet away from the next. The light comes from electric lamps between them.

"Looks like a hotel," Tam mumbles next to me.

I pull the door as close to shut as it will get behind us. Tam's right. Most liners are a lot like hotels on the inside.

And that gives us a big problem. There are about twenty doorways in the hall. Judging by the width of the ship, each deck probably has two or three halls, and judging by its height, there are probably three or four decks like this one.

Behind most of the ship's doors, there should be nothing.

Behind some of them, there will be pirates.

Behind one to three of them, if we're lucky, will be Nic, Thom, and Mrs. Trachia.

"How in Goshend's name are we gonna find them?" Tam whispers.

I close my eyes. *You can do this,* I tell myself. *Be brave.*

"Follow my lead," I whisper to Tam. "And make sure nothing happens to me. We have to be fast."

I reach for the Panpathia.

It's hard to find. There's so much noise, so much metal, so much dead wood. I have to fight through the pounding behind my eyes. The little threads of lifebond that tie cloud gardens together are almost invisible, but the *Remora*'s garden, high above us, shines like a lighthouse in the fog.

Once I find it, I find the web too. There are a bunch of strands coming out of the *Remora*'s cloud balloon. Some of them run to other ships on the Cloud Sea. Some of them lead to the *Orion*. And some of them lead into the *Remora* itself.

There are two of the last kind. I let my mind crawl along them, and I start walking. There's no sign of the purple stuff that made me stick to the web before, no sign of the monster on the horizon. Whatever it is, it must be hunting somebody else right now.

I move as quick as I can, but it's hard with my eyes closed. I have to shuffle, let my feet test the floor in front of me before I take a step. Every so often, I feel Tam's hand on my shoulder, guiding me in one direction or another. I turn left, then right. I take a staircase down. I lead us along a hallway, and then we turn left and go down another set of stairs.

The strands I'm following feel bigger and more real as I get closer to the people they're attached to. One of them has the warm, comforting feel of Mrs. Trachia. When I let my mind touch it, I can almost smell the cinnamony scent she dabs on her neck. The other strand smells worried, but it's bright and strong. I wonder if it belongs to the kid who saved me on the Panpathia.

The two strands split. The small, bright one leads through a doorway to my right. Mrs. Trachia's continues down the hallway.

I stop. This kid helped me earlier. We should help him too, if we can.

"Is this it?" Tam whispers.

I shake my head.

"Then why're we stopping?"

"I think there's somebody in here." Maybe that kid got kidnapped too. *Hello?* I ask. *Are you there?*

Something shifts on the Panpathia, far away. Something big and dark and cold. Like it heard me talking and maybe it's interested in finding out what made the noise.

No more talking on the Panpathia then. I've gotta stay quiet and small, too far away for whatever that thing is to notice. "Open the door, Tam," I whisper.

"Is Mrs. T, Thom, or Nic inside?"

"Just open it."

Tam huffs. I feel him raise the sledgehammer.

And then he lowers it.

"No," he says.

I curl my fingers into my palms. "Tam—"

"No. Listen, Nadya. There could be alarms, or traps, or pirates sleeping in there. Sal, Pepper, and Tian Li are getting shot at, *right now*. We owe it to them to get in, get the others, and get out before someone gets hurt."

I take long, deep breaths. "It's a kid, I think. He helped me. We should help him too."

Tam grinds his teeth. "Are you absolutely sure?"

I frown. I listen as hard as I can, try to get a sense of where he is, exactly. But I can't. He could be through that door, or the strand he's attached to could keep going. He could be on the other side of the ship, for all I know. "No," I admit. "Not for sure."

"Then we can't do this," Tam says. "It's too dangerous."

I think about Tam's lecture. *Bad things happen. We know stuff you don't.* "Okay," I say. I bite my tongue. I'm still trying to be quiet, but my mind drips my thoughts onto the Panpathia. *I'm sorry*, I think.

And as we walk away, I think I hear a voice whisper back, *It's okay.*

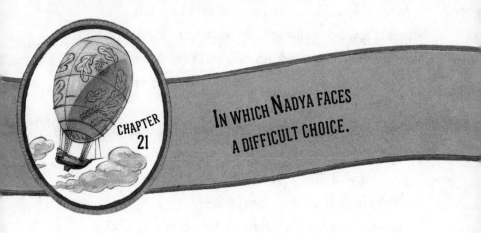

IN WHICH NADYA FACES
A DIFFICULT CHOICE.

We find Mrs. T in the next hallway over.

There's a heavy padlock on her door, so Tam bashes the sledgehammer against the door's middle until it gives way.

"Hurry," he whispers. The sound of him breaking down the door was pretty loud. Hopefully, the pirates are all still firing at the *Orion*, and nobody's wandering around the halls listening for break-ins.

I let go of the Panpathia, feeling like I just got away with sneaking out in Vash Abandi and nearly getting spotted by its night watch and a pack of prowlers alike, and scoot through the hole in the door left by Tam's sledgehammer. The room beyond is dark as the inside of an eagle egg.

A set of chains rattles in the corner.

"Mrs. T?" I call softly.

The chains stop moving.

"Nadya?"

The voice that calls back is unmistakably Mrs. T's. I stumble toward it through the darkness. My hands find her face, her hair, her shoulders. She pulls me into a hug.

"Nadya, child," she says. "What are you doing here? How did you—?"

"Where're you chained?" Tam steps up behind me. He's got his crowbar and hammer ready.

"At the wall, Tam. But honestly—you two should be far, far away from here, with everyone—"

She stops talking and pushes my shoulders back. My vision's adjusting to the darkness, and I can see her face. She looks tired, with big bags under her eyes and more lines than I'm used to seeing. As she talks, those lines get deep and serious.

"What are the pirates shooting at, Nadya?" she asks.

I swallow. Tam's hammer bangs the crowbar into the wood. He cranks back on it and there's a loud *crack*, and then the bracket that Mrs. T's chained to breaks free.

"No time to break the chains, Mrs. T," Tam says. "We've gotta move fast. Where're Thom and Nic?"

Mrs. T puts a hand to her head. "I don't know," she says. "I haven't seen them since the pirates brought us aboard. They only let me go up to the cloud balloon."

Tam turns his frown on me. "Can you find them, Nadya?"

A line of sweat trickles down my neck. I didn't feel them at all on the Panpathia, and I don't want to go back on it again.

The voice from the room we didn't enter reaches into my mind, high and childlike. *I know where they are!* it sings. *I know,*

I know! You go down and left and three doors in. One of them is chained to a wall and the other to a floor. You should help them! Free them! Free them!

I swallow again and look at Mrs. T, but she's just gathering her chains. She didn't hear the other voice.

"Mrs. T," I ask quietly, "do you know if there's a cloudling on the ship?"

She blinks. "There's somebody else, but I haven't seen them or been able to contact them." Her eyes narrow. "Why?"

"There's a kid down the hall—I keep hearing his voice . . ."

"Nadya!" Tam barks. "Can you find Thom and Nic, or not?" He's sweating. His face shines in the light leaking through the broken door.

Go! Go! Help them! Save them! cheers the voice in my mind. *Then you can come back and bring help!*

"Yes," I say.

Mrs. T stares at me like she's not sure how that's possible. I'll tell her later. For now, I just lead us back into the hall.

Thom and Nic are right where the kid says they are. Nic's chained to the floor and Thom to the wall. The room around them's a dingy, darkened place that smells of stale urine. Both of them look weak, and I wonder how often they've been fed and given water. Or if they've gotten much of either at all.

Thom leans on Tam after he's broken free of the wall. Nic struggles to his feet and rests against the wall itself, breathing heavily. Thom has bruises and dried blood on his face.

"Zelda," Nic rasps. "How—what—?"

"Can you walk?" I ask. It feels a little weird to be leading them around, but we're the ones with the plan. We got here. We know how to get out again. They don't, and they seem willing to trust us. "We've got a bunch of stairs to climb."

Thom nods. So does Nic. I put Nic's arm around my shoulders and help him.

"Nadya," he wheezes as we step into the hallway. "Why did you come back?"

His skin looks paper thin and bony. He coughs after he finishes speaking. His whole chest shakes and rattles.

Goose bumps prickle on my skin. "Do you remember where you found me?" I ask.

He says nothing for a few seconds. We reach the stairs at the end of the hallway and turn up them.

"Yes," he croaks at last.

"And Salyeh? And Tam? And Pep? And Tian Li?"

He coughs again, hard, then wipes his hand over his lips. "Yes."

I hear someone slip below us and look down and see Thom on one knee. Mrs. T slides underneath his left arm, and she and Tam half carry, half help him stagger the rest of the way up the stairs.

"We couldn't just leave you, Nic," I say. "You saved our lives."

We take a few steps. He wheezes.

"You don't—" Nic pauses to cough loud and long. "You don't owe me anything, Nadya."

All those thoughts about Thom, Nic, and Mrs. T I couldn't

keep straight before come clear, like the sun breaking through a day of clouds and lighting up the whole big sapphire sea. "It's not about owing, Nic," I say. I grin and plant a kiss on his cheek. "It's about caring, and doing what's right."

Nic's face softens and warms. He looks like he's about to say something else, but then he doubles up with another coughing fit. "Thank you," he rasps when he can talk again.

I share a worried glance with Tam and Mrs. T. Whatever he's got, it sounds pretty nasty. *We'll deal with it later,* I think. *After we're safe.*

I just hope we make it.

Miraculously, we don't run into any pirates on the way to the cabin we broke in through. But my back starts to hurt from holding Nic up, and my legs burn from taking his weight on the stairs, and my shoulders feel like spiny balls of dancing starlight. When we get to the cabin, I let Nic slide down the wall near the door. He leans against it. A grateful look crosses his face, and then he grimaces as another coughing fit takes hold of him.

Tam drops Thom into Mrs. T's lap and starts uncoiling the rope from his shoulder.

"Sal must be doing a heckuva job keeping them busy up there," he mumbles.

"He's a good pilot," I say.

Tam nods and starts fumbling at his belt.

Are you out? Are you out? the kid in my head whispers. *Are you safe yet, Nadya?*

My gut churns some more. I wonder how he knows my name. I wonder whether it's any safer for him to be talking over the Panpathia than it was for me. I hope that thing doesn't find him. "Can I help you, Tam?"

Tam shakes his head. His mouth opens, but I don't hear his words.

The lines of the Panpathia flare sudden and bright in my eyes. My mind runs along them, through two hallways, down two flights of stairs, halfway down another hallway, and through a door.

And I see.

The kid who's talking to me has an iron collar around his neck and manacles around his wrists and ankles. His skin's even paler than Pepper's. He looks thin and underfed. Short, curly dark red hair in tight whorls clings to his scalp. He's leaning against his chains, shaking them as he roots for me. He's so much younger than I thought he was. Just a little kid, the age I was when I first got on the ship.

The churning in my stomach becomes a steel fist.

"Nadya?" Mrs. T asks. "Nadya, child, what's wrong?"

I look at the floor. Tam has set down the crowbar and hammer to focus on setting up a belay point.

"Are you okay?" he asks me. "I need you to belay while we get Nic and Thom down to the Flightwing."

My heart speeds up. I see the kid with the chains again and again. The kid who saved me on the Panpathia. Who helped us find Thom and Nic. Who wants us to escape and bring back help. If I heard the pirates on the *Orion* right when

I was in the hiding place, he's gonna get sold to some scum-bucket.

I can't just leave him.

"I'm sorry," I whisper.

"That's okay, Nadya—hey!"

Tam reaches out to stop me, but by then I've grabbed the hammer and the crowbar and I'm gone.

I run as fast as I can back down the hallway, heading for the room where the little kid's chained.

The carpet barely muffles the sound of my feet. My heart races.

What are you doing? the kid's voice shrieks. *You have to run! Go, run! Run for help! Please, run!*

I run. I run and I run and I run.

The first hallway sails past, and I thunder down the stairs and turn down the second. My lungs start to burn. My legs get wobbly. My stomach threatens messy revolution.

But still, I run.

By the time I reach the door to the kid's cell, my arms and legs are shaking. My body's covered in sweat. My heart's pounding so fast I worry it'll beat its way right through my chest.

I place the teeth of the crowbar in the gap between the door and the jamb, raise the hammer, and swing at the rounded end of the crowbar with every ounce of strength in my body. *Ping!* the metal sings as I pound the crowbar into the gap. *Ping! Ping! CRUNCH.*

I lean my full weight on the crowbar. The door splinters and cracks, and I pull the crowbar free and switch to the hammer again, smashing it into the wood until there's a hole in the door big enough for me to crawl through.

"Kid?" I call into the darkness. I don't bother whispering. I've been loud as a train, and something tells me we're running out of time.

"H-here," a thin voice whispers back.

I rush forward. A pair of bony arms tries to push me away.

"You h-h-h-have to run, Nadya! You can't f-f-free me. I can't leave. Th-they won't let me! Go bring h-help!"

"Hush," I tell him.

My eyes adjust to the darkness. I can see him now, just as clear as I could in my head. Pale boy. Red hair. Bony arms. Ragged clothing. His eyes are bright, like a blue, fast-flowing stream.

I can see where he's chained to the wall. Five brackets. One for each wrist and ankle and another for his neck.

I step past him, place the teeth of the crowbar under the first bracket, and start swinging.

Hurry, Nadya! Hurry! the kid calls in my mind.

I grit my teeth and focus on swinging. The bracket comes free. My arms feel like soggy noodles. My lungs feel like dried-up, raspy paper.

You can do this, I tell myself. The second bracket pops away from the wall. *There's still fire left in your boiler.*

257

I swing the hammer and crank the crowbar. The third bracket falls away. I turn to the fourth and start hammering. My shoulders are screaming.

Think of the garden.

Swing.

Think of Pepper, falling in the dark.

Swing.

Think of Salyeh and his promise. Think of Tian Li and her dreams, getting shot at to buy you time.

The fourth bracket breaks off. I set the crowbar against the wood above the fifth.

Think of Tam, waiting for you.

Swing.

Think of Nic, and Thom, and Mrs. T.

The last bracket comes free.

"Come on," I say. I grab the kid's hand. "We've gotta—"

A shriek fills the air. It's like a ship's whistle but higher, more penetrating somehow. It reaches into my mind and stabs my brain with little needles. I scream. I put my hands over my ears. I fall to my knees and bang my head against the deck.

Stop! my mind shouts. *Stop! Stop! Stop! I'll do anything! Just stop!*

But it doesn't. It goes on and on, until I feel like my ears must be bleeding and I can't see straight.

A thin hand touches my neck.

The shrieking stops.

I kneel on the floor, sobbing. My ears feel like they've

been stabbed with skewers. They ring as loud as they would if a firecracker had just gone off next to them. *There could be alarms,* Tam said, and he was right.

It's time to run, but I'm so tired and everything hurts. I'm not sure I can do it.

"Come on, Nadya—"

The hand on my neck goes to my arm and tries to pull me up, but it can't. It's small and weak, and I'm big.

And strong, I tell myself. *C'mon, Nadya!*

I struggle to my feet. I grab the crowbar and hammer in one hand. I wrap the other around the kid's wrist.

And then we run.

We're almost to the cabin Tam and I broke into when the kid leans back and jerks on my hand.

Stop, Nadya! his voice shouts in my head. The sound of it brings tears to my eyes. Everything in my mind feels raw and swollen, like my brain's been bruised.

"Sorry," the kid whispers. "But it's not safe."

I look ahead. The hallway's empty and quiet in its bright electric light. I can't see anything wrong. "How do you know?" I whisper back.

"There's something on th-th-the web."

I shiver, thinking of ice on the back of my skull and that monster over the horizon.

"We'll stay off it then, okay? But we have to go that way to get out."

"But—"

"No buts." I squeeze his hand in a way I hope is reassuring. "We'll be careful, okay?"

He doesn't say anything, but he squeezes my hand back.

My arms and legs are still quivering, and I force them to move slowly and quietly. I pad down the hallway, listening for trouble, but there's nothing. The door to the cabin ahead is shut. The lights on the walls glow harshly. The sound of the *Remora*'s engines fills the air.

I'm nearly to the door when I hear a man's voice.

"I'm only going to ask you once more, boy. *Where's the cloudling?*" The voice becomes a furious roar, as though its owner's hammering words into someone like nails.

I freeze. The voice doesn't belong to Tam or Thom or Nic. It's deep and cruel and sharp.

"I don't know what you're talking about," Tam says.

My dinner threatens to jump up my throat. The pirates have found Tam, and it's my fault.

He told me not to rescue this kid. He told me there'd be an alarm. I ran off on my own and did it anyway, and now Tam's suffering for my mistakes.

I can't let this happen. I have to make it right.

I let go of the kid's hand. "Stay here," I tell him. I shift the crowbar into my left hand. I keep the hammer in my right.

"The boy doesn't know anything, Darkpatch," a second man says. He sounds a little younger and a lot less angry. "It must have been someone else. One of the crew, maybe, taking advantage of the commotion—"

"The boy knows more than he's telling!" the first voice snarls. I hear a muffled *thump*. Tam moans. "And I'm gonna teach his friends down in that flying machine what it means to lie to me!"

I know the Panpathia's dangerous right now, but I have to risk going onto it one last time. I have to see what's happening in there so I can get the jump on the pirates.

I reach out with my mind, like I did to find Opal and talk to the gormling in the hold, and I can picture the pirate who was just talking, see him perfectly. He's a big man, wearing a pale blue jacket with silver embroidery that used to be nice but has gotten threadbare. Tall black boots. Long, messy hair. Scars all over his knuckles, a black patch over his left eye.

And beneath that patch there's something strange and awful. Not a damaged eye. Not even a socket. Something dark and wriggling, made of shadows. A creature that looks back when I look at it. There's a dark, purple thread running from it off to the north, where I feel something huge and dark and cold turning and scuttling toward me so fast it shakes the whole of the Panpathia.

I jump off the Panpathia as quick as I can. I feel ice on the back of my skull again, but it hasn't gotten far. I tighten my grip on the hammer and crowbar. The kid squeezes my wrist, and the ice melts faster.

"You hear that?" the voice shouts. "This is what I do to liars!"

Keep talking, I urge the voice, shivering and trying not to think about the creature made of shadows. *Keep talking, so I know where you are.* Over the sound of the engines, I hear a pistol cock.

I yank the door open.

I see three figures in the foggy darkness. One of them's lying on the ground, curled up in a ball. The second, crouching over the first, turns to face me. There's a pistol in its hand. The third, a man, stands close to me, facing the other two shadows.

The pistol swivels toward me. I start to throw the hammer. There's a flash and a bang, and the hammer leaves my hand and crashes through a window.

My heart thunders, but I don't feel anything hit me.

I swing the crowbar at the man standing next to me. He catches it and spins me so the claw of the crowbar presses against my neck, then shoves me against the wall.

I hear a wretched gurgle.

The shadow that was crouching over Tam slumps over. Something falls out of its pocket with a heavy *thunk*. Tam drags himself away across the floor.

I don't understand. Tam couldn't have taken down that pirate from the floor. So who did?

"Easy, sky child," the other pirate's voice whispers in my ear. I struggle until I hear the pistol cock again. Then I freeze. Tam shouts and lunges toward us, but the man spins us out of the way and kicks Tam in the back. He crashes to the floor and moans.

"Settle down, both of you," the man says. His words crack across the fog like a whip. "You're wasting time."

"Tam," I say. "Calm down." The hot iron of the pistol presses against my temple.

Tam drags himself to his feet and holds a hand against his ribs. There's blood on his face. His left eye looks swollen.

The man holding me lets go and pushes me forward, yanking the crowbar from my hand. "Let me congratulate you two on killing Captain Maladrew Darkpatch, Scourge of the Cloud Sea and commodore of the infamous Darkmist Pirates," he says.

I look at the pirate slumped on the floor. A spreading pool of blood beneath his threadbare blue jacket glistens in the light from the hallway.

"Of course," the man continues, "it's a shame that I couldn't stop you from doing it. But that's life, don't you think?"

I turn around. The man holding the pistol has a cheerful, youthful face. A long pink scar races along his scalp and ends in a deep hook under his left eye. He wears brown breeches, a crushed-velvet coat with too many pockets, and boots that go up almost to his knees. His hair's tied back in a ponytail. A short, forked goatee juts forth from his chin like two fingers.

The man grins. "You've done me a service with your theatrics tonight," he says. "Darkpatch had to go. And I'm feeling generous enough to let you keep your lives as repayment." He frowns. "Of course, if the crew comes down before you're off, I'll have to shoot you. It wouldn't do to be seen as soft. Not yet, anyway."

"You're letting . . . us go?" Tam wheezes behind me. It sounds like talking hurts him a lot.

My eyes linger on the blood and the corpse on the floor. *He killed him. Killed him cold as ice.* The pistol shot cracks in my memory. He could've killed us too. In the shadows, I think I see something small and dark scuttle away from Darkpatch's body toward the mirror. I feel the kid I rescued jump onto the Panpathia, full of sunshine and fire like he was when he helped me on the *Orion*, and there's a bright flash and the smell of summer rain, and then the little shadow's gone.

"Yes, if you're smart enough to take advantage of it." The man's laughing eyes harden. "I don't like killing children, I don't like kidnapping them, and I smell a rat in this deal that Darkpatch made." He spits on the floor in the direction of the dead captain, then gestures toward the window with the pistol. "Staying alive as a pirate means knowing when you're outgunned. These people Darkpatch sells kids to, they're first-class rotters. We keep dealing with them, eventually they're going to eat us up whole." He looks at me and quirks an eyebrow. "If you do have the cloudling, you can keep him. He's more trouble than he's worth."

Trembling, I walk to the door and hold my hand out. The kid's fingers grasp mine.

Did you do something to that shadow? I ask him over the Panpathia. It feels safer now. The thing of shadows and ice is milling around somewhere over the horizon, like it can't find the way to us, and whatever I felt in the room before is gone now.

Yes, he says. *I had to.*

Our nameless, ponytailed savior grins and I have to stop

talking to the kid for now. "I thought you'd have him nearby." The pirate steps forward and rubs the kid's head a little. "Going off on your adventure now, eh, Aaron?"

"Yes, Mr. Robles."

The man, Robles, winks and steps back. "Good boy," he says lightly, but his pistol hasn't wavered.

"That's it?" I ask. The rope that the others must've used to get back to the Flightwing hangs out the broken window, our last chance at freedom.

"Almost," Robles says. "I'm afraid I still need a skylung to keep this boat running. Our last one jumped overboard a couple weeks after Darkpatch came back from the desert, and your Mrs. Trachia was doing such a fine job. I'd hate to lose her."

The wind puffs a bit of fog in through the window. I hear sporadic shooting above the drone of the engines. Tam stiffens behind me.

"I'm a skylung," I croak. "I'll stay." I don't want to. I'm terrified of this ship and these people and their strange, huge cloud garden. But this is my fault. I've gotta make it right. I've gotta make sure the others can get away.

"You most certainly will *not*," says a voice from the window.

Mrs. T pulls herself through it, dragging her skirts behind her. She cuts her hand on the broken glass, but she doesn't seem to notice. She steps gingerly into the cabin, her hair swimming around her head in massive, untidy curls, her eyes baggy and tired. But the strength is there in her arms and legs, and her back is straight.

"I will remain and keep your ship afloat, Mr. Robles," she says. Her chin swims high in the air. Blood drips silently from her fingers. Her eyes blaze. "Will that be quite sufficient?"

Robles chuckles. "Quite," he says. He levels the gun at me. "Now you kids get out of here. Won't be too long now before someone comes looking for old Darkpatch and me."

My throat goes dry.

"Nadya, Tam, go out the window," Mrs. Trachia says. She stands like an oak tree, rooted and immovable.

"Mrs. T—"

"This isn't up for discussion, Nadya Skylung! Every second you stay here puts everyone in terrible danger!"

Tam limps toward the rope. "Come on, Nadya," he says. "She's right."

I look at Mrs. T, a yellow-chiffon soldier standing statue straight in the darkness. I look at Robles, all signs of humor gone from his squinting eyes. I look at the dead captain on the floor. I look at the blood. I look at Aaron. I look at Tam.

My stomach grabs hold of my heart and shakes it for dear life. I promise myself I'm not going to cry, but when I hurl myself forward and bury my chin in Mrs. T's dress, I do it anyway.

"Hush now, *rybka*," she says, more softly this time. "Go. Keep the others safe." She strokes the back of my head, gently, twice. "Stay off the Panpathia, and tell Nic I said it's time for you to know everything. Find Raj. He'll teach you."

Every part of me wants to stay. I can't leave her. I can't.

Until Aaron sniffles behind me and Mrs. T nods in his direction, and I realize she's right, like always.

I shuffle Aaron toward the window. "Can you climb a rope?" I ask him, choking, and he nods. "Okay," I whimper. "Stay close to me, just in case." My chin's trembling. Tam's still holding his ribs. "How about you?" I whisper.

"I'll be all right."

I look back at Mrs. T. My mouth opens and closes. I can't find any words.

"Thank you, Mrs. T," Tam says.

I nod. There's a lump in my throat the size of a mountain.

Mrs. T returns the nod briskly. "I'm so proud of you both. Go," she says.

There isn't time to haul in the rope and climb down safely. I grab hold of it and walk myself backward out the window. My face feels numb. I'm crying. The Flightwing sits on the engine housing below me. Thom and Nic are slumped in its spare seats, neither of them moving. Dark fog swirls behind them like a hungry ghost.

Aaron slips out of the window above me. I walk down, and he follows. A few seconds later, Tam comes down as well. My chest is bursting. My head pounds, my body hurts, and I feel like I might throw up.

Focus, Nadya. Focus. We still have to get airborne and back to the *Orion.*

My feet hit the hard, slick metal of the engine housing. I take Aaron's hand once he's down and guide him as carefully as I can over to the Flightwing. I don't think about how we're not roped into anything. I don't think about how one missed step could send us sliding to our deaths.

I think about how we're leaving Mrs. Trachia behind.

I settle Aaron into the Flightwing's back seat between Thom and Nic. Thom's head lolls forward over his chest. He's breathing, but other than that he's not moving a bit.

"Where's Zelda?" Nic rasps. He looks like he's barely conscious.

"She—" My voice catches. *Focus, Nadya.* "She—"

Nic doesn't make me finish. He just nods.

"There's a kid between you and Thom," I choke out. "Take care of him, okay?"

Nic nods again. He grabs Aaron's hand.

I turn back and find Tam getting into the Flightwing beside me. We're still hooked to the *Remora*.

"You have to get the barbs free," Tam wheezes. "I can't do it. I think they cracked a rib."

I look at the hooks and swallow. In my mind, I'm falling, falling . . .

I grit my teeth and climb out of the Flightwing. I grab one of the safety lines and fumble to get it tied to my belt, and then I set off for the barbs.

They're big, each one the length of my forearm and as wide as three of my fingers put together, and Tam banged them into the *Remora*'s hull pretty deep. *It's not gonna work,* I think. *I'll never get them out. We'll never get free.*

"Nadya!" a voice calls above me.

I look up. It's Mrs. T.

Robles is standing by the broken window. He's still got a pistol pointed at Mrs. T with one hand, but his other hand is dangling a machete over me.

He drops it. It tumbles toward me pointy end first, and I have to scramble out of the way. It lands with a loud clang, and I snatch it before it can slide away.

I look up, thinking wildly that maybe I can get Mrs. T back with this thing somehow, but she and Robles are gone again, and Tam and the others are counting on me, so I turn to the ropes. The machete hacks through the rope attached to the first hook in three chops. I slip and slide my way to the second.

Shouting erupts in the cabin above me.

I get to the second rope and swing once, twice. I hear the *chuff-chuff-chuff* of the Flightwing's main rotor over the drone of the *Remora*'s engines. Tam has it running. All I have to do is cut us free and get to him.

I hear a shot. Something pings off the engine housing next to me and hits my calf like a snakebite.

I hack through the second rope. Mrs. T shrieks above me. Another shot cracks into the air.

I don't know where it goes. I drop the machete and half run, half limp toward the Flightwing. Every step sends needles of pain stabbing up my leg.

More shrieks. Another shot. More shouts. A snake bites my shoulder and nearly jerks me off my feet.

The Flightwing starts to slide off the back of the engine

housing. I'm running toward it, but everything's in slow motion. Everything hurts. My body screams. My heart fills with panic.

Tam pedals harder. The Flightwing slides farther backward, then falls off. I reach the edge of the engine housing and jump.

The Flightwing rises up to meet me.

My chest slams into one of the metal bars in the Flightwing's nose. My hands wrap around it and cling for dear life. My legs kick above the foggy, endless sky.

My arm feels like it's on fire. There's something sticky leaking down it.

"Hang on, Nadya! Hang on!" Tam's working the hydraulics frantically and pedaling like a madman. A shot pings off the metal near my head.

The rotor roars. We soar into the darkness and the mist, leaving the guns behind. The shadow of the *Remora* disappears below us. There's only the lights around her deck rail to show us where she is.

"Easy," Tam says. "That's it. Easy . . ."

He grabs me under my good armpit. He sucks in a sharp, pained breath when I lean on his arm, but with his help, I manage to swing my legs onto the bars. My calf hurts deep. Putting weight on it is agonizing.

I manage to pull myself into my seat.

"Goshend's teeth, Nadya," Tam says. His face looks gray in the light seeping through the fog.

I look down at myself. My shirt's soaked with blood. There's a hole a quarter inch wide in my calf.

Focus, Nadya.

"Get us back to the *Orion*, Tam," I croak. My throat feels dry and scratchy. "Get us home."

"I'll need your help," he says.

I nod.

We work the pedals together, me on elevation again, him on steering. Every time I pedal with my hurt calf, it feels like someone's dropping an anvil on my shin. Tam takes us over the big dark blob of the *Remora's* cloud balloon so that we're out in front of it, where the *Orion* should be.

I can't keep my eyes open. I'm so tired, and everything hurts—everything—

"Bit lower, Nadya," Tam says. "I can see her."

Guns bark *pop pop* in the blackness. I can't see. I can't think. I just want to stop pedaling and sleep.

"Bit lower. We're almost there."

My legs ache. My right shoulder's on fire. There's blood all over my hands.

"Steady . . . steady . . ."

I hear a gentle *thump*. The rotor spins down above me. I lean back in my seat.

My body starts to shake.

Voices surround me. Tam shouts something. I feel hands undoing my safety belt. Hands lifting me up. Hands carrying me and setting me down and probing my shoulder and leg. The voices grow soft and distant. They sound worried.

Hang on, says a bright voice in my head.

Aaron? I think.

In my mind, I see him walking out of the darkness. He holds my hand and smiles.

Hang on, Nadya, he says. *Just hang on.*

I have terrible dreams.

A bright light shines in my face, and there are voices yelling and screaming. A nest of thick shadows rises out of a palace of ice and swallows me. Mouths snap and snarl in the darkness, nipping at my face, my ears, my eyes, my tongue. A spider the size of a mountain races toward me on the Panpathia, high over the emerald sea, and bundles me up with sharp feet in sticky purple webbing. Tian Li's words echo slow and deep over everything, like she's a hundred times too big and speaking three times too slow.

Shadows and cold. Shadows and cold.

. . . swallow us . . . swallow us . . . swallow us . . . swallow us . . .

Something moves in the distance. A firestorm of sunset light chases the darkness away. Briefly, I see Nic's sweating face and smell the metallic tang of ether.

I wake up in my bed.

The sun pours through my porthole windows. The *Orion*'s engines hum gently outside. White spirit-moss wisps of cloud trail over the side of my cabin.

Everything hurts. The right side of my chest is on fire. I'm thirsty as a tree frog in a desert. My left leg throbs and pulses.

Someone's fingers are curled around mine. When I turn my head to see who it is, she yelps, and I stare into Pepper's blue eyes. Her hair looks like it hasn't been combed in days. Her shirt's wrinkled and dirty.

"You're awake," she says softly.

I try to say something back, but my throat's too dry. I hack and cough for a few seconds. Pepper hands me a tiny glass of water, and I guzzle it as fast as I can. My head's killing me.

"More," I croak when it's gone, and I hand it back to her.

Pep shakes her head. "Thom said you've got to take it slow when you wake up. You can have another in ten minutes."

I don't bug her about it. I feel too weak for a fight. "What happened?" I whisper. "I remember the Flightwing landing . . ."

Pep swallows. Her hand closes over mine again. "You were bleeding pretty bad. Tam and Tian Li pulled you out of the Flightwing and rushed you down to the sickroom." Pep's face turns pale, and she starts rubbing my hand. She smiles as she talks, though. "You should've seen them, Nadya. I've never seen anybody move so fast."

She looks at me, but she won't meet my eyes.

Something went wrong, I think. I wait for her to tell me what.

"Sal and I had to stay up and get the *Orion* safe. We dove

274

under the *Remora*, then dropped farther and ran back the way we came. Once we were as low as we were gonna get, I left the cloud balloon and came down to the sickroom."

She swallows again. "It was bad, Nadya. There was a lot of blood. Tam cinched a belt around your leg and it stopped the bleeding, but your calf turned a nasty shade of white. They were holding bandages to your shoulder and wrapping them tighter and tighter. You were pale as a sheet."

I nod and swallow. My throat feels raspy and dry again. "Can I have another glass yet?"

Pepper checks her watch and shakes her head. "A few more minutes, Nadya."

She takes a deep breath and lets it out. "We got you fixed, eventually. Tian Li dug the ball out of your calf and everything. Sal stayed up on deck the whole time, keeping us safe. I guess Nic was sort of conscious, but Thom didn't wake up till the next day in his cabin."

"What about Aaron?"

Pepper rocks back and forth. "Aaron was fine. He just sat in the Flightwing. Sal didn't even know he was there until Nic said something."

"How's he now?"

"Still fine. He likes to sit out in the sun. He doesn't talk much, but he smiles all the time."

I nod. That's good. I shift my weight off my left side. My leg's on fire, all the way down to my toes.

"So what happened next?"

Pep takes a deep breath. "Well . . ."

The door to my cabin opens. I look up and see Thom standing in the jamb. His bruises have turned a little green, and there're bags under his eyes, but he seems a lot better than when I saw him last. He limps in and stands next to Pepper. Nic and Tam are behind him. They're pretty banged up too. A second later Salyeh and Tian Li walk in, leading Aaron by the hand.

They look like they're heading into a funeral, so I crack a smile. "Why so glum?" I ask. "I'm fine. Everything's all right."

Except that Mrs. T's gone, I remind myself. But somehow I don't think that's why they look so sad. *How long have I been sleeping?* I wonder. *And what in the world could've happened?*

"Nadya," Nic says, "the first thing Thom and I did when we were strong enough was check on you. I want you to know that. The very first thing." His voice is hoarse, and he coughs a few times.

Thom's smokestack-shaped head bobs up and down. His mouth drips chinward in a deep, craggy frown. There's a scabbed-over cut just to the left of his nose, and his lips still look a little puffy.

My stomach twists up. I stare Nic straight in the eye. "What happened?" I ask.

Nic lays a hand on my right foot. "There was an infection in your calf wound. We could see it streaking up your leg."

He keeps talking, but I don't hear him. My eyes are on my blankets. Underneath Nic's hand, there's a little bump where my right foot pokes up.

On the other side, there's nothing.

I grind my teeth together and wiggle my toes. I can feel them moving, but I don't see anything happening under the covers.

Tears fill my eyes. I remember waking up to agony and blood and metal. I remember screaming my head off. I remember Thom holding a cloth over my nose and mouth until my dreams pulled me back down again.

I yank my hand free of Pepper's and dig my fingers into my bed. My chest moves in and out in ocean-sized swells. I feel like throwing up. *Move,* I tell my left foot. *Move!*

I feel it moving, but still, I don't see anything.

"Show me," I whisper. Pepper puts a hand on my right wrist. Tam moves to the other side of the bed and holds my left. Nic stands, sighs, and pulls down the covers.

There's an enormous bandage around my left knee. Below it, the lower half of my leg is gone.

It's okay, a little voice in my head—my own, not Aaron's—says. *It's okay, it's all going to be okay* . . . But I don't listen.

I try to sit up and hit something, kick something—make something, *anything* pay. Tian Li pounces on my right ankle. Tam and Pepper hold my wrists. Nic hovers his hand over my left thigh, but it hurts so bad the first time it hits the bed that I stop flailing and just curl up in a ball.

I scream.

And I scream.

And I scream.

• • •

I spend a week crying.

Nic comes in and takes care of me. He asks how I'm doing, checks my wounds and bandages, makes me get out of bed and do some exercises with my shoulder—where the ball went straight through the muscle and out again—and what's left of my leg. He says I'll appreciate them later, but right now they just feel like needles sticking into my stitches and make me want to shout him out of my room. I eat but I don't taste anything. I try to read and write, but I can't focus on the words. I can still feel my missing shin and foot, like I have a ghost leg, and Nic says a lot of people who lose limbs get those feelings. The pain gets worse unless Nic gives me medicine that makes my head fuzzy and my body dull. Mostly I stare out the window and think about all the things I'll never be able to do again. Never run. Never climb up the rafters inside the cloud garden. Never play tag or foot hockey or broomball with Pep. Never be first mate or captain.

My whole life was set up around being able to move. How am I gonna take care of the plants in the catwalks and the cloud balloon? How am I even gonna get *up* to the catwalks and the cloud balloon? Once, when Nic has me moving, I look at the ladder and try to imagine climbing it, but my ghost foot buzzes like it's asleep and my stitches are full of fire and my right leg's weak and woozy. That ladder I've been up and down a million times looks like a cliff a thousand feet high, with water pouring down it in a hurricane.

People come in and out and try to comfort me—Tian Li, Salyeh, Nic, Aaron—everyone but Tam and Thom. I let Pepper wash me and feed me and I let Nic change my bandages. Sometimes I let Tian Li hold my hand while I cry. I listen halfheartedly when Sal talks about taking our time getting to Far Agondy so Nic and Thom can get better. But mostly whenever someone visits me, I turn my head away from them and look at the wall. I don't want to talk. I don't want to listen. Sometimes I get caught up in big whirlpools of guilt, thinking of everything I could've done differently—not gone off on my own, zigged instead of zagged when I was running away, cut the Flightwing loose faster, not tried to be a hero and rescue everybody in the first place—and I convince myself it's all my fault. Other times I blame Tam, or Nic, or even Mrs. T. A few times I feel a bit better, but it never seems to last long. I've lost a part of myself, and all I want to do is mourn it.

On the eighth day, Tam comes into my cabin.

His bruises have gone yellow and green. His clothes are dirty and torn and covered in grease. His skin sags, and his eyes look bloodshot.

He's got a cloth-wrapped bundle under his arm.

He doesn't say anything after he opens the door, but I can't bring myself to turn away from him. He takes a seat in the chair at the side of my bed, sets his bundle down and licks his chapped lips, opens his mouth, closes it again.

And then he speaks.

"I'm sorry, Nadya," he whispers. His voice is hoarse. I

look at his hands and see that his knuckles are scabbed and bruised, like he's been hitting something.

"It's my fault," he says. "If I'd gone with you to get that kid or thought of getting him on the way back—if I'd been strong enough to get the barbs out or I made them better or if I pedaled faster . . . Maybe we all coulda made it out. We coulda faced those pirates together instead of separate. You never woulda gotten shot. You never woulda . . ."

I just breathe. Somewhere in my heart, there's a part of me that says it's nobody's fault, and that we're pretty lucky all we lost to the pirates was Mrs. Trachia and part of my leg. That voice gets louder every day, but I'm not ready to let go of blaming yet. So I say nothing.

Tears run like little rivers over the grease-stained wasteland of Tam's cheeks. He looks up at me, and the fire's back in his eyes.

"I swear I'll fix it someday, Nadya. Even if it takes the rest of my life. I'll make sure you can do everything you ever wanted to. Everything you ever dreamed. I'll make sure this doesn't—"

I turn away from him and close my eyes. I don't want to hear those words. I don't want to hear him make promises he can't keep.

I hear the sound of metal clanking behind me. It sounds like Tam's unwrapping something and taking it out of the bundle.

"I got out all my books, Nadya. I've been working nonstop.

Thom's helping me understand the engineering, and Nic's helping with the anatomy. When we get to Far Agondy, I'll get Gossner to help me too. You'll walk again, I swear it. You'll run. You'll climb."

Somewhere in my heart, a little candle of hope flares to life.

Don't listen to him, say all the dark things in my mind. *It's just going to hurt worse when you find out it's all a lie. Keep staring at the wall. Don't roll over. Don't take the risk. You've given too much. You hurt too much. Don't get hurt again.*

I roll over and look at Tam.

He's standing next to my bed. In his hand he's got what looks like a long, straight rod of aluminum. It's attached to a padded cylinder that looks like it might fit around my thigh at one end, and on the other there's a complicated mess of little rods and springs and sculpted metal that looks almost like an ankle joint and a foot.

I swallow.

"I know it looks weird," he says, holding it out so that I can see it clearly, "but I think I can get it to work. It sorta flexes when you put weight on it. The cylinder takes your weight on your thigh so the hurt part of your leg doesn't touch anything."

The sun touches the back of Tam's rat's nest of hair and sets it shining. I think of him and Thom down in the hold, working. I think of Nic and Pep and Sal and Tian Li taking care of me. I think of how even though I'm in the middle of the biggest fall of my life, they're all there, trying to catch me.

Then I think of being able to get around on my own again, and I take a deep, shuddery breath.

The bulb in Tam's throat bobs up and down. "Nadya, will you come be a part of the crew again?" His eyes glisten. "We miss you." He looks at the floor. "*I* miss you."

My chin trembles. A bunch of memories wash over me all at once—the fall from the cloud balloon, the scramble for safety under the *Orion*, the fight with the pirates, the Flight-wing, the lead snakebite that cost me my leg.

And rolling along behind the memories like a clear sky after a thunderstorm, there's hope. I look at his metal leg, and I see how maybe, *maybe*, it could work. There's enough of my leg left below the knee that I can still bend it, and if I had something to attach to it that didn't hurt too much and that could hold my weight, and if it flexed at the ankle and the foot, and I learned how to use it, maybe I could move around on the catwalks again, and get back up in the cloud balloon.

And when I think about that and really *believe* I could do it, I start to feel better.

I sit up. It hurts. It's hard. Tam helps me. While he's close, I wrap my good arm around him and give him a hug. His body feels stiff and awkward, like he's not sure what he's supposed to do, so I squeeze him as hard as I can and he figures it out. He winces, then squeezes back. It hurts my shoulder, but I don't care.

"Thank you," I whisper.

"You're welcome, Nadya. You're *always* welcome."

We break apart. I wipe the tears from my eyes. "Can you get me a crutch?" I ask. I think it might be a long time before I'm ready for his metal leg.

He smiles and turns away, and then his footsteps thump rapidly over the deck.

He runs.

I squeeze my eyes shut and try not to cry.

Tam walks back in a minute later. He's got an old crutch tucked under his arm—one we picked up after Nic twisted an ankle on the stairways in T'an Gaban last year. I slip its wooden V under my good armpit, even though it's too big for me, and Tam gently lifts my bad arm and puts it over his shoulders. We have to turn sideways and do an awkward shuffle, but together we squeeze out of my door and onto the deck.

The sun's setting over a turquoise ocean to the west. A few clouds hang on the horizon. We're still awfully low—less than a thousand feet, I reckon. I guess it's possible we're still trying to avoid the pirates, but I worry a little about the cloud garden. It can go for a while on its own, but everybody must be pretty scared.

I shut my eyes and reach for it. It feels sick with anxiety.

I'm gonna be okay, I try to tell everyone. *Everything's gonna be okay. I got hurt, but I'll be back soon, I promise. My friends are helping me.*

It takes a second, but Butterbeak and Mudwumple whisper back, *Okay,* in relieved chorus.

I open my eyes and stand on the deck for a minute or so, looking at the sun and feeling the wind on my face. The engines both seem to be running again. My missing leg hurts like I stepped on a nail with my ghost foot, but talking makes it easier to ignore the pain, so I talk.

"What happened to the pirates we caught?" I ask.

Tam coughs. He gets a funny look on his face, like there's more to the story than he wants to tell me. "Nic and Thom put them in Mrs. T's cabin. They're keeping them chained up and the fireminder sedated. We're going to turn them in to the Cloud Navy when we get to port to tell them Mrs. T was kidnapped and we need her back."

I nod. I get real angry when I think about the pirates. I wonder if that's why Tam looks so weird. They hurt him too.

I do my best to push those thoughts away. I'd rather just pretend the pirates don't exist, and I figure that's okay for a while. I've earned it.

You're up! says a bright voice in my mind. I look down and see Aaron sitting with his back against the ladder that leads to the cloud balloon. Shyly, he waves at me. He looks like a new chick in the cloud garden meeting its skylung for the first time. *I've been taking care of your plants and animals a little,* he says. *I can keep doing it, if you want.*

My stomach churns a bit. On the one hand, I'm glad someone's taking care of them. On the other, I wish it was me. I feel a little jealous.

But his smile's so big I can't help but smile back after a

second. *Thanks,* I say. *That'd be great. Make friends with Mud-wumple, and everybody else will listen to you.*

He nods, then looks down and blushes, sort of like I do around Amber on the *Emerald Dream* sometimes.

Thom's at the wheel on the aft deck. He raises a hand to me in greeting. I do the best I can to wave back with my good hand, but I can't move it very well without losing a grip on my crutch. The motion sends a wave of fire up my hurt shoulder, and I wince. My left knee starts throbbing. I bet all the blood's pooling in it now that I'm standing again.

"Can you take me back to my bed?" I ask Tam.

He nods, and we limp into my cabin. He helps me lie down. I'm breathing hard by the end of it, my stitches are back on fire, and my ghost foot falls asleep again. I get frustrated and sad and angry for a second, but it fades quicker this time. My heart feels stronger than it has since I woke up.

"Thanks," I say to Tam. I think about being down in the cargo hold with him, fixing the Flightwing in the moonlight and . . . "What happened to the gormling?" I ask. We must've run out of food for it days ago.

He glances out toward the deck and rubs his head. "Aaron can talk to it. He helped us figure out some stuff it can eat from the stores, and we dropped down by the ocean and switched out the water in its tank bucket by bucket. Nic took us way off course to make sure the pirates couldn't find us, so we're a long way from Far Agondy still. But the gormling's fine."

I breathe a sigh of relief. Tam looks at me for a second,

then reaches slowly into his pocket. "I've got something else for you, Nadya," he says.

He pulls out my doorknob and hands it to me.

I stare at it and swallow. I'd forgotten all about it with everything that's been happening, and seeing it now, I feel real bad about that. It looks pretty roughed up. There's a dent on the left side of it that wasn't there before, and a couple new scrapes. I lean in to sniff it, and it smells like solvent and metal—the scent of home is still there, but it's fainter than it used to be. "Where was it?" I whisper, rubbing my thumb over the tree embossed on the front.

He swallows. "You remember Darkpatch?"

I nod. I don't think I'll ever forget.

"It was in his pocket. It fell out when he got shot, and I grabbed it before we left."

My heart freezes. I stare at that silver tree reaching toward the sky, its roots plunging deep into the earth. I have a sudden memory, a new one: my mother yanking the doorknob off a big silver safe buried deep in the wall of a cloudship's ironroom before she gave it to me. My father shouting a warning in the background. "Why did he want it?" I whisper.

"I don't know," Tam says. "Makes you wonder, doesn't it? I had to clean it a bit. I'm sorry if it ruined the smell."

I look up at him. He seems nervous, like he's afraid I'll get mad at him.

My heart thaws again. Everything that was happening on the pirate ship—he was hurt, scared—and he still grabbed my doorknob for me.

"Don't be sorry, Tam. Thank you. For everything." I reach out my arms to give him another hug, and he leans forward so I can.

Afterward he coughs and shuffles his feet a little awkwardly, and I put the doorknob on the other side of my bed. I stare at it for a second, rubbing my thigh to distract myself from my ghost foot, and I feel like it's time to get some answers.

"Can you ask Nic to come see me?" I ask.

A few minutes after Tam leaves, there's a knock at my door. I figure it's going to be Nic like I asked for, so I wipe my eyes and make sure my doorknob's next to me so I can show it to him.

"Come in!" I shout when I'm ready.

The door opens a crack, and then Tall Thom shoulders it the rest of the way. He's carrying a tray. With cookies. And a cup of tea.

My jaw falls open.

"Ouch," Thom grunts, and then he kicks the door shut. "Nic's on his way, but I wanted to talk to you first. I figure I've waited too long already. How you feeling?"

I shut my mouth and frown. "Everything hurts. I don't like looking at my leg. I'm sad or mad a lot. This is awful."

Thom grunts again and sets the tray down on the chair by my bed. He hands me the cup, and I inhale. It's chamomile, just the right temperature. "One and a half spoonfuls of honey, I believe, was the recipe," he says with a grin.

I take a sip. It tastes just like the cups Mrs. T used to make me.

Thom looks around the room, then starts tidying things up a bit. He shakes the dust from the curtain over my porthole, tosses some dirty clothes into a basket that Pep's been taking down and washing for me. "Zelda and I used to talk a lot, you know," he says as he cleans. "And we all try to look after you kids in our own way, but that doesn't mean we can't switch roles every once in a while." He sighs, his hand on the edge of my desk. "You miss her?"

I nod and rub my thigh some more. I do. A lot.

He leans on the desk and crosses his arms. "Me too. How's the tea?"

I take another sip. "It's great," I say. "Thom . . ."

"I'm not trying to take her place," he says, getting up and starting to pace around the cabin. "We'll get her back, anyway. Just trying to cheer you up a bit."

I nibble one of the cookies. It's walnut and chocolate chip, soft and sweet and delicious. "Did you make this?" I ask around a mouthful. I didn't know he could bake.

"Er, yeah," he says, rubbing the back of his neck. "Don't tell the others, all right? They'll be after me to make 'em all the time."

I nod, and he clears his throat. "Look," he says, "I wanted to talk to you about being first mate."

My heart sinks like a punctured cloud balloon. All those dreams, all that hope, they just wither, and I'm back to feeling like my life's ruined again. "I know," I mumble. "'Cause of my leg, right?"

He scoffs. "Your leg's got nothin' to do with it, Nadya."

I look up, and he's staring out the porthole. "I served on a lot of ships before I came back to this one," he says. "Saw a lot of people missin' legs or arms or hands gettin' along just fine. You'll get it figured out, and we'll help you." He turns his eyes back to me. "But after all that's happened, I'm gonna be staying on as first mate for a while. We've got a lot to do, and the world's more dangerous than we thought. It's no time for me to be going off on my own."

I take another bite of cookie, my stomach and my heart doing a funny dance of relief and happiness and worry. "What's so dangerous?" I ask.

He scratches the half day's growth of beard under his chin. "Nic's the one to ask about that. He knows it better 'n me. But look, first mate." He stares straight at me, hard, like he does when he scolds me, except this time he's not scolding. "It woulda been you, Nadya. I heard from the other kids on the ship how everything happened while we were gone, and I'm impressed. Real impressed."

My chest clenches. My heart soars. I look down at my legs, one there, one half missing, and my throat closes up and I feel like crying. I did it. Even though I fell off the cloud balloon, even though I was scared, even though I screwed up so much. They were still gonna pick me, except it all got messed up by the pirates. "Thanks," I say. I squeeze the edge of the bed. I *did* it. "What about Tam?"

"Talked to him already," he says. "He agreed with me. Thinks he still has a lot to learn and you're ahead of him." He gets up and puts a hand on my good leg, pats it like a father. "Look, it doesn't matter much who wears the title of first mate on this ship. What matters is who people turn to when the crudcloud soaks the boilers." He leans back, smiling again. "For a long time, that's been me. But when I wasn't here, it was you. And if something ever happens to me and Nic again, let's just say I feel real good having Nadya Skylung around to take care of things."

He squeezes my leg, leaves the cookies and tea near my bed, and walks out with the tray he brought in. I stare after him, dumbfounded. My ghost leg gets some shooting pains, and I jiggle my real foot absentmindedly to try to get them to go away. Slowly, everything Thom said settles over me, like the sun breaking through a bank of clouds and lighting up my face on the morning after a long, cold night out at sea, and I feel as warm as the cookies and tea he brought me.

Nic shows up shortly after Thom leaves. He walks stiffly over to the chair by my bed and coughs a couple times. He's a lot better than he was when we found him on the *Remora*, but he doesn't look anything close to as strong as he was before.

"How are you feeling, Nadya?" he asks. He sits gingerly on the chair and stretches out one of his legs in front of him, then closes his eyes and rubs his temples.

My heart pounds. "Fine," I say. Actually my stitches are stretching and pinching and my ghost toes are itching, but I don't want to talk about how I feel. I did plenty of that with Thom. From Nic, I want answers. "Nic, Mrs. T said it's time for me to know about everything. She said to tell you that." I swallow hard and brush cookie crumbs from my shirt, afraid he won't believe me. Afraid he'll never tell me anything.

He opens his eyes again. They're narrow at first, and he looks hard at me like he's making sure I'm not lying, but whatever he sees there must convince him, because his face crumples after a second. "All right," he says slowly. Out on deck, where the sun's warm and golden, Pepper and Tian Li laugh about something. They seem very far away. "We agreed it would be her job to decide that." He looks at my legs. I curl the injured one up protectively under the covers, out of instinct. "What do you want to know?"

I take a deep breath. I've been waiting for this for so long. There's so much to ask I barely know where to start. I shift on the bed, and my doorknob rolls toward me, and I figure I'll start there. "Do you know anything about my parents, or my doorknob?"

Nic frowns. "A little," he says. "Not as much as I'd like." He pauses and rubs his chin, like he's thinking hard. Like maybe he's still trying to figure out how to tell me the truth.

But I can't wait to find out. "Captain Darkpatch had the doorknob," I burst out. "In his pocket. Tam got it back for me."

Nic curses and stands up, then winces. "Let me see it," he says, holding out his hand. I fish it out from my blankets. Carefully, he runs his fingers along the rod with all the slots that sticks out of its back. He pulls out his glasses and puts them on, then holds the doorknob up real close to his eye and inspects it. After a few seconds, he sighs softly and hands it back to me. "Zelda and I have never been sure what this is," he says, returning his glasses to his pocket, "but I suspect it's very important—or more accurately, that the door it was once attached to is. Do you see the tree on the front?"

I nod, looking at the back of the doorknob, trying to figure out what he was checking. I can't see or feel anything unusual—it's just the same as it's always been.

"That tree is called the Tree of Whispers, and it sits at the heart of the Roof of the World. It's the anchor for the Panpathia—all those minds, all that big web, they all lead back to it." He raises an eyebrow. "Did Zelda tell you about the Panpathia?"

I nod again, trying to imagine all those strands of light coming together in one place.

"It shone like a second sun, Nadya, at the center of the world's most beautiful city, on an island in a lake surrounded by an ancient forest with tall mountains on every side. It was a big part of what made the skylung civilization possible. In the cities up there, everybody talked on the Panpathia. Between houses. Between towns. It drew people closer together than they are in the rest of the world."

The way he talks, so sad, makes my stomach clench. "What happened?"

He clears his throat and sits down again, rubbing his head and his chest. "Something dark and cold came to the Roof of the World, and it poisoned the Tree of Whispers and everyone who came in contact with it. We called it the

Malumbra, and we knew something was wrong—people were acting strangely, getting cold and sick and then better all of a sudden—but we didn't understand what it was doing until it was too late. That monster—it possessed whole cities up there. Turned people into mindless drones. House by house and town by town, it hunted down the minds on the Panpathia and took them over. Just a touch from it, a breath, a whisper, could spread the shadow. We lost thousands of people."

For a second, I can't breathe. I can't move. All I can think of is feeling stuck on the Panpathia, ice crawling along the back of my skull, my body moving without me telling it to. My mouth opens and closes. I can't speak.

Nic frowns. "What's wrong, Nadya?"

I take a deep, quivering breath. "What kind of touch from it?" I ask.

Nic's nostrils flare, like he gets why I'm asking right away. He stands up and comes toward me. "What happened?"

"On the Panpathia," I start. I try to get the rest all out in a rush, because I think if I stop talking I'll be too scared to keep going. "I was looking for Mrs. T and I felt something awful on the horizon, and then my head got all cold and I got stuck and my body started moving without me making it." I close my eyes. "What's going to happen to me, Nic?"

Nic breathes out slowly. "Open your eyes," he says.

I do, and he leans down and holds my face still. He puts on his glasses again and stares deep into my eyes, like he's searching for something.

"You're okay, Nadya," says Aaron's voice behind him. "I burned it out of you."

I jump when I hear Aaron's voice, but Nic doesn't budge. He stares into my eyes a little longer, then lets out a long sigh, straightens up, and takes off his glasses again. "I think he's right," he says. "We learned to see it, in the eyes. A darkness that the light can't touch, very small at first but always growing. Eventually it takes over the whole eye, then the whole body, turning a person into a shadow of their former self."

I stare at Aaron. I feel confused but relieved, like I'm a baby cloudbird that just got back into its nest after falling for the first time. "Darkpatch was like that," I say, remembering the thing behind his eye, the way Aaron went after it on the Panpathia. "Aaron burned the shadow that came out of him too."

Nic turns around. "Aaron," he asks, "how can you do that?"

The kid shuffles his feet. He's standing outside my cabin, like he doesn't want to leave the sunlight. "Th-th-they taught us in Cloudlington, before th-the shadow came. To protect us."

Nic frowns deeply. "Cloudlington is a little town outside Far Agondy," he explains to me. "Many cloudlings who escaped the Roof of the World fled there." He turns back to Aaron. "Is that why someone's buying kidnapped cloudling and skylung children?"

Aaron flinches. He looks over his shoulder at the sun, like he wants to be reassured it's still there, then shrugs. "Maybe."

Nic sighs and sits in his chair again. He rubs his hands

295

over his face and looks up, then back down at me. "There's a lot we don't know, Nadya. It's not safe to go to the Roof of the World anymore. Everybody who's tried never comes back again. We're afraid the Malumbra wants to come south into the rest of the world, and there've been signs. Sea creatures getting more aggressive, like something's hunting their minds. These kidnappings. Little settlements like Cloudlington disappearing."

"Who's 'we'?" I ask, my mouth dry. I hope, even though I know it's wishful thinking, that "we" means my parents too, that secretly Mrs. T and Nic and Thom have just been taking care of me while they're off on some big important mission to save the world.

"We call ourselves the Diaspora," Nic says, and I remember the secret ledger Salyeh found. Nic coughs, then runs a hand over his bald head. "Some people—skylungs like Zelda, cloudlings, and immigrants like me—escaped from the Malumbra on the first cloudships, and we've been trying to lay the groundwork for someone to go back and fight it ever since. Your parents . . ." He sighs again and looks at me apologetically. "I never met your parents, Nadya. But there was a rumor that one of the escaping cloudships had something that could stop the darkness, drive it out of the Tree of Whispers for good. When we found you, we were looking for that ship."

I swallow, hard, thinking of my mother and the safe, my father shouting. "It crashed, didn't it?" I whisper. My stitches bark as I shift my weight, and I wince.

Nic nods.

"Were they . . . ?" I can't bring myself to finish.

"Dead?" Nic asks. He shakes his head. "I don't know. Not that we could see. Your balloon was caught on some rocks at the edge of a deep crater outside Vash Abandi. The ship must have fallen in. We tried to go down and find it, but it was too far for the ropes we had, and we could feel the darkness there, watching us. We didn't want to chance getting touched by it." He takes a deep breath. "I'm not sure what happened to your parents. I—" He coughs again, a long fit, like he can't stop. I hand him the water glass by my bed, and he drinks it all. "That's all I know, Nadya. I need to rest. We'll learn more—" He stops and coughs until his face turns red. "In Far Agondy. There's a meeting, with some of the others . . . in the Diaspora." He sounds almost like he's choking.

He gets up and walks out. I hear him start coughing again almost as soon as he's gone.

Aaron stays a little longer.

Where's your family? I ask him, thinking about what Nic said.

Gone, he answers. *And my friends.* He shuffles his feet and looks back at the sun again. *Some of them disappeared when the shadowy men came to town. Some of them got away, but I don't know where they are anymore. I got caught by the pirates when I was walking to Far Agondy, but I still want to find them. Can you help me?*

I look at him. An orphan, just like me and the others. I remember what Tam said about everything everybody's been through, how lucky I was that Mrs. T and Nic found me when they did. I don't feel quite as lucky after what happened to my leg, but I still want to pass on what I can. *I think so,* I say. I wave at my sheets, the crutch Tam left behind for me, and the bandage on my knee. *Y'know, once I get all this stuff with my leg figured out.* That part's gonna be hard, I think. Real hard.

He smiles. Tentatively, he walks in and touches my good leg, like the others have been doing. *Thanks, Nadya,* he says. *It's good not to be alone anymore.* He looks like he wants to climb up and hug me like I'm his big sister. Maybe he has one. Maybe he misses her.

After he leaves, there's silence for a while. I sit on my bed, my ghost leg feeling like it's got red ants nipping up and down it, and I rub my hands over my doorknob and think. I feel sort of hollow inside. For so long I convinced myself that Mrs. T and Nic would know what really happened to my parents, and in the end, they never even knew them. Maybe that's why Mrs. T wouldn't answer when I asked her about them. Maybe that's what she was figuring out how to tell me. Maybe she was waiting until I was grown-up enough to handle a hard answer instead of an easy one.

There's so much to do now. A lot more than there was a week ago, when all I was worried about was whether I'd become first mate or not. I've gotta figure out how to live with just one and a half legs. We have to get Mrs. Trachia back somehow. We have to figure out what the Malumbra's doing and why. Somewhere in the desert, there's an answer to the question of what happened to my parents in a crashed ship at the bottom of a crater. And I want to help Aaron too.

But I think we can do it. I've got my friends, and I've got the *Orion*. We'll get that new leg made, and I'll learn how to walk on it. We'll go to Far Agondy and meet these friends of Nic's. Whatever tore apart my homeland and took my parents away and tried to take me too, we'll beat it.

My name is Nadya Skylung. I keep the cloudship *Orion* afloat. My friends and I faced the Darkmist Pirates and a monster made of shadows, and we won. We're not gonna let anything stop us.

But first, I need to eat.

Dinner shows up at my door a little after the sun sets. I figure it's just gonna be Pepper bringing me some food like usual, but this time it's everybody, even Nic, who still looks tired but isn't coughing so much.

"Surprise!" Pep says, grinning like a moonbear. "I thought we could all eat together tonight!"

I smile. Tian Li comes in and gives me a hug and says she's glad I'm feeling better. Salyeh does too, and Aaron smiles at me. He's carrying a tray of food when he comes in. I bet they've got him helping around the ship, feeling part of the crew like the rest of us already. Tam seems pretty pleased with himself for getting me out of bed, but his smugness doesn't bother me, just this once. I'm glad he's feeling better too.

Nic has baked us all stuffed-bread sandwiches filled with

our favorite foods. Mine has pepperoni and spinach and onion and olive and cheese and tomato sauce. The bread's moist and buttery and spiced with garlic and oregano. There's a salad too, with crumbled goat cheese, croutons, and a creamy garlic dressing splashed over it. We even have chocolate cake for dessert.

We talk. We laugh. We tell jokes and swap stories. Even though I feel like crying sometimes when I think about my leg and Mrs. T, my chest feels lighter than it has in days. Except for the fact that we're eating in my cabin, I'm in my bed, and Aaron's sitting in Mrs. T's place, it feels like a normal dinner, and I forget to worry about my parents or shadows or anything.

I'm a little sad again by the time I go to sleep that night, but I feel like I can handle it. Under the sadness and the pain, I'm still me, and I'll always be me, and that's good enough for now.

Everything'll be all right, I tell myself. I hold my pillow like it's another person. I remember the feeling of Mrs. T tucking me in, and even though she's not here in person anymore, it feels like somehow she's still around. She helped me pick out my clothes, bought me my books and my journal and pens, sat on the chair and the bed. She's everywhere, if I think about it the right way, and no matter how far from this place she is, she'll always be right where I need her when it comes to my heart, smiling and touching my cheek and telling me she's proud.

• • •

That night I dream again, of darkness and cold. The nightmares aren't as bad as they were when I was being operated
on, but there are still teeth in the shadows, nipping and biting
at my mind. I wake up in the middle of the night, sweating,
my stitches throbbing.

And I hear a voice in my thoughts, calling for help.

I sit up in the shadows of my cabin, heart pounding. I try
to separate the dream from reality, try to figure out if I really
heard anything.

Help me! the voice shouts a second time. *Someone! Please!* It
sounds far away.

It's like Aaron's but different, a little older, a little deeper.
I send my mind racing over the Panpathia, tearing past the
starlike gardens of warships, traders, and liners bearing hundreds of minds across vast fathoms of sea and sky. I cross
miles of ocean, see the bright lights of Far Agondy on the
horizon, pass through walls and buildings and sewers and
alleys until I see a girl with skin like Tam's and big brown
eyes, being grabbed by two shadowy figures in the night.
She shouts again, her voice reaching hundreds of miles over
the Panpathia. She doesn't have gills, so she's not a skylung.
Another cloudling, then. She must be.

The vision disappears, but not before the girl screams for
help one last time.

Somewhere in the heart of Far Agondy.

Acknowledgments

This book took more than five years to go from first draft to publication, so there are a lot of people to thank. First, Mary Haas, without whose prodding it almost certainly never would have been written. Next, my wife, Cass, who has been my sounding board and biggest true believer for nearly a decade now. Third, Wes Davis, Adrien Pauchet, and Anna, Fred, and Marggi Seymour, who read the first draft and suggested that this story might be something special. Thank you to the many other readers who helped as well!

Beyond that, lots of people provided technical help. Dave Goldberg gave me advice on the climbing sections. Jeremy Sim, Geoffrey Glover, and Kati Gardner helped with characterization. Jennifer Foehner Wells, Brandon Stenger, and Wendy Hammer provided last-minute reading and reassurance. My dad pointed out places I'd diverged wildly from the physically possible. The usual caveat applies: If there are mistakes, they're all mine (and some of them may not be mistakes anyway—playing with physics is part of the fun). Cindy Howle, Rob Farren, and Anne Heausler made the copyediting process downright enjoyable. Cecilia Yung and Marikka Tamura did an amazing job directing the art and designing the book. Brett Helquist deserves special mention for his fantastic artwork; at several points his sketches led me to better descriptions. My agent, Danielle Burby, made great suggestions, found the book a perfect home, and provided incredible support throughout the publication process. Katherine Perkins, Stephanie Pitts, and the team at Putnam shared my vision for the book and the world, helped me expand on it, and put together a dream package for the story I wrote.

Finally, there's Cass again, who really ought to be thanked on every page. I could not do this without you. And, of course, Oren, who graciously waited until two days after I turned in the manuscript to be born and turn my world brilliantly, wonderfully upside down so that I could see it better.

Jeff Seymour makes his middle-grade debut with *Nadya Skylung and the Cloudship Rescue*. In addition to writing speculative fiction, he works as a freelance editor. Jeff lives in Indiana with his wife, their son, and two energetic cats.

Visit him online at jeff-seymour.com.

Brett Helquist has illustrated many books for children, including the bestselling A Series of Unfortunate Events by Lemony Snicket. He lives with his family in Brooklyn, New York.

Learn more at bretthelquist.com.